GIPSY
MOTH

GIPSY
MOTH

AVIATRIX

WILLY MITCHELL

iUniverse®

GIPSY MOTH
AVIATRIX

iUniverse books may be ordered through booksellers or by contacting:

iUniverse
1663 Liberty Drive
Bloomington, IN 47403
www.iuniverse.com
844-349-9409

Cover art by Kathrin Longhurst.

ISBN: 978-1-6632-1033-3 (sc)
ISBN: 978-1-6632-1279-5 (hc)
ISBN: 978-1-6632-1034-0 (e)

Library of Congress Control Number: 2020921311

Print information available on the last page.

iUniverse rev. date: 11/05/2020

To my mother, my wife, my daughter, my
sister, and all the women who strive to change
the world for the better and for good.

The Song of the Ninety-Nines

In the air, everywhere,
It is the song of The Ninety-Nines.
Wings in flight, day, and night,
With the song of The Ninety-Nines.
On the line, fliers fine,
Ships and spirits tuned in rhyme.
Keep that formation, over the nation,
With the song of The Ninety-Nines.

—Dick Ballou, 1941

Wings of Gold

I have seen your soul at dawn,
the invent of a new morn.
Above the clouds, from the skies,
deep into those beautiful eyes.

Even the watchful purple hills,
and those dreaded purposeful mills.
The stain of the evening, creeping from my heart,
each day I awake, and each day I start.

To think of those less fortunate than I,
as I adventure up in the sky.
Looking down, golden fields of corn,
to you my dear, I do adorn.

In moments many, I sustain the goal,
in thought of those that take the toll.
I sit up here proud as can be,
I hope for a world that one day will see.

Cracking icicles and brittle branches,
I sail above your homes and ranches.
I think of stories never told,
as I steer on these, my wings of gold.

—Emil A. Harte

CONTENTS

ACKNOWLEDGMENTS

Gipsy Moth is dedicated to my uncle Tommy Mitchell, who passed away earlier this year, in 2020. Here's a toast to you, Uncle Tom. See you on the other side.

This book is also dedicated to all the amazing women I have met or who have influenced my life so far.

To my mother, my wife, and my daughter; my amazing grandma Maggie Mitchell; my aunties May and Margaret; and my sister, who deserves a knighthood for her contributions to children's needs and lives over the years.

To another Maggie, former prime minister Margaret Thatcher, one of the greatest leaders of our time, and, going back in history, to Joan of Arc; Mary, Queen of Scots; Marie Curie; Florence Nightingale; Emmeline Pankhurst; and Rosa Parks for their refusal to give up or surrender and for their will to carry on in the face of adversity for their causes.

To my friend Georgina, who is one of the most inspiring people I have ever had the pleasure to meet and privilege to know, an adventurer, a world traveler, a leader, and a true inspiration.

To the Ninety-Nines, a group set up in 1929 with the mission of advancing women in the world of aviation and beyond (www.ninety-nines.org).

To the amazing artist Kathrin Longhurst, who grew up in East Germany and now lives in Australia and produces amazing portraits, including her extensive series of aviatrixes (www.kathrinlonghurst.com). A huge thanks for the cover artwork for *Gipsy Moth*.

To all those who have supported me on my writing journey so far: Charles, Jay, Hans, Prentiss, Jimmy, and Jeff. To fellow writer and historian Andrew Hemmings and to teacher and creative writing coach Alta Wehmeyer.

Finally, to all the beta readers who graciously gave their time to read drafts and iron out some of the early continuity and do fact-checking for *Gipsy Moth*.

The list is long. Thank you to all I have mentioned and all I have missed.

AUTHOR'S NOTE

I've always admired early aviators. The idea of taking to the skies in a plane constructed from wood, canvas, and wire captivated my imagination as a boy, and that fascination didn't disappear when I began my own adventures as a kid in the Air Training Corps, flying Bulldogs and Chipmunks and doing barrel rolls and loop-the-loops.

Then, later in life, in the British military, I was a passenger in the giant Hercules, jumped from Chinooks and Wessexes into the Arctic tundra below, and rode in Gazelles, hedgehopping dangerous terrain below on full alert.

Thus, writing this novel based on the exploits of my aunt Nikki, Amy Johnson, Amelia Earhart, and other early pilots seems inevitable.

Many of the first pilots back in the 1920s loved a specific aircraft known as the Gipsy Moth. The de Havilland DH.60 Moth was a 1920s two-seat British touring and training aircraft developed into a series of models and specifications by the de Havilland Aircraft Company.

The first flight of the Cirrus-engine-powered prototype DH.60 Moth was piloted by Geoffrey de Havilland at the company's airfield on February 22, 1925.

The Moth was a two-seat biplane of wooden construction. It had a plywood-covered fuselage and fabric-covered surfaces, with a single tail and fin. Its folding wings were a useful feature, as they allowed the aircraft to be stored in much smaller spaces than other alternatives.

The Gipsy Moth became a mainstay for the pioneers of flight in both civil and military aviation.

It's also useful to know that the term *gypsy moth* has another level of meaning that pertains to the plot of the novel. Not every individual can be counted upon to act with honor and integrity. You can be a gypsy moth in humanity as well as in nature. The name in Latin is *Lymantria dispar*. *Lymantria* means "destroy," and *dispar* means "to separate."

Along with the red fire ant, the crazy yellow ant, the razorback wild boar, the Singapore daisy, the black rat, the blue rat, the house rat, the roof rat, the ship's rat, Dutch elm disease, the cannibal snail, the walking catfish, and the Asian tiger mosquito, the gypsy moth is listed as one of the world's one hundred worst invasive alien species.

What does that have to do with this story? The answer to that question resides in the pages that follow.

PROLOGUE

I never had liked funerals, and this one was no exception: the passing of my own father from the earth. Just a week before, I had been in Sydney, Australia, heading to a friend's house for a barbecue, when I received the call from my sister.

I had been in Sydney for nearly two years by that time. I was in my thirties and was enjoying life between marriages and all the fruits of life that the city and Australia had to offer—probably, in hindsight, a little too much.

I was living in Davidson, across the Sydney Harbor Bridge, which was close to French's Forest and to Manly and its beautiful beach. The day of the barbecue, I drove past Taronga Zoo, onto the Harbor Bridge, through the city, and across the eastern suburbs to Randwick.

As I drove across the bridge, as I often did, I was amazed at the foresight of the people responsible for such a design. At the time of the bridge's construction in 1923, there hadn't been a lot to the north of the city, and their creation of a construction that managed the modern volume of cars, commuters, and trains blew my mind.

I admired the pioneers of yesteryear, such as those who'd had the vision to create telegrams, electricity, the lightbulb, television, and the motor car—those who'd turned the impossible into reality and pushed the envelope, no matter their field of passion.

As I continued, I recalled another time on the bridge. I left my office in Glebe, heading home earlier than usual, and on that afternoon, the bridge was like a ghost town. I was nearly the only one on the bridge. On the opposite side, I saw a cavalcade heading toward me: motorcycle outriders followed by a black vintage Rolls-Royce with a Union Jack flying high on its front wings. I realized it was none other than Queen Elizabeth II herself, my queen. I wound down my window and slung up a salute: "The queen! God bless her!" *Old habits die hard*, I thought, smiling to myself. "Queenie."

Australians talked a lot about removing Betty Two Strokes, as they irritatingly called her, from the Aussie dollar but at the same time had a love affair and affection for the monarchy. Regardless, she was my queen. I had served for Her Majesty, and I was proud to be a royalist.

I passed the Sydney Opera House, in all her resplendent and iconic beauty, on my left and Circular Quay on my right before heading through the Royal Botanical Gardens, yet another clue to the royalist heritage of Australia.

I had decided to take the scenic route.

My first year in Sydney, I lived in the eastern suburb of Randwick, and I knew the route well. I took the turn off the Eastern Distributor at Paddington and headed toward Oxford Street—more reminders of the city's colonial past and connection with the motherland. Once up to Bondi

Junction, I looked down onto Double Bay, Rose Bay, and the glorious Sydney sunshine glinting on the rooftops and Sydney Harbor beyond. Then I went onward to the world-famous Bondi Beach.

Just two years previously, I'd been on a Singapore Airlines flight, looking down on the predawn lights of Sydney for the first time, anticipating my arrival to my new life down under.

Recently and involuntarily divorced, I missed my wife and my son. I spent many an hour traversing the eastern beaches of Bondi, Tamarama, Bronte, Clovelly, and Coogee, which was where I was headed. I was going to my favorite local haunt, the Coogee Bay Hotel, to pick up steaks from the meat counter at their novel make-your-own-barbecue service.

I had a nice bottle of Yalumba Signature in the back and a six-pack of Victoria Bitter. I knew Michael liked wine; the Yalumba would hit the mark, and he would have plenty of beers on ice. Michael had been my host upon my arrival in the city, until I'd gotten my bearings and found my feet. He had always been more than generous in his welcome and his hospitality.

A short time later, I reached my destination, parked, and headed to the meat counter. Then, with Australian prime rump steaks secured in the cooler, I drove straight to Michael's. I was pulling into the apartment block on Cowper Street, when I received the call. It was my sister. My father had departed the earth.

I just sat in the car. I didn't know how long. My world wasn't turned upside down. Death wasn't like that for me anymore—my ten years in the army had seen to that. I just sat there thinking through the practicalities of the next steps. I would raise a glass to toast my father later that day—and many times over the years to come.

A week later, I was back in Yorkshire after my mammoth return from the other side of the world. I had no luxurious layover in Singapore, just a two-hour wait before I was back on the plane. I faced London Heathrow, the Heathrow Express, and a train from King's Cross via York and into Harrogate. The trip was twenty-two hours in the air and thirty-six hours door to door—plenty of time for reflection.

The last time I had spoken to my father had been two weeks before. He had been in the care home, as my mother no longer was able to care for him at home. I'd heard the nurse rolling the portable phone to his private room, where he'd sat in his armchair, watching television.

"Hello, Dad. It's Willy. How are you today?"

"I'm good. Thank you, William. I enjoyed our lunch together earlier."

"Lunch together? Dad, I am calling from Australia."

"Don't be so bloody silly. You were here with me earlier."

"That wasn't me, Dad. I am ten thousand miles away in Sydney."

"Anyway, Son, whatever you say. I'm busy now, and I have to go."

I'd heard cricket on in the background; it had sounded as if someone had just hit a six. He'd put the phone down on me.

That was the last time I spoke with my father.

Although some might have found that sad, I found it the opposite. I found it quite amusing. That was my dad, still a version of his former self. He always was busy and had to go. Busy doing what exactly? Watching television?

Anyhow, he never had even liked cricket anyway. To me, that made it doubly amusing.

I was back home now for the funeral of my father, Walter Baxter Beattie.

The service was at Saint John's in Shaw Mills. It was a quiet little church atop the dale, where, over the years, we had been to many services of remembrance, christenings, and weddings—happy times for the most part. This was my first funeral there—and hopefully my last, but I was not sure that was a realistic hope.

My ex-wife turned up with my son to pay her respects, but that did not really help, as there was clearly no reconciliation in sight, as I had once hoped.

Our former next-door neighbors, whom we called Auntie and Uncle, turned up with my cousin Julie, who was drunk and asleep in the car. I looked at my watch; it was 10:30 a.m.

My uncle John showed up with his wife, Betty. Uncle John and my father had not been close since John, on his return from Beirut, accused my father of fraternizing with his wife. Dad was only trying to say hello and let her know her husband would be home soon, but John's jealousy once again got the better of him.

I smiled at John and Betty. That was about it. I had no time for my father's brother.

I propped my mother up as we walked into the church. I stood on one side, and on the other was my sister. We got the formalities over with and headed down to Hampsthwaite for the wake.

I did not much like wakes either but felt obliged to stay. It was my own father's funeral, as my sister kindly reminded me.

My parents had kept us away from funerals when we were children. My cousin Susan's funeral had been my first. In her prime, in her thirties, she'd been taken by cancer, and I recalled all the sadness and heartbreak on display. I remembered my best friend's mother, Mrs. Agnes Mackay, and her send-off in the Highlands of Scotland—the wind, the rain, the pipers, the dour Scotsmen, and women and children looking on, stoic in their remembrance under the weeping skies and with the mountain of Ben Loyal behind.

Well-wishers came over and talked politely about my father, bringing back memories, and asked after my mother, me, and my life down under, managing to avoid the touchy subject of my ex-wife and her appearance for the funeral. She was now gone, and I'd barely had a chance to talk to my son, William.

Dad had grown up in a golden age. His father, my grandfather, had owned a Rolls-Royce dealership in the north of England and then built tanks during World War I. Father had been fascinated with the cars, spent many a day at his father's garage with the mechanics, and built versions of his own at home.

He'd followed in his own father's footsteps, and by the time I'd come on the scene, he'd had two garages of his own for sales, repairs, and service. As he had with his father, I'd spent weekends and holidays at the garage, in my mechanics coveralls.

Dad always had had some project or another in the works, often one going on in our garage at the bottom of the garden. I had been the message runner sent to call him in for dinner or take him a mug of tea, and I also had helped him, passing a spanner, a screwdriver, a spark plug, brake calipers, or some other tool or part to complete what just looked like a giant, impossible puzzle to me. My dad had been able to fix anything, I'd learned as a child.

After an hour of tiptoeing around family and friends not sure what to say to me, I went to find my mother's brother, Uncle Tommy. He was nursing a Liddesdale whisky in the corner alone.

As I sat down beside him, he grabbed the bottle and poured me a glass.

"Is there any ice?" I asked.

He grinned at me with his tooth-missing smile. One of his teeth had been knocked out in a fight with a fellow sailor many years ago. He had never bothered to replace it. I'd always thought he looked meaner with the missing tooth, and maybe he wore it like a badge of honor.

"Och, I forgot. On the rocks nowadays, eh?" he said, referring to my international-traveler status, mocking me as only Uncle Tommy could.

"Just the way I prefer it, Uncle Tom—that's all," I said, smiling right back at him.

He went to the bar to get some ice.

Uncle Tommy was one of my favorite uncles. Although he was sometimes a hothead and had been a bit of a fighter in his day, he was a former Mariner and always had a great tale to tell, and he knew I always enjoyed a good story.

I had worked out over time that there were plenty of family secrets and things we did not talk about on both sides of the family.

I discovered that as a young man, prior to World War II, my father married for the first time. His first wife was one of the biggest mysteries. She was twice his age and wealthy, and upon my father's return from the war, she replaced him and hooked up with an Italian prisoner of war.

I did not know about my father's first marriage until my uncle John blurted it out one day. I did not know that my mother and father were not really married while I was growing up, despite the wedding picture taken in the back of some fancy car way back then. I did not know that at some time when I was in my teens, they eventually did get married in secret.

Like my grandfather, my own son, and me, Dad was in the army. He was in the Royal Electrical and Mechanical Engineers, was at the Normandy landings, and returned home after five long years' separation but with the benefit of a generous monthly allowance from his now estranged wife.

With plenty of disposable income, he hung around Europe for a while with his pal Jules Constantine, the son of a wealthy Greek shipping magnate, driving around in his SS Jaguar 100 ERB 290. Its license plate is etched in my memory.

My father was having a time similar to my time in Sydney. He was also between marriages and making the most of it.

He had a good run in his time.

I had no complaints about the way he had lived his life, and I thought to myself, *Nor should he.* I was sure he was content with his life and all his experiences, certainly more than most.

I did not know until after his passing that my grandfather on my mother's side was in a Glasgow pipe band and wore steel-toed boots and had his pipe laced with lead.

I did not know about my father's parents' tragic demise.

But I had learned that all secrets had a habit of coming out, especially with the passing of time.

Apart from his memory and his wise words and teachings, my father had not left us much at all, just some trinkets from his past, the war, his life, a couple of sketchbooks, old car manuals, an oil painting of Scottish poet Robbie Burns, a watercolor of a hazy castle above a waterfall, and some old photographs, pictures of various racing cars of the era, including one of a blue Riley 9 with its number 21 racing badge on the doors.

He'd always lived in the now, and I put that down to his experiences during the war, when he never knew his chance of survival for the next hour or twenty-four, never mind the next year or years to come. My dad had lived in the moment.

Maybe that was it, or perhaps there was more to it than that.

Among the items bestowed to me, he had left me his collection of old color prints of twelve historic planes of the golden age of aviation, from the initial flights of the Wright brothers to the quick evolution of flight through World War I, the 1920s and '30s, and into World War II. The prints had adorned the walls of my father's study for years, and I had admired them from as early as I could remember.

Each colorful print showed a flight machine, including its year of service, manufacturer, horsepower, engine, maximum speed, ceiling altitude, and armaments. One of the prints was of the 1907–1909 Wright Flyer. Another was of a 1917 Sopwith Camel, familiar with its red, blue, and white of the Royal Air Force. Another image was of a 1913 Gordon Bennett.

But center stage was a biwinged plane, a world-famous Gipsy Moth, a de Havilland DH.60. It had room for the pilot plus one. It was twenty-three feet in length and had a wingspan of thirty feet. It weighed 920 pounds unladen. Its four-cylinder 100-horsepower piston engine got it to a top speed of 102 miles per hour, and it had a ceiling altitude of 14,500 feet and a rate of climb of 500 feet per minute.

According to the print, this plane's name was *Jason*, and he was a handsome young craft for his time. Built in 1925 and dressed in a British racing green, *Jason* had his name autographed on the engine panel, behind the single propeller. The wings and tail were pale gray, and on the fuselage was his call sign for all to see: G-AAAH.

Jason was a thing of beauty, and I knew the photo was my father's favorite in his collection.

Uncle Tommy returned with a pint glass full of ice and a spoon. The whole on-the-rocks thing was still a foreign phenomenon in England, especially in the north and especially in Yorkshire. The old men would look on mystified as they drank their whisky neat, with no ice and maybe a splash of water.

I spooned three cubes into my Liddesdale.

"To yer father!" Tommy toasted.

"Aye, to Dad!"

We clinked our glasses and fell silent for a moment in our memories.

"He was a cracking fella, yer father."

"Aye, I know."

"A wise man. He'd been around."

"That he had."

We raised our glasses again.

My father's boxes of trinkets were in the closet at the back of his study. In addition to the plane prints, there were photographs of his beloved SS Jaguar 100, prints of race cars and Le Mans, and various owner manuals of the myriad of cars my father had owned at one point or another. Cars had been his life. He had inherited that love from his father, my grandfather, whom I had never met, as he was gone long before I arrived.

The ERB 290 was built on January 20, 1938, and was the supercar of its day. After World War II was over, my father purchased it and converted the former race car from black to cream with brown leather upholstery, and its new two-and-a-half-liter engine powered it from zero to sixty miles per hour in less than nine seconds and gave it a top speed of 101 miles per hour—a significant performance for its time.

Dad was used to fast cars; he had grown up with them. Sometimes he broke them, fixed them, bought them, sold them, and raced them.

Dad toured the Jaguar around Europe with his friend Jules.

In the closet was a journal of his adventures, including photographs of him and Jules in Paris, Nice, Menton, Monte

Carlo, and Juan-les-Pins, France; Pisa, Portofino, Rome, Naples, and Palermo, Italy; and Barcelona, Spain. The locations were all neatly documented on the back of the photographs, in my father's distinctive scroll of handwriting.

There was a picture of Dad with a girl. She was playing the maracas and showing far more midriff than I imagined was socially acceptable back in those days.

In another box was a trove of World War II memorabilia, including a black leather-bound copy of *Mein Kampf*, with its chilling title and author etched into the leather in gold leaf. There were an array of German Nazi medals, insignia from the SS, and an Iron Cross. I wondered about the circumstances in which my father had managed to gather those prized possessions from the Germans and if the Germans had been alive or dead when he did so.

There were a pair of field binoculars and, carefully folded up, a set of my father's field maps issued to guide the soldiers from Normandy to Germany on their campaign of liberation.

There was an old chess set dated from 1868, and another travel chess set in a small wooden box had my father's name branded into the wood. I could imagine Dad and Jules sitting in the depths of the troop ship on their way back from their stint in Iceland, betting their way through the long, damp, dark journey and escaping from their boredom amid the drone of the engines reverberating throughout the ship.

Then there was a picture of a fetching woman in what looked like a Royal Air Force uniform. She appeared again in a photo with my father in one of his Savile Row suits.

"He left me his old plane prints, yer know," I said.

Uncle Tommy looked at me, giving me his Uncle Tommy look.

"What's the history there? I never really understood," I said.

"What do yer mean?"

"Well, he was in the army and into cars but never really talked about airplanes apart from the ones in his office."

Tommy took a long sip—giving himself time to think, I suspected. "Och, it's a long story, Willy." That was Mitchell code for "Not now" or even "Not ever."

"What do yer mean?" A long story meant there was indeed a story. "What is the story?"

Theatrically and comically, he looked around as if to make sure no one else was listening.

"Don't worry, Tommy; he's dead." I was a bit callous in my prompt, but Tommy had been around a bit too and was not too worried about airs and graces.

"Well, son, it's like this. Yer dad would want yer to know, and that's maybe why he gave yer them old planes."

I knew this was going to be good. Another family secret was about to be revealed.

"Did you ever meet yer aunt Nikki?"

I thought for a moment. "Yes, I think so. I vaguely remember her." I cast my mind back. "We went to her house once when I was a kid, with Dad." I remembered that it had felt like a hunting lodge, with heads of lions and elk and foxes, and I remembered a tiger skin on the floor in front of the fire. "Somewhere down south, I think?"

I delved into my memory bank and recalled the quaint old stone longhouse on the corner, in a village somewhere. The impeccable and eclectic yet eccentric furnishings.

I remembered the back garden. Aunt Nikki's maid had prepared afternoon tea in the late-summer sunshine. I recalled the birds, the bees, and the scent of the flowers. I remembered the tension between my father and my aunt as they wrangled over the Earl Grey or the Darjeeling and the sparks of an argument debating the origins of each. The tea itself, in individually packaged bags of silk, looked both exotic and expensive.

It was clear from their looks and demeanor that they were siblings. There was clearly something between the two of them, and I never had understood why, but I had never really thought about it too much.

Now apparently widowed, Aunt Nikki had clearly done all right for herself, marrying above her rank to a distinguished officer of the RAF Bomber Command who was retired on his pension. They traveled the world, picking mementos from around the globe, many of which adorned her home as if it were a museum.

"That was the last time I saw Aunt Nikki," I said.

Tommy looked at me and nodded with a smile. "She was a character all right for sure," he said, taking a sip of his whisky.

I was glad for this distraction from the wake and all the sadness, memories, and sympathy.

"Yer aunt Nikki was a pilot, yer know," he said as I listened. "And a bloody good one at that, as was her best friend."

"Okay." I recalled the photograph of the woman in dad's secret chest.

"They went to the Boulevard School in Hull together."

"And?"

"Then university in Sheffield."

"What? Dad did?"

"No, no, Nikki and Johnnie. Yer Dad would visit for sure."

"Okay." This was arduous work, but by nature, I knew it was going to be big.

"You see, that's when yer dad fell in love for the first time."

"What? Yer mean that old spinster he married?"

He shot a look at me. I had seen a similar look on Tommy's face before. My mother described it as the *Tommy head*. "No, not that bloody woman," he snapped, and he shook his head, took a sip of whisky, lit up one of his Player's Navy Cut cigarettes, and threw the packet to my side of the table.

I looked at its distinctive white and blue and the emblem of the old sailor on the front.

"I didn'ay even know you knew about her," he said. His annoyance had passed. "Yer dad wasn't in love with her. I was talking about his first love. I was talking about a real love."

I saw the reaction and recognized the nerve I had obviously hit. Uncle John, the now openly bitter and jealous brother of my father, had shared the secret of my father's first wife, named Esme apparently, but that was all I knew. That secret was well locked away in the depths of the family archives.

"So Dad was in love?"

"Aye, this one was the One."

"Who? Johnnie?" I asked, dumbfounded and confused.

He nodded his confirmation, taking another sip of his whisky.

"My father was in love with a bloke?" I asked in disbelief.

"No, no, yer silly bugger. Johnnie was a girl. A proper woman, a good old Yorkshire lass." He laughed at my confusion and took a few moments for the giggles to subside.

I sat there annoyed that the joke was on me. Uncle Tommy knew I had a short fuse and also had been a bit of a fighter in my time. We both had a recognized respect for each other as two former fighters. Tommy had retired from the pursuit much longer ago than I had myself.

"Well, what happened, Tommy?" I was eager to get to the point.

"You promise not to tell yer mother?" He added suspense to the story.

"Another secret of the Mitchell family?" I smiled sarcastically, getting my revenge for his earlier joke on me. I actually resented all the mystery and secrets and, therefore, Uncle Tommy, who, by implication, was part of that complex web.

On the day of my father's funeral, Uncle Tommy told me the story: at school, my father had fallen in love with my aunt Nikki's best friend; he had kept in touch with her as Nikki and his love went to university together, then went to London, and started flying; over time, they had drifted apart; and she had gotten married, breaking my father's heart.

"Between them, they became the first women in aviation in the land."

"Really?"

"Pioneers, Willy. One record after another and another."

I was suitably impressed. I never had known, but then again, I did not know many of the stories of our family's past. I knew about Jock Half Lugs, my great-grandfather, and his horse in the Grand National and now about my aunt, a pioneering aviator.

"I had no idea. Why didn't he ever mention it?"

He did not answer. According to Uncle Tommy, Nikki and her friend were the first British women to be licensed ground crew; get flying certificates; and then, shortly afterward, become full-blown pilots. That was a time of pioneering in aviation, especially for women. They had the opportunity to progress, take the lead, and soar like never before.

"The very first, Willy. With flying colors—literally. The plane pictures were a present from yer father's first love. That's probably why he never talked about it too much."

I took a sip of my whisky, giving myself a moment to pause and think. "So what happened? Where is she now?"

It was Uncle Tommy's turn to take a sip and some time to think.

I could tell this was uncomfortable for him. "I saw the framed picture of another woman in Dad's things. There were other loose snaps of her. A good-looking woman with a pilot's skullcap and goggles on her head. Was that Johnnie?"

"That'll be her, Willy." He had sadness in his face. "A very interesting woman. Very sad."

"Who? Aunt Nikki?"

He shook his head. "No, the whole bloody story."

I changed direction and listened patiently and attentively as he told me the tale of my aunt Nikki's part in the golden age of aviation and of the heroes, the Wright brothers, Lindbergh, Alcock and Brown, William "Billy" Mitchell, the Red Baron, and the women, including an American named Amelia Earhart and a British woman, a Yorkshire rose, named Amy Johnson.

"Billy Mitchell? Was he a relative?" I looked over at my own uncle Billy, who was across the room, talking to my mother.

"Aye, lad, he was a cousin of sorts, an American cousin from across the pond. But ultimately, Willy, we all go back to the same place." He grinned.

I was not sure if that meant he was a relation or not, apart from the name.

"There are plenty of us Mitchells out there, you know, Willy."

I thought of my own adoption of my maternal family's name. I had grown up as a Mitchell Beattie but had dropped the Beattie at the start of my writing career. Willy Mitchell was much easier to remember than William Baxter Mitchell Beattie. At least that was what I had thought at the time. Now, with the passing of my father, I sort of regretted that decision.

Tommy went on to talk about Amelia Earhart and her adventures and achievements. I knew of her, of course; she was famous, a female pioneer of aviation, the original aviatrix. He went on to explain her mysterious disappearance in the central Pacific while she was trying the first circumnavigation, close to a far-off place called Howland Island.

"They never did find the plane wreck or her body, yer know. Disappeared from the face of the earth."

As Tommy talked, I remembered an awkward moment when I'd spotted a picture on the wall at my aunt's house of my father and two women. One obviously was Nikki. I had asked if the other woman was another aunt of mine in the picture. My father and my aunt had looked away quickly, moved the subject on, and gotten us out of the house into the garden. In hindsight, I realized they'd done it to avoid any more potentially awkward questions.

"And what about Dad's girlfriend?" I got Tommy back on track. I used the term *girlfriend* deliberately and provocatively and smiled as I asked.

"Och, it all ended in tragedy, Willy. A great tragedy. Yer know, life is a bloody tragedy, Willy."

"What the hell happened?"

He explained she had moved to London, pursued her aviation career, and eventually lost touch with my father. "Yer see, we didn't have email, mobile phones, or texting back then, Willy; it was all much more analog in them days. They would still exchange notes now and then. I remember yer dad the day he received the note telling him she was to be married. Some guy called Morrison or Mollison—I cannay quite remember now." He looked at me and shrugged in a "That's life" kind of way. "That's when he married. His first marriage before yer mother." Tommy nodded.

"So that was that then? Did yer meet her?"

"Who?"

"Either of them."

He looked away, and I sensed the pain again.

"What is it? What is it you're not telling me, Uncle Tommy?"

"Look, Willy, it's a long story. Maybe for another day." It was a statement, not a question. "Yer see, son, life was different back in them days. Yer father made some tough choices. Life was different back then. Yer aunt Nikki and her friend were strong; they knew how to stand up on their own two feet and get things done, just like yer grandma." It was a great diversion from my wily old uncle Tom.

I thought of my grandma Maggie Mitchell, who had been fiercely independent, had a bottle of stout and a nip of whisky each day, and lived to the grand old age of 101. I raised my glass. "To Maggie Mitchell!"

We both remembered her with admiration, one as a son and one as a grandson. "To Maggie!"

The bar was emptying, the wake was coming to an end, and the stream of well-wishers were leaving and passing on their best. My mother caught my attention. She was sitting in the corner alone, staring blankly into space. I felt guilty for not paying her my full attention on that day, of all days.

"Hey, Tommy." I nodded over to my mum.

"I'd better go." He smiled and nodded.

"Thanks for taking my mind off things."

"No worries, Willy." He reminded me of his own worldly adventures, including the land down under.

I smiled back at him. "What ever happened to Aunt Nikki?"

He shrugged. "Don't know. She disappeared into thin air. Haven't heard sight nor sound for what must be thirty years. Thought she might have been here today."

"And my father's love?"

He just shrugged again and raised the palms of his hands like an elementary pupil saying, "It wasn't me."

"And the spinster?"

The moment was over. We hugged and said our goodbyes.

"Until next time." I knew there were further installments to this story, and I also wanted to learn more about my father's first wife, whom he married despite apparently being in love with someone else.

A week later, I received a note from Uncle Tommy. It was a brief note with little explanation, although it did not need one.

> Willy,
>
> I heard from your aunt Nikki the day I got back home after your dad's funeral. She had read the obituary in the *Yorkshire Post*. She wanted me to pass on her condolences to the family. Go see her. She would like that. She has a story to tell!
>
> > Nikki Beattie-Baxter
> > Back Ends
> > Chipping Camden
> > Gloucestershire
> > GL55 6AB
>
> Her number is (01451) 810990.
> Look forward to reading the next book!
> Till next time.
>
> Uncle Tom

I read the note, made a cup of tea, and made plans. I would call her.

Flight

Up in the clouds I yearn to be,
the birds, the bees, just you and me.
Looking down on field and pasture
on our way to our next adventure.

Flying above high in the sky,
not a care or a question why.
Go far enough, and we will see the sea,
and with a fair wind, we will be back for tea.

—Nikki Beattie, 1912

I

GOLDEN GIRL

May 24, 1930
Darwin, Northern Territory, Australia

NIKKI STOOD ON THE AIRFIELD. She was waiting for her best friend, Amy, to arrive. Amy was the first female pilot to fly solo from England to Australia.

Nikki glanced over at the throng of reporters. As one of the few licensed female pilots herself, she knew how it was to be the object of attention and understood the associated pressure to succeed. She and Amy had been on a long journey together since childhood. They'd met at the Boulevard School in Kingston, and their friendship had flourished and sustained. She was proud of Amy. The epic flight that was about to end in triumph marked just the latest feat in Amy's book of accomplishments in the world of aviation.

It was late May and, thankfully, cooler; the wet, humid season was already past. Still, beads of sweat formed at her hairline. She ran her right hand over her auburn hair, which was tied up in a bun and topped with a forage cap. A slight smile lit up her face as she considered how she looked—almost like a man dressed in her khakis, trousers, military-style shirt, and pair of suede boots. She was dressed for the country she was in, Australia; for the climate; and also for the aviation world.

She almost laughed. Nobody who got close could have mistaken her gender—she was tall and slender, with high cheekbones and bright steel-blue eyes.

Breaking into that world was hard and even more difficult as a woman. Her dress code was deliberate and designed to counteract the resistances she had seen that would potentially block her from the man's world she desperately wanted to be part of. Besides, her dress was also practical for the lifestyle she led.

She walked away from the crowds gathered to watch Amy land. Looking up to the skies, she grabbed her water flask, took a long gulp, dampened her handkerchief, and wiped her face in the early morning heat.

After university, Nikki and Amy had both moved to London for work and opportunity. Her friend's father had secured them both secretarial jobs at a reputable law firm in the city with William Charles Crocker. As she stood there on the airfield, waiting, she had time to reflect.

London was worlds apart from where they had come from. The first half of the Roaring Twenties had been a time for celebration and jubilation after the war, a time of hedonism. Women had experienced a new kind of freedom and newfound independence. London was full of temptation, parties, nightclubs, and cocktail bars.

They'd been two no-nonsense, straight-talking Yorkshire girls having fun in the capital and gaining the attention of many and certainly not just for their looks. They'd had so much fun together in those days, discovering the world beyond Yorkshire, and nowadays, they were discovering the world beyond the shores of Old Blighty. *Who would have imagined?* she thought to herself.

But in the late 1920s had come the bust. Poverty was spreading through the lower classes, and unemployment was rising. It was a decade of opposites, and they were grateful to be on the boom side of the bust.

They'd joined the London Aeroplane Club, and under the tutelage of Captain Valentine Baker, they'd found their wings.

First, they'd obtained their ground engineer's licenses. The pride she'd felt then resurfaced as she continued to scan the sky for Amy's plane. She and her best friend had been the first British women to receive such a license. Then they both had passed their aviator exams and gotten their pilot's licenses—numbers 1979 and 1980—becoming known in the London social circles as the Flying Foxtrots.

They had gone to the same school, the Boulevard School in the East Riding of Yorkshire, and despite Nikki's family's relocation to the West Riding, they had been together again at Sheffield University, studying Latin, French, and economics.

Although they hadn't been in the engineering class, they had gate-crashed, much to the disagreement of the professor at the time. They'd been the first women to ever do so, determined to carve their own path and buck the status quo of the era.

Nikki had been through a torrid time: first her mother's illness; then her father's departure; and then, tragically, her mother's passing. Her best friend and soul mate had been there for her throughout, just as Nikki would be there for her. That was why she was in Darwin that day, on the other side of the world.

Nikki had arrived at the airfield first thing that morning, at six thirty local time, as the sun was rising in the Northern Territory skies. Amy, at the controls of her Gipsy Moth, *Jason*, had set off from Timor at around the same time, and Nikki was going to be there for her friend, or as close as she could be, through the final leg of this world first. Amy was the first woman to fly solo from England to Australia—eleven thousand miles and nineteen days of solo flight.

From London to Istanbul was plain sailing, but the next leg across the Taurus Mountains was more challenging.

The mountains were at an elevation of 11,800 feet, and the Gipsy Moth, fully laden, could only get up to just more than ten thousand. Ingeniously, through the fog, Amy spotted the Baghdad Railway Line and followed that route, at a lower elevation, all the way to her next stop: Aleppo, Syria.

In the next stage, she was on her way to Baghdad, and almost there, she ran into a sandstorm that was so severe it forced her to land and lie low for three hours until it passed. She arrived in Baghdad safely a few hours later.

In Baghdad, Imperial Airways engineers completed some needed repairs and maintenance on *Jason*.

On to Karachi the following day, Amy was ahead of Australian aviation pioneer Bert Hinkler's world record by two days. The news excited Amy's family, friends, and fans. To be the first woman to achieve the feat but to beat the time of a man too? Nikki was thrilled at that prospect.

The press was building up a frenzy, and due to her work at Crocker's law firm, Amy was dubbed the Flying Secretary.

When Amy landed in Allahabad, a whole posse of journalists received her. Maybe her dream was becoming real.

With her pilot's license under her belt for less than a year, the lass from Yorkshire was set to rival the more renowned almost superstar status of American aviatrix Amelia Earhart.

Amy's journey continued from Rangoon on to Singapore and Java and across the Timor Sea.

Nikki knew this last leg was around an eight-hour flight, and Amy had lifted her wheels at six thirty in the morning in Timor, so that would bring her in by probably between three and four o'clock in the afternoon local time, depending on the tailwinds across the Timor.

Nikki anxiously checked her watch; it was 3:10 p.m. She scoured the horizon with her field binoculars, looking across the flat landscape dappled with scrub trees, her anxiety getting the better of her. The crowd happily murmured away, with the buzz of excitement growing in the crowd. She looked out toward the northeast, looking for Amy.

With a couple of false sightings from the crowd, stuttered cheers went up around the airfield. Nikki thought to herself that the entire population of Darwin must have been gathered there that day. She could not believe what a huge thing the flight had become, even on the other side of the world. She wondered if there was the same level of excitement back at home.

Nikki scanned the skies once more. She paused, still, listening intently. For a moment, she thought she could hear the drone of the hundred-horsepower four-cylinder de Havilland beyond the landmass in front of her. She caught her breath and closed her eyes, and after a few more minutes, she did hear it. It was *Jason*!

At precisely 3:18 p.m., she checked her watch and jumped into the air. "She's here! She made it! She's on her way!"

The crowd looked over, trying to comprehend Nikki's screams of delight. They were silent for a moment and then broke out into mass cheers and celebrations as Amy landed the plane. Nikki made her way to the front, determined to be the first to greet her best friend and congratulate her.

The de Havilland pulled up to a stop, the engine turned off and sputtered as it wound down, and the smell of oil fuel and the feel of the heat from the engine were familiar and welcome sensations for Nikki.

Out popped the pilot from the cockpit, complete with flying jacket and leather cap. Amy pulled her flying goggles onto the top of her head and, with a big smile and bright eyes, stood up in the cockpit with arms aloft, waving to the crowd amid the rapturous cheers. A brass band started playing traditional ceremonial celebrations.

As Amy stepped down out of the cockpit, Nikki rushed up and embraced her childhood friend.

"Oh my God, you made it! I am so bloody proud of you," Nikki said. "How was it?"

Amid all the celebrations around them, Amy related that when she'd sighted Melville Island, she'd known she had made it. She had stood up midflight and cheered to herself, victorious. She had cried and laughed simultaneously at the relief, the excitement, and the achievement and then picked up on Point Charles Lighthouse and turned toward Port Darwin and her goal.

"Thanks for being here, Nikki. It's so lovely to see your face and your smile."

Amy captured Nikki in that moment. Despite all the noise around them, it was as if they were the only two in the field. Amy stroked her face with the back of her fingers, looked into her eyes, and smiled that Amy smile. Nikki knew how much pressure she was under and hoped her friend would not get overwhelmed with all the attention.

Amy was quickly engulfed and whisked away to the dignitaries, the celebrations, and the formalities. Nikki knew they would have time to catch up later but also knew that just the next morning, Amy would be heading out of Darwin again to continue her journey on to Brisbane and then Sydney. Nikki would be aboard one of the three accompanying planes on those final two legs of the journey.

The rest of the day and evening passed in a blur. Nikki beamed with pride as telegrams streamed in from around the world. King George V sent a telegram from Buckingham Palace to the governor general of Australia and then on to the reception that evening in Darwin in honor of Miss Amy Johnson, aviatrix.

> The queen and I are thankful and delighted to know of Miss Johnson's safe arrival in Australia and heartily congratulate her upon her wonderful and courageous achievement.
>
> *George RI*

There were many telegrams and good wishes from all around the world, so much so that the Commonwealth government assigned a team of expert stenographers to cope with the volume—more than five hundred congratulatory messages.

All around the world, the press engaged with her pursuits, and front-page stories were rife. One said,

> A golden-haired English girl dropped out of the sky in Darwin, Australia, this afternoon, completing an achievement unprecedented in aviation history.
>
> Amy Johnson, who prefers to be known as Johnnie, flew alone in her tiny Moth plane all the way from England to Australia, boldly facing a thousand perils and winning out in the face of seemingly unbeatable obstacles.

The article went on to explain how demanding the flight was, including her landing in the desert near Baghdad after running into the sandstorm and being scared witless in Timor when she landed at night and was greeted by "a lot of black men who ran out from their little huts near the shore with knives, swords, and spears."

The mayor of Darwin, that night at the banquet, joked, "Every man in the world will be proposing to you." It was a humorous but potentially realistic warning. At the dinner, Amy revealed her preferred nickname of Johnnie to put off some of the potential suitors.

Sitting next to her best friend, Nikki saw Amy smile and brush off the comment in her typical no-nonsense Yorkshire way. She would not let anyone slow her down, let alone a male of the species. That would be too much of a distraction. Besides, she already had found her love a long way from there a long time ago.

Amy wore a pretty silver necklace with a silver-and-gold globe pendant. Nikki had noticed earlier that as Amy pulled up at the airfield, Amy kissed the globe as if it were a rosary or a good-luck charm. Nikki was sure there was a story there; she had never seen the necklace before.

For her world record, Amy Johnson received much praise and recognition and many awards, including a number-one civil pilot's license under Australia's Air Navigation Regulations, the Harmon Trophy, and Commander of the Most Excellent Order of the British Empire (CBE) at the king's birthday honors.

Nikki knew from the newspapers about the check for £10,000 that was on its way; Amy did not. Her father had signed an exclusive deal with the *Daily Mail* without Amy's knowledge. Nikki knew she would not be happy about that, although the money would no doubt come in useful, more than covering her father's investment in the trip.

The aviatrix from Yorkshire had arrived.

2

GOD SAVE THE KING

September 7, 1914
Boulevard School, Kingston upon Hull,
East Riding of Yorkshire, England

AS NIKKI SAT IN THE backseat of her father's Rolls-Royce, she knew her life was about to change, as she was starting at her new school: the Boulevard School in Kingston upon Hull. However, she had not contemplated a war breaking out in Europe. The war had already changed the world forever. The unthinkable had occurred just a couple of months earlier, when the summer had ushered in violence that had spooled out of control, and now the world seemed poised to plunge into a prolonged state of hell.

Yet the war seemed far away at the moment.

The rear window on her side of the car was open. She could feel the wind in her hair as they made their way from Kirk Ella to her first day at school. The school welcomed the families and the children with a church service at Saint Matthew's Church, which was right next to the school. Then they went into the reception and the classes beyond.

Starting at a new school was always difficult, but at least Nikki knew people at the Boulevard, and she also had her two brothers in tow, which she figured would help. She looked over at them in their new school uniforms—caps, blazers, and ties—and thought how cute they looked. They were not nervous, as Nikki was, or at least they didn't show any signs.

Nikki's father drove them in his Rolls-Royce, the latest 1914 version, which had thirty horsepower and six cylinders, with their mother at his side. Nikki wished the car could go just a little faster, but she loved the smell of the fuel, the oil, the manifold, and the exhaust fumes. She felt like a warrior as they passed down the tree-lined Boulevard Street, with its plain brick houses on either side, and onto Malm Street, to the daunting big redbrick building the size of a battleship, their new school. It was a far cry from their little school in Skelton.

Nikki kept a close eye on the news and the developments in Europe. The war not only fascinated her but took her mind away from the challenges in her own life.

Nikki gazed out the passenger-side window at the lush green scenery all around them, and she felt a pang of sadness and fear for all the men who were heading off to fight in the war.

That summer, the whole of Europe had been on tenterhooks. Archduke Franz Ferdinand and his wife, Sophie, had been assassinated in Bosnia, and the backlash had caused a ripple effect across Europe. At the end of July, Austria-Hungary had declared war on Serbia, and the tenuous peace between Europe's great powers had collapsed. Within a week, Russia, Belgium, France, and Great Britain all had lined up against Austria-Hungary and Germany. World War I had begun, and the killing had already started.

Back in Skelton, before they'd left, they'd celebrated local heroes Frank and Ernest Wild's departure on polar explorer Shackleton's *Endurance* to conquer Antarctica from one side to the other. At the annual summer fair, the Wild family and local dignitaries had paid tribute to Shackleton's right-hand man, Frank Wild, and the Imperial Expedition, which would win back the explorers crown' for the empire. A number of the explorers had connections to her new home, the city of Hull. Shackleton's latest expedition was a big thing.

Her father was a Rolls-Royce dealer in the northeast corner of England—everything south of Newcastle and down as far as Sheffield. He was well connected, as the only people who could afford those vehicles were the wealthy: the landowners, mill owners, industrialists, and wealthy fish merchants of Hull.

Daddy had sold a couple of cars to the mayor, William Hodge, and then been introduced to various local businessmen, including John Johnson of Andrew Johnson Knudtzon Company. That was where Nikki had first met Amy. As she sat in the back of the Rolls, she remembered the scene just six weeks earlier.

Her father slowed the car down as he steered up the final stretch leading to the school. Nikki fought back an onset of nerves, but she knew Amy would be there, and that comfort calmed her down. She recalled the first time they had met. Her father had been visiting Amy's dad on business.

Their fathers had sat in the study at the Johnsons' house, doing business. Amy and her sisters had greeted Nikki at the front door as they arrived. Nikki's brothers, Walter and John, had remained by Nikki's side as Amy, under the chaperone of Mrs. Johnson, escorted them to the back garden of the house. Nikki and Amy had gotten on famously well. Amy was a welcome female friend. Nikki often tired of her boisterous brothers, and Ms. Boswell, their nanny, was her only other female relief. Nikki and Amy had hit it off together at once, as, apparently, had their fathers, with Mr. Johnson signing up for two brand-spanking-new Rolls-Royces. Nikki's father had been incredibly pleased during the journey back home to Skelton. She smiled at the memory of the happy car ride home. Not all car rides or family times together were the happiest.

Amy and Nikki both had been born in 1903, the year of the Wright brothers' maiden flight. They looked similar, with the same height and hair color; liked the same things; and both had a dream to one day fly.

When Nikki's dad had announced they were moving to Hull in order for him to set up a new car dealership, she'd been thrilled, thinking rightly that the move would mean she could spend more time with Amy. She knew the move would also make Walter happy; she could see it in his eyes as the announcement was made.

Apparently, per school tradition, at the start of the term, the first order of the day was a church service, and as her father parked the car, with all its admirers, they stood outside the church's front doors, patiently waiting for their father. Dressed in their new all-green uniforms, the boys, with their ties and flat caps, and Nikki, with a bow and a straw boater, politely smiled and said good morning to the arrivals as they filled Saint Matthew's Church.

The Johnsons pulled up in their own brand-new Rolls-Royce courtesy of her father and parked it behind Nikki's father's, doubling the admiration. Amy jumped out and skipped toward Nikki and her brothers.

"What a fine day for a ride." Amy beamed at her new school friends, giving Nikki a big hug. "It's so nice to have you here. Welcome to Saint Matthew's and the Boulevard." She dragged Nikki by the hand, and the boys and Amy's sisters followed as they found their way to the front of the church and the allocated seating for the families of the richest and most influential families of the school. The Beatties were honored thanks to Mr. Johnson's lobbying to be included as such.

The congregation finally took their seats. Amy's grandparents and both girls' parents had arrived. Grandfather wore his livery collar of office as the mayor of the city, their fathers wore three-piece suits, and both mothers wore carefully selected haute couture of the day. Both were beautiful and demure, but Nikki's mother was quiet and a little shy, while Amy's mother was quite the opposite. Mrs. Johnson was tall and slender, and her dark hair framed a face of beauty with warm dark brown eyes and naturally olive skin. She wore little makeup—she did not need to wear any.

She was also called Amy, Amy Hodge, the granddaughter of the honorable mayor.

Nikki and Amy held hands. The church was full to the brim.

The vicar said his introductions, his welcomes to the church and the school, and his blessings for the world and for peace to soon prevail. The finale was a hymn, a song of unity, an anthem for coming victory.

The congregation stood up and sang, children, parents, grandparents, and all.

> God save our gracious king!
> Long live our noble king!
> God save the king!
> Send him victorious,
> happy, and glorious,
> long to reign over us.
> God save the king!

Nikki felt the hairs on the back of her neck stand up. It was the first time she had ever experienced this. It was exhilarating and exciting. With a cause, a purpose, together they were united in the pursuit of victory.

Still holding her hand throughout, she turned to Amy and smiled. Amy looked her in the eye and smiled back. Nikki liked Amy. They were like two peas from the same pod.

At the end of the service, the congregation made their way out of the church, dispersing from whence they'd come. The Beatties and the Johnsons took a few more moments to exchange pleasantries. The mayor left, and Nikki's mother went to sit in the car while Nikki's father continued laughing and schmoozing with his client and his wife, Mrs. Johnson.

Nikki thought how nice it was that their parents seemed to get on so well together.

If the war would soon end, all would be right with the world. The prevailing wisdom held that the conflict would end by Christmas, although Nikki doubted it would happen that way.

The Boulevard

The move from Skelton was oh so hard;
we ended up at the Boulevard.
Its big red brick and playing yard—
it seemed we had not traveled too far.

Then we met Betty, Wills, and Amy.
I thought then, *Well, just maybe*
Walter, John, my family, and I
might just give this place a try.

The war had started with great aplomb;
the troops be home before the next bomb.
Life is good at Lair Close.
I miss my father and my mother the most.

Once the enemy is defeated,
our previous life will be repeated.
Mother will return to the norm;
Father will return from the gathering storm.

—Nikki Beattie, circa 1915

Nikki stabbed another piece of her Cumberland sausage with her fork, lifted the morsel to her mouth, and slowly ate with all the pleasure her favorite meal had to offer. Lost in thought, she reflected on how bad the war seemed to be getting, and it was only January, just five months after hostilities had broken out the previous July. All in all, though, she and her brothers were living good, comfortable lives, and she was grateful for that.

They were settling in well in their new home in Kirk Ella and at school. Although they faced strict, harsh teachers and lots of repetitive learning, they had the Johnsons as friends, and the children were all friendly. On weekends, they would take turns visiting each other's house, under the care of the hired help, the family nannies.

Nikki and the boys liked their nanny, Miss Boswell. She was young, fun, and adventurous and was happiest when the children were having fun, and she often joined in their games. Miss Esme Boswell was from London and taught them Cockney rhyming slang and old Pearly songs, such as "Roll Out the Barrel," having a right proper royal knees-up.

She would organize puppet shows, and the children especially liked Punch and Judy. Each time they had sausages for supper, it would make them all giggle at the dinner table.

Miss Boswell was tall and slim, with chestnut-brown hair and mahogany-brown eyes, and was warm and kind. She looked as demure as any of the mothers at the church, including Mrs. Johnson, but Nikki knew that her Londoner accent would get in the way of her progress up the social scale. She knew that even at the age of eleven, nearly twelve. It was a shame, she thought. Maybe she could help that in some way. She liked Miss Boswell, and she would work on it.

Miss Boswell would put on parlor games, and hide-and-seek, dress-up pantomime, and imaginary games filled their days, weekends, and weeks, with the occasional reminder of the war and of the increasing suffering and death toll at the fronts.

"Miss Boswell, I thought the soldier boys would be home by Christmas. Where are they?" asked Walter over supper one evening.

The answer was not authoritative, and she quickly moved on to another subject. The truth was, nobody really knew the answer to that question. Things in Europe were getting much worse than even the might of the British Empire had realized or predicted.

The Johnson and Beattie children often were with each other, either at each other's house or on outings down to the shore. Miss Boswell kept them all entertained, and she seemed to like it too. All the children liked Esmerelda, or Esme, whom they of course always called Miss Boswell to her face.

Nikki especially liked her nanny, and each night, Miss Boswell would dress her hair after her bath, and they would talk. They talked about the weather; the day; school; lessons; boys; and her best friend, Amy, and occasionally, Nikki would pry for insights into her parents.

Both sets of parents were absent. Their mothers were distant in their solitude and place in the world. Amy's father was busy with the family business. As fish merchants, due to the war, they were busier and more challenged than ever. Nikki's father continued to schmooze and sell more Rolls-Royces to those who could afford them and often was away for lengthy periods. He would come back at night, often late, after bedtime, and, subsequently, had little interaction with the children at all. The parents seemed to have little time for the children, and that made Nikki sad. She loved both her parents dearly, and she craved that same level of love in return.

Nikki noticed that desire most in her brothers. They missed their father, and they yearned for more. With Mother absent most of the time in mind more than presence, their rivalry and animosity grew.

"Why can't we see more of Father?" Nikki asked one day.

Miss Boswell just shook her head and tutted.

"You see, I think Walter and John need him more than he realizes," Nikki added, looking for a bite.

"I am sure he is very busy," Miss Boswell said. "Look at this beautiful house, your beautiful school, and your life. You have it very lucky, young lady."

It seemed Miss Boswell was speaking from experience.

Nikki knew she was right. She understood the privileges they enjoyed—and not only the fancy Rolls-Royces and the reserved seating in church. She had seen some of the parts of the city that were far less affluent, where the children played on the streets with no shoes. She also remembered the poor farm workers in Skelton. Although they appeared to be happy, they had little but themselves.

She had also heard some of Miss Boswell's stories of her own childhood growing up in the East End of London. She had referenced street traders, the pearlies, and also Gypsies. Nikki got the general gist and decided not to expand the conversation.

"Do you think Mummy and Daddy love each other?" Nikki asked unexpectedly. It had been a concern of hers for some time now. "Father is hardly ever here, and Mother is here, but we barely see her; she's locked in her room all the time. And even when they are together, they barely talk. Is that what marriage is like, Miss Boswell?"

Miss Boswell shook her head again, and Nikki noticed her cheeks flushing. "I wouldn't know the answer to that, my dear. I have never been married." She turned and gave a shy smile to Nikki. "Besides, young lady, you shouldn't be even asking questions like that. Of course they love each other. They are married, they are your parents, they are churchgoers, and they are mighty fine people," she said, getting right back to her thick London accent.

Nikki had not meant to cross a line, and from the response, she sensed she had. "I'm sorry, Miss Boswell. I just have all these questions in my mind."

"There's nothing wrong with having an inquisitive mind, Nikki—nothing wrong at all. But sometimes there are certain things that are just—well, sometimes some things are just better left unsaid."

Nikki contemplated what that meant and deduced which topics were better left unsaid. Religion was probably out. School and the amount of homework for sure. Challenging the sense of war was maybe out too. Obviously, questions about her parents were off the table.

What about being a freethinker? A free spirit? What about one day adventuring the world, climbing a mountain, or going to Antarctica? What about flying a plane one day?

She sensed that now was not the right time to bring up any of that.

Nikki and Amy had become like sisters. They took every opportunity to be together. Like a release and escape, their friendship was sure to last, hopefully forever, Nikki often thought. She found her time with Amy much more fulfilling than time with her brothers; all they seemed to ever do was build things, break things, and then fix them. Nikki did not understand the logic, if there was any. She loved them both dearly, but clearly, they were different and had different interests.

One Saturday morning, Amy came around to Lair Close, and she and Nikki sat together in the bay window of the Beatties' home in Kirk Ella, looking out onto the lawn, where Walter and John were building their latest contraption: a car made from old milk crates and bicycle parts.

It was clear to see Walter had taken quite a liking to Amy. He would follow them around during playtime in the yard behind the big redbrick school. On weekends, he would occasionally join them to play dress-up. *Peter Pan* was their favorite, when both the girls and the boys could join in.

"Oh, your brother is so cute," Amy said all of a sudden.

Nikki paused for a moment and smiled. "I think he would be very pleased to hear that, Amy."

Amy flushed. "I mean, I like him. He's really kind and considerate." She changed the subject away from Walter like a counterpunch. "Do you like William?" she asked Nikki, and it was her turn to flush.

She was referring to William Sheppard, a boy in their class. He was the son of an army man and had aspirations himself to join one day too.

"He's sweet too," Nikki said. She smiled back at Amy. Both girls' cheeks were back to normal now. "What do you want to be when you grow up?" Nikki asked.

Amy looked out the window at the grounds, the lawn, and the iron gates beyond. "I really couldn't tell you. I think I want to be free like a bird up in the sky."

Nikki knew that both their mothers lived in bird cages. She hoped the same fate didn't await her or her friend. "What about an actress? A historian? An archaeologist? What about a suffragette or an explorer?" Her eyes twinkled as she looked out the window at the two budding engineers building a ramp down a hillock outside.

Like a sudden spark, Amy said, "I know—let's make a flying machine!"

Nikki loved the idea. They were kindred spirits; they both knew what their dreams might be, even if it meant challenging the norms, breaking out of their bindings, and stealing into another world—a man's world.

"That sounds fun. Where shall we go?" Nikki asked.

Then they both shouted out together, "Neverland!" They beamed at each other with admiration and love. They quickly had established themselves as soul mates. They both needed that bond in their lives.

Despite their privileged upbringing, just like Peter Pan, they felt loneliness, as if they were orphans. Amy was Peter Pan, Nikki was Wendy, and Walter and John were the Lost Boys. They needed their own adventures, and if they could not make them happen for real, they would dream them until they came true.

"One day, my darling Nikki, we are going to fly around the world together, conquering distant shores, discovering far-off lands, and making our way in this world."

They held hands and looked out at the lawn. The boys and the sisters played, smiling and dreaming about their future to come.

3

MIDNIGHT SNACK

February 1915
Kirk Ella, Kingston upon Hull, East
Riding of Yorkshire, England

THE WINTER MONTHS HAD COME, and Christmas
and New Year's had gone. It was February and a particularly
cold one at that. The trees were bare, frost was on the
ground, and even the fountain was frozen solid. Nikki was
looking forward to the signs of spring just a few weeks away
and hoped the new season would come soon.

Nikki was quiet and, some said, shy, but once people got
to know her, she was reserved but confident. She always
listened to her father and the teachings of the Yorkshire
way: "Don't engage tongue until you have put your brain
into gear." Nikki embraced that concept wholeheartedly;

it was a mantra she believed in, and at school, she would roll her eyes when her classmates did not abide by the same rules.

Nikki was also observant and possessed more emotional intelligence than a typical girl of twelve. She carefully watched the interactions between humans in the classroom at school, including between the teachers and between girls and boys on the playground. She observed her father's interactions with his clients, the lack of interactions and the behaviors of her mother, and the dynamic between her brothers, one the leader and one the follower.

She also watched closely the fleeting interactions of Mrs. Johnson and of Miss Boswell with her father, and those were the ones that concerned her the most. Perhaps it was female intuition, but she felt suspicious. She knew not of what; nevertheless, it made her uneasy, for what reason she was unsure.

Her mother was detached, and her father was absent most of the time. Even when they were together, they barely spoke. She wondered if they really loved each other or if they were together only for their children's sake.

On the face of it, they were a happy family and had all the material things one could have wished for, but there were dark undercurrents that Nikki had yet to fully compute. She more sensed them than understood their origins. Yet the underlying uneasiness permeated her existence, except when she was with Amy.

Father would have parties around at the house. The children would eat early, and Miss Boswell would take them up to their quarters before the adults arrived. As they listened to bedtime stories, they could hear cars crunching on the gravel of the driveway and music and laughter downstairs till long after bedtime.

The parties always followed a similar pattern, and that particular February evening, the festivities were well underway. Nikki imagined the high rollers. All the men were dressed in suits just like her father, and the women wore pencil cocktail dresses and coiffured hair and jewels. She imagined the band playing in the corner and the dancing of the latest crazes, including the Charleston, which she had mimicked at school with the other girls.

Later that night, Nikki and the boys looked out the window as the party wound down and watched the parade of cars, mostly Rolls-Royces, as they sped from the gravel driveway through the iron gates and down to the road and toward home.

At twelve o'clock, Nikki looked up from her book and ventured down to the pantry below; she could not sleep. All was quiet in the house as she tiptoed toward the kitchen. Glasses and empty bottles were everywhere; the maid would clean up in the morning.

She reached the kitchen and, from the larder, grabbed a slice of bread, a piece of cheddar cheese, and a smidge of Miss Boswell's homemade London chutney. Then she got a glass of milk.

She walked through the house with sandwich and milk in hand and wandered around downstairs, where the party had been just a few hours earlier. The smell of wine and cocktails, the occasional spill on the rugs, and stale cigar smoke lingered in the air.

She noticed a sound from the direction of her father's study and assumed it might be one of the cats. As she peered through the door, which was half ajar, she could see her father with a woman who had dark hair and olive skin. He was on top of her on his sofa. He was breathing heavily, and the woman was moaning slightly, seemingly enjoying whatever he was doing to her.

Nikki froze for a moment in the shadows, out of sight of the pair. The woman looked up. It was dark. She looked from a distance through the crack in the door. Nikki stood and stared for a second that seemed like an eternity and then turned and fled, dropping the milk and the sandwich onto the table on her way. She ran upstairs and back to bed.

She tried to sleep and erase the memory from her mind, regretting leaving her midnight snack on the table, and eventually faded off to sleep as the predawn chorus was just beginning outside.

She imagined one day being free, fulfilling her fantasy: Nikki and her best friend, Amy—just the two of them together.

Life was complicated, and it just got even more so, she thought as she drifted to sleep as the sun rose.

"I want to be free. Free like a bird," she muttered to herself as she fell to sleep.

Much to Nikki's relief, spring had arrived. It was April. Nikki sat in the children's room with Miss Boswell, embroidering a keepsake for Amy. They sat side by side; Nikki wore her favorite Wendy dress, and the nanny wore her usual attire of a dark skirt, double-buttoned bodice, and white scarf. It was not a uniform and never exactly the same but rarely deviated in terms of color or formality. Given how close they were, it was hard sometimes to remember that Miss Boswell was in fact the hired help and not family.

Miss Boswell had taught Nikki the fine arts and crafts expected of the female kind of the day. Nikki found them dull and pointless. She would have much preferred to be doing something fun.

Mother and Father were away in London; they had been summoned by Father's former commanding officer of the Corps of Royal Engineers, whom he had served during the Boer War. After that war, Father had returned to England in late July, and by the following July, Nikki had been born.

That had been twelve years ago. Now Nikki was growing up fast. She read her father's newspapers daily, keeping track of current events, politics, and the news.

World War I was raging across Europe. Allied troops were retreating from the disaster of the Gallipoli campaign in Turkey, which had left 100,000 dead and more than 250,000 injured. Winston Churchill, the first lord of the admiralty, hung his head heavily at what was considered not only a retreat but a victory claimed by the Ottomans.

The Royal Flying Corps was building their strength, with new squadrons being created one after another. German flying aces Max Immelmann and Oswald Boelcke were the first pilots to be awarded the Pour le Mérite, the Blue Max.

Nikki could imagine them flying far above the fields of France, battling above the clouds. She imagined their British counterparts, cunning and shrewd, impishly exacting their revenge. "Take that, you hound!" they would yell from their cockpits. At least that was how Walter and John had played it out the previous day in the garden.

She thought of the crews of the *Endurance* and the *Aurora* trekking across Antarctica to meet each other and how Shackleton would be the first to complete the journey across the frozen continent. She wondered if Frank Wild had been one of those chosen to make the final leg of the expedition.

Challenges were all around. They were living in truly unprecedented times.

"Did you see Mother and Father leave this morning?" Nikki looked up from her needlework.

Miss Boswell shook her head. "No, my dear, I did not."

"He was wearing his uniform."

Miss Boswell kept on with her embroidery, silent.

"Do you think he will have to go to the war?"

"I don't know, my dear. Many brave men have gone already."

Nikki calculated that her father was either forty or forty-one, and the first drafts had been young men, boys not much older than Nikki herself. In fact, she knew some of last year's sixth-formers who had gone off late the previous year, two of whom had been remembered at Saint Matthew's during their weekly service the previous week.

It was difficult for the children—in fact, anyone—to compute the level of killing and injured in far-off lands. They were detached from the pain, the suffering, and the loss but felt for those poor souls and the loved ones left behind.

"When do you think the war will be over?" Nikki asked. "They said it would be over by Christmas."

"Nikki, I have really no idea." Tears welled up in Miss Boswell's eyes.

Nikki was at first unclear about where the tears were coming from. It turned out that three of her brothers, her father, and two of her uncles were in the war, and one of them, her brother James, was missing in action, presumed dead.

"I just pray to God that your father doesn't have to go," Miss Boswell said with tears in her eyes—Nikki assumed from the thought of her brother.

The memory from a couple of months previously had been weighing heavily on Nikki's mind, and this was her first chance to address it. "I saw Father with a woman the night of the party," she said.

Miss Boswell sat up, suddenly alert. "Oh yes, dear? What did you see?" she asked, keeping her head down, focusing on the needlework before her.

Nikki explained her midnight trip to the larder and what she had seen in her father's study. "It was dark, so I couldn't really make her out. I know it wasn't Mother, though. Her complexion was much darker, and anyway, I think I would have recognized my own mother," she said, wanting to get it off her chest. She trusted Miss Boswell. "Were Mr. and Mrs. Johnson at the party?" Nikki asked.

"I think so, dear. Why?"

"I couldn't see properly—hardly at all—but I think it might have been her."

Nikki made a point of not looking at Miss Boswell directly but got a sense of her apprehension out of the corner of her eye. She thought it could have been Mrs. Johnson with her father that evening, but she had always been struck by how similar in appearance Mrs. Johnson and Miss Boswell were. Nikki had her suspicions but kept them to herself.

"Are you sure you weren't dreaming?" Miss Boswell asked.

Nikki thought about that. Maybe she had been dreaming. Maybe it had been a figment of her imagination, or maybe that approach was for the best even if it had been real. *Lock it away, push it to one side, and put it down to imagination.*

"Oh, my dearest Nikki, you and your inquisitive mind." Miss Boswell smiled and patted her hand.

They continued in silence for a few moments.

"Is there a Mr. Boswell?" Nikki asked, knowing there was not a husband but wondering if there was a man in her nanny's life. "Or a boyfriend maybe?"

Miss Boswell gave Nikki a look, and Nikki knew she was crossing a line.

"No, dear, there is no Mr. Boswell, apart from my father. I'm too busy here looking after you and your family." She smiled in a way that signaled the end of the conversation.

Conveniently for Miss Boswell and Nikki to avoid another awkward moment, there was a wild commotion at the front of the house, accompanied by what sounded like repeated gunshots.

Miss Boswell and Nikki dropped their samples onto the sofa, jumped up, and hurried to the bay window in the formal sitting room at the front of the house. The sight before them put them in complete shock.

Walter and John were in Father's Silver Ghost, driving around the fountain in the middle of the driveway in circles. John was tooting the horn, and occasionally, the Rolls-Royce's engine backfired like a gunshot at dawn. They drove around and around. Walter was hanging on to the big, heavy steering wheel, and it was not obvious who was in control, the car or Walter. Nikki suspected not the latter. Her fear was confirmed as the big British racing-green Rolls-Royce went crashing into the fountain, toppling it over. Water sprayed everywhere, and the car came to a halt right in the middle of the pond.

"Well, that's a bit of excitement for the day," Nikki said.

"Boys!" was all Miss Boswell could muster at the top of her voice.

The groundskeeper came running from his work in the gardens to rescue the boys and make the vehicle safe.

Walter and John were grounded after that incident. Their stunt was not just dangerous but potentially expensive too.

Thankfully, Father owned a dealership, and with a couple of discreet phone calls to Mr. Watkins, the foreman at Father's garage, Miss Boswell managed to get the minor repairs completed. Mr. Woodridge, the groundskeeper, hastily repaired the fountain. Nikki was with him as he completed the finishing touches on the fountain. The Silver Ghost was safely back in its garage, where it belonged, under lock and key to avoid any repeat incidents, not that Walter or John would have dared.

"As good as new," Mr. Woodridge said with his hands on his hips. He looked across at Nikki and smiled a wide, friendly grin with his half-moon spectacles on the tip of his nose. Nikki liked Mr. Woodridge. "No one would ever know." He winked at Nikki.

That night, as she was contemplating sleep, Nikki tried to emulate the wink, holding open her left eye with her fingers and closing her right. She fell asleep in her pursuit but would learn the trick over the next few weeks.

Her next crusade was to conquer the dark art of whistling. It was much more fun than needlework.

Mother and Father returned to Kirk Ella the following week. The boys had taken the wind out of their own sails and would be sheepish for weeks, fearing their father's rage if he ever found out about their antics. Mr. Watkins knew how to keep a secret and understood the dangers of the word getting out, as did Mr. Woodridge, and it was not in Miss Boswell's best interest to let the secret out, especially since she had been in charge. That was Nikki's assessment of the silence at least.

Nikki had secretly hoped her mother and father would have a nice time in London together. It was a rarity for them to do something together. She hoped they might come back renewed, refreshed, reinvigorated, and in love again.

Sadly, the only difference she noticed was in her father upon his return. He took to wearing his khaki uniform, which was normally reserved for his monthly meeting at the local barracks, on a daily basis: his polished brown leather shoes, his forage cap, his brown leather Sam Browne belt strap, and a crown added to his three pips on his epaulette. Nikki did not know what that meant, but he looked good in his uniform; it suited him.

There was a flurry of visitors to the house. Men in uniforms with chauffeur-driven cars would roll up onto the gravel at the front of the house. They usually arrived very early and often were gone again before breakfast. Her father then would leave for the day, off to plan something or other to do with the war.

Before, Kingston upon Hull had been a thriving fishing port, but the war had changed that. The fleet that once had anchored in port at the beginning of the war was four hundred strong and identified as ideal for minesweeper duties. Every trawler, save ninety, converted to their new role, along with every other available vessel, including even the ferryboats of the Humber. This new fleet of all shapes and sizes was now more than eight hundred strong and employed nine thousand men, safeguarding the oceans from the invisible but deadly enemy munitions lurking in the dark waters below.

Although army, Father, in the Royal Corps of Engineers, was leading the trawler fleet initiative with his apparent expertise in that area of dealing with munitions.

He was preoccupied, and to the relief of Nikki and especially the boys, the Silver Ghost incident was not mentioned at all.

In addition to the German navy attacking England's, German zeppelin airships started their campaign to bomb England, including London, Great Yarmouth, King's Lynn, and Kingston upon Hull. They were silent assassins dropping their bombs of devastation onto the sleeping nation below from far above the clouds.

Time passed quickly as Nikki and Amy further developed their deep friendship. On August 23, Miss Boswell summoned the Beattie children to the front porch. It was only seven o'clock in the morning and still dark. A light covering of dew was on the ground. A military-looking car was parked out front, and judging from the number of Father's cases and chests packed and stacked, he was obviously leaving for some time.

Nikki stood on the front porch with her mother, Walter, John, and Miss Boswell. Her heart sank. While she wasn't close with her father, she missed him whenever he was gone for more than a few days.

"Where are you going, Father?" Nikki was the first to ask the obvious question. "And for how long will you be gone this time?" she added, sensing the worst.

Brigadier William Beattie of the Corps of Royal Engineers instructed his driver to make the final arrangements before their departure as he turned to the farewell committee on the front porch. "Walter, John, I want to make sure you look after your mother, your sister, and Miss Boswell here." He looked up and smiled at the nanny, and she shyly smiled and looked at her shoes. "Nikki, keep studying hard. You are doing so well. When I get back, I want to learn all about your grade As and your flying machine." He winked at Nikki.

How on earth does he know about that? she wondered in disbelief, looking at Miss Boswell and realizing that maybe they were closer than she had thought. Miss Boswell must have told him about her ambitions.

"Walter, John, stay away from the Silver Ghost and the fountain. You understand?"

Although she felt sad, the looks on the faces of her brothers were priceless. Neither of them said anything. They just looked down at their shoes.

Nikki went to her father and hugged him. "Don't go, Daddy," she said with tears running down her face.

"Be brave, my little sweetheart," he said, his voice tender and kind. "Daddy has to help win the war, and he needs you to be brave here at home."

"I'll try," she said, stepping back and wiping the tears away. "Where are you going? Not over there! Tell me you aren't going to France."

He simply said, "Loose lips sink ships, my dear." Father turned to Nikki's mother and gave her a peck on the cheek. "Stay well, my dear." He then turned to Miss Boswell as she held out her hand and curtsied. Father took the hand theatrically and bowed. "And as for you, Miss Boswell, look after my family the best you know how, my dear. You are the rock to our family, and I thank you so very much."

Nikki could see Miss Boswell glance sideways at her mother and blush, but ultimately, Father was right; in the absence of their mother, she was the cornerstone of the family and probably more of a mother to the children than their own. She certainly was a more reliable pair of hands that Father entrusted with the welfare of his children.

Nikki watched as her dad got into the backseat of the car. The driver pulled away. She saw her father lean out the window and salute. Fighting back tears, she returned the salute, as did her brothers. The car continued toward their big iron gate and out onto the road, on its way to London or France or some unknown destination.

For Nikki, there was some sense of relief. At least he could not do whatever he'd been doing to Mrs. Johnson—or had it been Miss Boswell?—that night. One was her nanny, and that was unthinkable, but the other was her best friend's mother. If the latter, what if Amy ever found out? Or Amy's father or, heaven forbid, her grandfather, the mayor of Hull?

Nikki remembered the motto on her father's cap badge and translated it using knowledge from her Latin classes at school: *"Ubique* and *Quo Fas et Gloria Ducunt"* (Everywhere where right and glory lead).

She dearly hoped that to be true.

4

THE GIRL IN BROWN

October 15, 1918
Spadina Military Hospital
The Daniels Building, 1 Spadina
Crescent, Toronto, Canada

AMELIA "MILLIE" EARHART CHECKED HER pocket watch; it was 9:55 p.m. She was five minutes away from the end of her shift. It had been a particularly difficult one for them all; they'd lost another three patients to the dreaded Spanish flu.

The previous Christmas, she had visited Toronto with her sister and seen the wounded soldiers returning from the Red Fields of France, and she'd been struck by the sadness and the tragedy of it all and wanted to do what she could to help.

At the start of 1918, she had enlisted with the Red Cross, trained to become a nurse's aide, and begun her work with the Voluntary Aid Detachment at the hospital. That had been more than seven months ago, and over that time, the flu had overtaken the deaths from injuries on the battlefield.

Millie went to the restroom to get a glass of water, as she felt slightly faint. It had been a long night, after all. She would head home. She needed some rest, and she would be fine in the morning, she told herself.

Millie was a Kansas girl. She'd grown up with the rough and the tumble, climbing trees, hunting rats with her father's rifle, and belly-slamming her sled down the hill at the back of the family house in winter with her sister Grace Muriel, whom she'd nicknamed Pidge. Muriel had nicknamed her Meelie out of difficulty in pronouncing her real name.

They kept worms, moths, and a tree toad. She liked to wear bloomers instead of flowery dresses, and many considered her a tomboy. Though they never much played with dolls, they did have two special companions, Donk and Ellie. The pair were jointed wooden animals and went with the sisters on many of their adventures and journeys. Donk was Amelia's and was a donkey, and Ellie was an elephant belonging to Muriel.

The sisters often spent time in their backyard, playing with their pet dog, James Ferocious, and on the Flying Dutchman, a merry-go-round built by their uncle Nicey. Amelia also fashioned a roller coaster in the family's back garden after one she had seen at the local fair. On a wooden box, she flew down the ramp attached to the roof of the toolshed and crashed in a heap on the grass.

"Look, Pidge! It's just like flying!" she announced with a big smile on her face, despite her busted lip, torn bloomers, and bruises.

Amelia and Muriel had two imaginary playmates, Laura and Ringa, with whom they shared their great adventures. They were also part of their imaginary tribe, the Dee-Jays, made up of small black creatures whom Millie would use as an excuse for talking out of turn, eating the last piece of pie, or breaking or losing something.

She had been only seven years old then. Now a young woman of twenty-one, Millie was tall, slender, fit, and lean, and her blonde hair framed her good looks and beauty. She wore the nurse's uniform well.

She put on her coat and, exhausted, made her way home. The Toronto winter night was bitterly cold, and she would be glad to get to her fire. She would make herself a hot toddy and read her book—she liked reading—and then go to bed.

At the age of ten, at the state fair, she had seen her first ever airplane, a biplane. "A thing of rusty wire and wood and not interesting at all," she had said at the time. A lot had changed since then.

Henry Ford had set a new land-speed record in 1904, traveling more than ninety-one miles an hour, and the International Alliance of Women had been founded. *The Scarlet Pimpernel* had opened its doors in London's West End the same year the Automobile Association was founded. Mount Vesuvius had erupted, devastating Naples, and an earthquake in San Francisco had killed three thousand and left three hundred thousand homeless.

In aviation, the pioneers had taken to the skies, pushing the limits and the boundaries and turning the impossible possible. World War I raged in Europe, with more than seventy million people in conflict on the other side of the Atlantic, including half a million Canadians and three million Americans.

By the time Millie was seventeen, it had become clear that her father, Edwin, was an alcoholic. He was forced to retire early from his work at the railroad, and that was the end of his career. His drinking drained both the family's finances and their patience. The family home was auctioned off, and that marked the "final ending of her childhood," as Millie put it. She, her sister, and her mother moved to Chicago to live with friends.

Although she was generally a happy, gregarious, fun-loving girl, her yearbook at Hyde Park School at that time described her as "the girl in brown who walks alone," which was a testament to the fall from relative happiness the family had endured.

Growing up, Millie kept a scrapbook, collecting newspaper clippings about pioneering women in society as role models and inspiration in the male-orientated world, including film directors, engineers, and women in advertising, law, and business.

She got home that night, turned the key in the lock, opened the door, and went straight to her room. She shared a house with seven other nurses. Some were on shift, and some, like her, were finished for the night. She just wanted to be alone that night.

With the fire lit and a hot toddy made, she liked reading. That night, she deliberated whether she would immerse herself in her favorite book of sonnets by the poetic apostle of beauty himself, Dante Gabriel Rosetti, whom she remembered from her childhood library, or the aviation engineering textbook. She had borrowed both from the extensive hospital library, which once had been part of the University of Toronto.

As she sat reading her poetry by the warmth of the fire, Millie was conscious of her own growing symptoms; her cough was mild but was getting worse. She was not sure if she was being paranoid. She probably was, she decided, and she carried on reading.

She recalled her own poem she had written many years ago:

> Beauty is not the hue and glow of right,
> Nor for man's pleasure given.
> For hell itself is beautiful at night,
> From the far windows of heaven.

At the hospital, Millie helped in the kitchen, dispensed medicines, and helped the nurses with their duties, and although not on the front line, she had enough exposure to illness to be in danger.

She had seen the morgue at the hospital stacked to its limit and wondered at the tragedy of it all. Thirty one million had been injured or lost due to the war, and now many tens of millions were ill or dying around the world because of the flu.

It was estimated that five hundred million people worldwide had the virus, and somewhere between twenty and fifty million people had died or would die. It was the deadliest pandemic in the history of the world, potentially affecting close to a third of the world's population at that time.

It was one o'clock in the morning, the fire was on its last embers, and she headed off to bed to sleep.

She soldiered on, but two weeks later, she was hospitalized with confirmation that she had contracted the Spanish flu.

Luckier than many, she was released, having recovered, two months later.

After minor surgery, with lasting damage to her sinuses, and convalescing for almost a year afterward, Millie went to stay with her sister in Northampton, Massachusetts, and in addition to her reading and writing, she learned to play the banjo.

It was good to be in the comfort of her sister's home; she appreciated the love that surrounded her as she nursed her way back to health. She was in good company, but she was a free spirit, an independent thinker. She knew she wanted to be different. She wanted to stand up for women, and she knew by then that flying was a way to achieve that level of notoriety and, therefore, influence to affect the world and her cause.

She learned of her parents' reuniting in California, and although part of her was happy for them to be back together, part of her was sad too. Her father had thrown away their family through his drinking, and Millie was not sure he deserved her mother, but whatever made them happy she was okay with.

She was feeling better now and decided to make the trip to go see them, as it had been a while.

Reunited in California, Millie and her father went to visit a local airfield close to their home in Long Beach. They were meeting a pilot, Frank Monroe Hawks.

Hawks, an air racer and former air force pilot, was tall, handsome, and charming with his leather skullcap, goggles, and leather pilot's jacket. He greeted Millie and her father with a big smile, the smile of an actor. After all, they were in movie land.

Hawks agreed to take Millie up for a joy ride, and her father handed over the ten-dollar fee. It was a ten-minute flight—a dollar a minute. That was a lot of money.

Millie stayed in California and worked a number of jobs, including working as a truck driver, a photographer, and a transcriber, to save up enough cash—$1,000, to be precise—to take flying lessons.

She had done her research. At nearby Kinner Field, there was an instructor named Anita Snook. She was not only a woman in a man's world, but she held a handful of firsts in the world of aviation, and she was close by.

"Neta Snook is the right instructor for me," Millie declared over dinner with her parents one evening. She went on to explain why and her rationale for spending $1,000, the equivalent of four months' average wage of the day.

The next morning, her father drove her to the airfield, and Millie marched up to Snook with her hard-earned cash in hand and said, "I want to fly. Will you teach me?"

It was time for celebration: World War I was over. Thanks to Miss Boswell, the Johnsons were with the Beatties at Lair Close, along with many other from their school, celebrating the end of the war. Trestle tables lay out on the lawn, covered in white linen tablecloths and adorned with Nikki's favorite delights and an abundance of Union Jacks. Upon Nikki's request, they had also invited the groundsman and his wife and two sons, the housekeeper and her husband, and her class teachers too. All were dressed in their Sunday best to celebrate the end of what had been a tragic and bloody conflict.

There had been many casualties—in fact, more than thirty-one million. Seventeen million military and civilians were dead, and fourteen million had been wounded. It had been the bloodiest conflict in the history of the world, with Russia taking the brunt of the Allied losses, followed by France and Great Britain. More than one million lives had been lost: sons, brothers, sisters, mothers, and fathers of the empire. They never would return home again.

Nikki was astounded by the numbers, the deaths, the sorry souls, and the loss. She prayed this would be the war to end all wars. It made her sad indeed, as did the absence of her father.

Every month since he had left Kirk Ella more than three years ago, her father had sent a letter with the postal stamp of Dorchester, Dorset. The letters gave pep talks to Nikki, Walter, and John and made little to no reference of what he was doing or where he was doing it. The postal stamp was the only clue. He had been back home only a handful of times and only for fleeting visits, just enough for them to remember his face.

Miss Boswell visited her family in London every couple of months and occasionally would see their father to update him on news of the family and bring back letters and presents. The children were excited to hear how their father was doing, what he was up to, and when he was coming home next or for good. Miss Boswell also seemed to enjoy that connection between the children and their father.

One morning, midmorning, the postman arrived as usual, and Nikki and the boys were ready, hoping for their monthly letter. They could hear the postman as he whistled his way up the drive on his bicycle with the packet of letters in his basket and pushed them through the letter box of the front door. The envelopes fell into a basket behind the door to collect them neatly.

Nikki rifled through the letters until she saw the one she was looking for, recognizing the postal stamp. She grabbed it, took it to the family room, and started to open it carefully, closely watched by Walter and John by her side. They were all eager to hear of any news and if Father was coming home. After all, the war was now over.

> November 7, 1918
> Lair Close
> West Ella Road
> Kirk Ella
> Kingston upon Hull
> East Riding of Yorkshire
> England

Dearest Nikki, Walter, and John,

As no doubt you will have seen, the war is all but over, thanks to God, and I am writing this letter to you as I will be leaving my post here in the coming weeks.

It's hard to contemplate where the past three years have gone, and only now can I share with you the nature of my work here: developing armored tanks for the soldiers on the front line.

Thanks to my experience with Rolls-Royce, we managed to create these machines, and thankfully, they were put to good use and were one cog in the huge engine that steered us to victory against our enemy.

While a success on one hand, on the other, the demand for Rolls-Royces for anything but war and royalty all but dried up over this time, and I have decided to relocate the business and the family to Ilkley in the West Riding of Yorkshire.

To that end, I have made the necessary arrangements to move the family in the next two weeks and will meet you there when I am finished here.

Please be patient, be brave, and help Mother and Miss Boswell as they manage the move.

I will be home for Christmas.

God bless you all.

Your loving father,
Brigadier William Beattie
Royal Corps of Engineers
Bovington Camp

Nikki finished reading the letter aloud and let out a big gulp with tears welling up. She blinked them away, conscious that the two boys were looking at her and that any sign of weakness would affect them.

She kept a brave face, but her mind was racing. *We are leaving?* She thought about their family home where they had grown up, she thought of school and her friends, she thought of her friend William, and she thought of her best friend, Amy.

She ran to Miss Boswell, waving the letter. "Is this true?" she demanded. "Are we really leaving? Did you know, Miss Boswell?"

Nikki was fifteen years old now and was a freethinking young lady, and having grown up with two brothers and two absent parents, she was determined, independent, straight to the point, and not shy to share her opinions. She was a true Yorkshire lass, as Mr. Woodridge described her.

Miss Boswell gave one of her head-shaking reactions, which by now Nikki knew meant she did not want to talk about it. Nikki saw the signal and went off to find her mother, who was probably in her bedroom, where she spent most of her time.

Nikki burst into her mother's bedroom unannounced. It had been months since she had been in there. Her visits to the room were rare, as her mother liked her privacy and spent much of her time alone, away from the world and away from the children, occasionally joining them for meals.

Even before Father's departure, Mother had been distant, and she was even more so now. Her bedroom was strewn with various brown bottles of substances obviously medicinal in nature.

Nikki walked into the scene, and as she did so, she let the letter drop to her waist in a gesture of bewilderment and disbelief, trying to compute what she was seeing. Her mother lay on the bed, not moving, with a half bottle of gin on her nightstand and a half-empty bottle of pills.

"Mother? Mother!" Nikki said.

The body on the bed was unresponsive, not moving. Nikki pushed her shoulder. Nothing. Then she shook her. Again, nothing. By that time, Miss Boswell and the housemaid, Mrs. Brunswick, were both at the bedroom door. Mrs. Brunswick went straight to her mother, and Miss Boswell dialed the phone beside the bed, calling the family doctor.

Leaving Mother, who was still unconscious, with Mrs. Brunswick in the bedroom, Miss Boswell escorted Nikki downstairs and to the family room.

The fog in Nikki's mind suddenly cleared, and what she had seen upstairs made sense now, as did the behaviors and the distance of her mother over the years, almost as long as she could remember.

"Is she all right, Miss Boswell?" Nikki asked, knowing the answer to her own question.

"No, my dear, your mother is most unwell and has been for some time."

"Has she ever been as bad as this?"

"I am sure Dr. Farrell will attend to her accordingly." Miss Boswell tried to avoid the question and offer at least some level of reassurance.

If only she had waited for Father's letter and his news that he was coming home! Nikki thought.

Two weeks later, the house was packed, and the two wagons on the driveway were laden with their worldly possessions. Mr. Watkins drove one to take the items into storage, and Mr. Woodridge drove the other, heading to Ilkley with a crew of men to help them at the other end. The Silver Ghost carried Miss Boswell, Nikki, and the boys. Mother would join them later, as she was convalescing in the local Broadgate Hospital. According to Miss Boswell, no visitors were allowed.

The journey from Kirk Ella to Ilkley was a long one: seventy-five miles west to Leeds, up to Wetherby, past the horse races, south of the spa town of Harrogate, on through the market town of Otley, and then on into Ilkley under the shadow of Ilkley Moor.

Nikki remained silent for much of the journey. She stared out the window as the countryside and sights passed by, thinking about their demise, their abrupt relocation, and their mother and hoping Father would return sooner rather than later.

Nikki recollected her goodbye with Amy. She and the boys had been invited to the Johnsons', where they'd had reception sandwiches, including egg and cress, coronation chicken, and ham and English mustard, and a selection of cakes, including scones, strawberry tartlets, and Nikki's favorite, Battenberg cake: pink and yellow square logs of sponge with raspberry jam to hold them together, wrapped in marzipan and sliced to give the perfect checkered slice.

Amy's sisters and the boys got along as though everything were normal, while Amy and Nikki were more attuned to the gravity of the situation. As the afternoon tea finished and the others went outside to play, Amy and Nikki sat together making pledges to stay connected, write to each other, and come visit during the holidays.

It was sad to part, but somewhere deep inside, Nikki knew they would be best friends forever.

As the Silver Ghost arrived to collect them, they all gave each other hugs. Amy and Nikki embraced with tears in their eyes but with the good old British stiff upper lip, with no place for too much emotion. *Until next time, my friend.*

Miss Boswell was more and more like a mother to them nowadays. She was their safety blanket, their matriarch, and the single adult constant in their lives.

They passed the sign for the town limits of Ilkley, sat up, and paid attention to their surroundings and their new hometown.

The occupants of the car broke out into a familiar song Miss Boswell had taught them upon news of their relocation. Miss Boswell led the way in her cockney accent, supported by the Beattie children in their best Yorkshire accents:

> Where hast thee been since I saw thee, I saw thee?
> On Ilkley Moor bar tat.
> Rat, tat, tat.
> Where hast thee been since I saw thee, I saw thee?
> On Ilkley Moor bar tat.
> Rat, tat, tat.

Miss Boswell, who had done her homework, took them through each of the verses one by one.

> Tha's been a-courtin' Mary Jane, Mary Jane,
> on Ilkley Moor bar tat.

It was the first on an interesting journey of lyrics and a welcome to their new town, the entire car singing as they rolled past the town limits and on to their new home.

> On Ilkley Moor bar tat.
> On Ilkley Moor bar tat.
> On Ilkley moor bar tat.

Miss Boswell explained that *bar tat* meant without your hat, which made the rest of the lyrics a little easier to understand.

In the song, the worms then followed, they would eat you up, the ducks would then eat the worms, and people would eat the duck, coming full circle.

The song took Nikki's mind off things for a few minutes. She appreciated the thoughtfulness and planning of Miss Boswell.

"This seems like a pleasant enough place," Nikki said, trying to stay positive for the boys. The boys rolled their eyes and just shrugged.

They pulled up outside Riverside House, a property on Bridge Lane that overlooked the River Wharfe. Although half the size of Lair Close back in Kirk Ella, it was certainly pleasant enough.

"This looks nice," Nikki said. *On Ilkley Moor bar tat!*

5

HOME

December 1918
Riverside House, Ilkley, West
Riding of Yorkshire, England

NIKKI SAT AT THE TABLE, in the bay window overlooking the river, with her father's letter in hand, rereading as if to make sure she had not made a mistake the first twenty times. *Father's coming home,* she whispered in her mind. It was early evening; the skies were dark, and the lights of the house shone out, showing the light snowflakes coming down and dusting the paved walk of the riverbank in front of the house.

Putting the letter down on the table, Nikki stood up and stretched. She walked up to the window and continued to look outside at the gently falling snow, the snow-covered trees, and the streetlights on the road out front. Her thoughts wandered as she reflected on the move to a new town and on Christmas, which was two days away.

The move had uprooted the family, but Miss Boswell had done a good job of organizing all their things, getting the furniture in place, putting the familiar pictures on the walls, putting out the ornaments, and bringing their life from one home to this new one down by the River Wharfedale in Ilkley.

Mother had been back home for a couple of weeks, mostly confined to her room. Nikki and the boys had filled her full of love, and to be fair, she had tried to perk up a touch. Nikki deducted that whatever medications she was taking must have been pretty strong. It was visibly hard for her to concentrate sufficiently to show even a distant smile, and the art of conversation was more difficult than it should have been.

Nikki and Amy kept their promise to each other, and their letters to each other arrived the same day. Nikki was excited to hear from Amy and relieved that only two weeks had passed. That meant, to Nikki, she had not been forgotten already. She knew they had a special bond, but in that life of uncertainty, who knew?

Nikki thought of the brave soldiers who carried on regardless, even with a sense of humor intact despite the adversity. She thought about all the pain and suffering around the world. She thought about Shackleton's men who were stuck on the ice and in the Antarctic for months with no complaints and then went straight to war on their return without question.

Nikki looked out the window, and despite the cold and the dark, she could see couples walking past and taking in the river amid an inch of fresh snow on the ground, with more falling out of the clouds above. Sighing, she sat down at the table and reread the letter.

Miss Boswell came downstairs and into the kitchen to make some cocoa. The boys were in bed, reading themselves to sleep—probably some car manual or something similar, Nikki thought to herself.

She thought of her father, who had been away for so long. She thought of her mother and the scene in her bedroom just a few weeks ago in Kirk Ella.

Miss Boswell sat down opposite her and passed her a mug of freshly made cocoa.

They sat together and stared out the window. Their relationship had changed into a friendship, Nikki thought. Both were lonely and probably the closest thing they had to companionship.

"Will Mother be all right?" Nikki asked.

Miss Boswell cupped her cocoa in both her hands and looked Nikki in the eye. "I hope so, my dear," she said unconvincingly.

"What's wrong with her?"

Miss Boswell shook her head slowly and looked out the window before returning her gaze. "She is doing very poorly, Nikki. She needs a lot of love, help, and support."

"Will Father be coming home help?" she asked hopefully.

Miss Boswell paused. "I hope so, Nikki. I hope so." She smiled warmly.

They talked about school, friends, Amy, and Nikki's dreams. Nikki was fifteen now and starting to think about life as a young adult and what that might involve for her.

She had kept in touch with the studious William in Hull but not quite with the same level of enthusiasm and vigor as she had with Amy.

"In the new year, I may go visit Amy in Hull," she said.

"And that young man William?" Miss Boswell teased.

Nikki blushed. "Maybe."

"What about you, Miss Boswell? Going down to London again soon?"

Nikki suspected Miss Boswell's regular journeys home involved more than just going to see her parents. Now in her early thirties, Miss Boswell was in her prime, and she was a good-looking woman with her dark hair, pretty brown eyes, and olive skin. She did not need makeup; she was a natural beauty, Nikki thought.

Nikki remembered thinking the same about Amy's mother. Either way, she didn't blame her father. In fact, she understood. She felt a level of neglect from her mother's absence. She tried her best to understand her detachment, but it was difficult to understand and make sense of. Why couldn't Mother show them all more love and be less self-absorbed with whatever demons she had in her head? In Nikki's own Neverland, her mother had become her version of Captain Hook, a once likeable character who had lost his way somehow and was misguided and certainly misunderstood.

Outside, the snow was now coming down heavily, and the walkers had made their way safely to the warmth of their homes. It was time for bed. Nikki said good night to Miss Boswell, her companion and friend.

They embraced.

"Night, my sweet Nikki."

"Night-night, Esme!" Nikki shouted back as she started up the first flight of stairs to her bedroom, using her nanny's Christian name for the first time. Nikki liked to push the envelope.

The next morning, it was Christmas Eve, and someone had been busy through the night, making the final arrangements to the house. There was a plate of freshly baked mince pies on the table, along with eggnog in a jug with glasses, and Christmas presents were under the tree. Nikki and the boys, now eleven and twelve, came downstairs in their jimjams, excited at the sights and smells of Christmas.

Outside, the sun was out, with blue skies, and a covering of snow was still on the ground from the night before. Even Mother made it down that morning, and they sat in the bay window together, eating the warm mince pies and sipping their alcohol-free eggnog.

"Well, just a splash!" Miss Boswell admitted to applause from the children.

They could hear carol singers outside making their way to rehearsals at the church nearby, warming up their voices as they trudged through the crunchy snow underfoot with the sunshine above.

"It really feels like Christmas, Mama." Nikki smiled at her mother, who smiled back and gently patted Nikki on the head.

"What time is Papa coming home?" Walter asked.

Miss Boswell looked at her watch. "Should be here mid to late morning," she said excitedly.

When they returned from church, Miss Boswell sent them up to their rooms with strict instructions to tidy up.

"Shipshape and Bristol fashion," she reminded them as they ran upstairs. They were to wear their Sunday best for their father's homecoming.

Nikki was excited, as were the boys. Father was actually coming home, and even Mother looked a little better. At least they hoped.

The morning went by slowly as they sat playing card games. The clock ticked in the background, reminding them of every second that passed by.

Finally, at 11:10 a.m., they heard the toot of a horn outside. The children stampeded to the door and looked out the window, and there was the car pulling into the drive. In the passenger seat, there he was: with no khakis, Father sat waving and smiling at them.

They ran out of the house, jumping, dancing, and shouting, "Father's home!"

Nikki was the first to reach the car. She threw herself into her father's arms as soon as he closed the car door and turned to face her. Moments later, the entire family mobbed him.

After the happy reunion, the driver carried stacks of presents in from the car, all wrapped up in gold paper and red bows. The *Harrods* labels indicated that whatever was inside was going to be pretty special. It was the same place Miss Boswell had brought presents from after her trips to London.

After Father settled in, Nikki joined her siblings at the dining room table. She helped herself to roast ham with boiled new potatoes, broccolini, and glazed carrots, followed by Miss Boswell's special raspberry pavlova. It was a perfect pre–Christmas Day delight, substantial enough but sufficiently light to preserve their capacity for the following day's traditional feast.

Full and satisfied from the sumptuous Christmas Eve dinner, Nikki relaxed on the sofa in front of the fire burning brightly and crackling in the fireplace at the far end of the study. The evening, in her view, was a success. It was good to have the family together again, even as Mother began to fade as Miss Boswell read Christmas stories to the gathered few. So much had already changed since the war ended, and Nikki was certain that much more was about to change in her life.

By nine o'clock, as Mother was waning, Father called it a night. Nikki stood up, yawned, and considered going to bed as well. Nikki walked past the tree one last time and took a side look at the presents underneath.

"Night-night, Mother. Night-night, Father." She leaned back and blew a kiss. "It's really wonderful to have you back home, Papa."

"It's good to be home, my little peewee," he said.

Mother looked tired. She'd had a checked-out look on her face all day. Her vacant eyes were not really seeing, just staring out as if she were a bystander to the Christmas scene, and she'd barely said a word all evening. But she had tried. She had kept a smile on her face for most of the evening, although Nikki was not sure what exactly she was smiling about.

Nikki went upstairs to bed, but she tossed and turned for the rest of the night, unable to sleep deeply, because she was so excited to have her father home for Christmas.

In the morning, she hurried downstairs with her brothers. As she expected, the presents from London were fabulous.

Nikki got a beautiful dress in black and gold and some bows for her hair, and she was thrilled with *The Aviation Pocket-Book*, an aide-mémoire of facts and details and all a budding aviatrix needed to know.

She beamed as she kissed Father on the cheek, tightly gripping the leather-bound book in her hand. She knew he had thought hard about this gift, and she took it as a sort of blessing of her dreams.

"Thank you so much, Papa."

Mother's demeanor stayed the same for most of the day, and then, after Christmas luncheon, her usual pattern of detachment and isolation returned.

Nikki lurched awake from a deep sleep, suddenly aware that her father was screaming. Her mother hadn't been doing well. She'd barely gotten through the holidays, and now, in mid-January, her mental state had gone downhill. Bleary-eyed, Nikki and her brothers stood in the hallway in their pajamas, trying to work out what all the commotion was inside the bedroom, peering through the door as Miss Boswell rushed in.

Three minutes later, Miss Boswell rushed back out the door, as white as a sheet and with bloodstains on the sleeves of her nightdress. "Into your rooms, children!" she barked in a voice they had never heard before, and at once, they followed the order.

Nikki hurried into her bedroom and closed the door. She stood behind it and strained to hear what was being said. She'd heard her dad shout before, especially during the holidays, but somehow, his voice sounded more urgent, almost panicked. She glanced at the clock on the nightstand beside her bed, noted it was about eight o'clock in the morning, and gingerly opened the bedroom door. She crept out and stood at the head of the stairs. Her father was down there with Miss Boswell. She heard loud knocks. Her dad opened the front door, and a man she recognized as the family doctor rushed in. Nikki hurried back inside her bedroom and closed the door behind her. She heard rapid footsteps outside, and then all went eerily silent.

Thirty minutes later, there was an ambulance outside, and as Nikki looked out the window, she saw her mother being taken by wheelchair into the back of the white wagon with the big red cross on the side. Two men in white nursing coats secured her mother in the back, took a few moments to speak to the doctor and Father, and then turned around in the driveway and headed out and up the hill to High Royds Hospital.

Nikki fought back tears as she sat down on her bed. She stared at the wall, and then the tears came. She sobbed, wondering what was going to happen to her, to her brothers, and to her mother and father.

A short time later, Miss Boswell opened the bedroom door. She came in and sat beside Nikki, resting her right hand on Nikki's shoulder. "I know it's hard, sweetheart," she said. "I know. Sometimes people have a hard time in the world, and they can't handle it. Your mother is going to be okay. She just needs some time to sort things out."

"I wish I could believe you," Nikki said, "but I don't."

Miss Boswell sighed and shook her head. "I understand. Now, come on. Let's get you and your brothers something to eat."

Nikki followed Miss Boswell out of the bedroom. A short time later, she and her brothers were seated at the table adjacent to the bay window. A plate of eggs, sausages, and toast sat untouched in front of her.

Eventually, Nikki broke the silence. "Is Mother all right, Father?"

He looked across at her with the deep, sad eyes of someone who had been up all night and, she suspected, had been crying too. "No, dear, your mother is not all right." His stark response confirmed the reality at hand. "The doctor signed a detention order this morning to send your mother to High Royds for her own protection."

"For how long?"

He sat there staring into space and eventually turned to Nikki. "I have no idea, my darling."

It was harsh news indeed, and clearly, Father was not taking the situation well at all. Miss Boswell, who sat with the family, reached out and held Father's hand and squeezed his fingers visibly three times.

It was Friday. Miss Boswell had already told them no school that day, and that would give them the weekend to work out what happened next.

On Saturday morning, Nikki joined her brothers in front of the house. She returned her father's hug and stepped back. He looked terrible. After he finished hugging them, he turned to Miss Boswell and hugged her as well. Nikki's eyes widened at the sight. She'd never seen her father hug Miss Boswell. Indeed, the tenderness of the moment made a big impression on Nikki. Something didn't seem quite right.

Father left with his suitcase as Nikki and her brothers waved goodbye once again, this time from their new home, Riverside, in Ilkley. His departure was sudden. Nikki had no idea where he was going or when he would return.

"Hope to see you soon, Father!" Nikki shouted after him hopefully, but something deep inside her told her that wish might not come true. They were now alone.

6

ALCOCK AND BROWN

June 14, 1919
Lester's Field
St. John's, Newfoundland, Labrador, Canada

NIKKI AND AMY BOTH HAD been fascinated by the advancements in aviation ever since Amy had planted the seed of flying the world one day. Both had been born in the year of Wilbur and Orville Wright's first powered flight, and Nikki felt it was perhaps her destiny. Her birth date was a coincidence in the passage of time. She followed the various advancements and the latest milestones, attempts, and achievements, and one story in particular caught her attention: the story of Alcock and Brown. As she read the newspaper article, her mind escaped and took her to Lester Field, where they had set off on their pioneering flight. Using her vivid imagination, she conjured up a mental image of what had gone on between the two men as they prepared to take off on their epic flight.

Teddie sat in the open cockpit of the Vickers Vimy, next to his friend and pilot Jack Alcock. They were going through their final checklist before takeoff on their adventure to conquer the Atlantic.

As they finished their checks, they both looked up from their clipboards and smiled at each other, knowing they finally had their dream in front of them. This was their moment. Just two thousand miles lay between them and their prize.

"Well, old boy, this is it!" Jack said. They beamed at each other, and then Jack shouted to one of the ground crew, "Chocks away!" He always loved to say that in his exaggerated accent of aristocracy, from which he was not.

Arthur Brown radioed his first message of their record-breaking flight attempt: "All well and started."

They lifted off from the field up and over the still, icy ocean below. They were off on their quest to be the first pilots to fly nonstop across the Atlantic.

Back in 1913, the *Daily Mail* had offered a £10,000 reward to the victors, but the Great War had gotten in the way of that endeavor, and the competition had been postponed till the war was over.

Nikki had done her homework. There was little she and Amy didn't know about flight, aviation, and the race for the next big prize or milestone. Nikki knew that back in 1913, there had been no aircraft even capable of achieving the feat. However, war had accelerated innovation. World War I had fueled the development of flight, allowing pilots to contemplate such a historic feat. The Vickers Vimy was an example of that progress, and although released too late for the war, the long-range bomber was the perfect choice for John "Jack" Alcock and Arthur "Teddie" Brown to make the attempt.

With goggles on and engines running, raring to go, Alcock and Brown sat in the open cockpit, still grinning.

"We're off, old boy! Looking forward to that pint of Guinness on the other side!" Alcock grinned at Brown, already freezing cold in the bitter temperature.

"Hold on to your hat!" Brown replied with their typical humor of the day in the face of the peril ahead and an endeavor no man or woman had ever achieved.

John "Jack" Alcock, from Manchester, England, had been interested in flying as a boy, and by the age of twenty, he'd been a pilot and a regular competitor at aircraft competitions, until the war inconveniently had gotten in the way. He'd become a military pilot instead but had been taken prisoner in Turkey after his Handley Page bomber's engines failed over the Gulf of Saros. "Bloody nuisance," he would say as he told his story.

Arthur "Teddie" Brown had been born in Glasgow, Scotland, to American parents and moved down to Manchester before World War I. He also had been a pilot taken as a prisoner of war after he was shot down over Germany.

Six months before, in Manchester, Jack had rushed into the Oxnoble on Liverpool Road, close to the train station, with a copy of the *Daily Mail*. "This is it, Teddie! This is the one, our chance," he'd said, throwing the newspaper down onto the bar in front of his friend.

Teddie, in the middle of taking a sip of his creamy Boddingtons ale, had looked at Jack with foam on his lip, wiping it off with his hand. "What is it, old boy, that's so important to get in the way of a man and his Boddingtons?"

"Look!" Alcock had pointed at the open newspaper as they both read the advertisement together, Alcock for the sixth time that morning.

£10,000 Prize: First to Cross the Atlantic

The aviator who shall first cross the Atlantic in an aeroplane in flight from any point in the United States of America, Canada, or Newfoundland to any point in Great Britain or Ireland in seventy-two continuous hours.

"I guess that calls for another round!" Brown had grinned from ear to ear.

"Come on, Teddie. That ten thousand pounds has got our names on it." Jack had started writing in the air and said theatrically, as if an announcer, "Ladies and gentlemen, I have no other than the pioneers of flight, the conquerors of that mighty ocean itself, the death defiers, the pioneers, the heroes of the empire, the one and only—drumroll, please."

They'd chorused together, "Alcock and Brown!"

"Hold on a minute. Why not Brown and Alcock?" Teddie had asked.

"It doesn't have the same ring. Besides, it's alphabetical, as in *ABC*."

"Look, if we win ten thousand pounds, I don't care what you call us."

"Come on. Let's have a beer to celebrate."

"Celebrate what? We haven't done anything yet!"

They'd cleared the rest of the afternoon for Boddingtons and planning.

Six months later, they had been in St. Johns, Newfoundland, waiting for their plane to arrive from England.

Alcock and Brown had waited, frustrated, as they saw the best fields being taken by the other crews. They also had been anxious because many of the other teams were ahead of them. They had not even had their plane yet. Jack had sensed that their opportunity was slipping away.

By mid-May, one of the rival crews had flown twenty hours east across the ocean but had to ditch due to engine failure. Fortunately, there had been a ship nearby to pick them all up safely.

Another had crashed on takeoff, not even getting off dry land.

A third, a United States Navy Curtiss seaplane, had made it to Portugal but after a ten-day stop in the Azores, so it didn't count.

"If we're not careful, this thing is going to overtake us," Jack had said of the string of failures before them. "It's only a matter of time before someone will succeed, and that will leave us high and dry."

Teddie Brown had nodded; Jack was saying aloud what he and the entire crew already knew.

"Stiff upper lip, old boy" was the staple British response whether facing a thousand warriors at Rorke's Drift, stranded on Antarctica, or waiting patiently for a plane to arrive to cross the Atlantic.

Jack Alcock had looked up at his friend Teddie from his steaming mug of tea and just smiled.

"She'll be here soon enough," Teddie had said reassuringly.

Sure enough, on May 26, the Vickers Vimy finally had arrived. There had been celebration as they hauled the crates to their patch of grass and their designated assembly point.

"Now we've just got to build the bloody thing," Jack had said, his frustration deepening.

"We'll be done by lunchtime," Alcock had said, humoring him.

Alcock, Brown, and the crew had taken the thirteen freight crates and started assembling their plane like a Meccano model-building set, working night and day to get her ready for the skies.

The Vickers was a large airplane. Twin twelve-cylinder Rolls-Royce engines pumped out 350 horsepower each, and it had a wingspan of sixty-seven feet. They'd modified it to remove everything, including the bomb racks, replacing them with added fuel tanks for the mammoth journey. The plane now was capable of carrying 865 gallons.

With a weight off his shoulders, Jack Alcock had leaned back on his heels with hands on his hips, standing next to Teddie Brown, beaming. "She's ready, my friend."

"And that she is, sir!"

"Let's sit through this coming storm, and we'll be on our way."

Another final delay had been upon them, but by the afternoon of June 14, they'd been ready to leave. After the storm, the forecast had been good, and their window of opportunity had opened.

Alcock taxied their way to the farthest end of the field to give them the longest possible runway to get the big beast off the ground.

The crew looked on with big smiles and pride. There was little more they could do now; it was down to Alcock and Brown.

Jack felt the weight of responsibility; their feat was in his hands now, and he wasn't about to let anyone down on the last leg. He looked down at the crew with his big beam and saluted. "For the king!" he shouted above the engine noise. There was no hope of them hearing, but they all saluted back regardless.

With the Rolls-Royce engines on idle and the twin props whirring, Alcock pulled back the throttle to maximum. Jack held his foot on the brake to get maximum power, pausing for a moment. The rumble and grumble of the engines sounded like the roar of a pride of lions standing off against each other. After a few seconds, Alcock released the brake and could feel the thrust as it pushed them down the field, rattling, bouncing, and floundering their way to flight.

"I hope you secured those bolts securely." He cranked a smile over at Brown, and Teddie looked at him, concerned about whether he meant it. Actually, he did mean it.

The Vickers groaned, creaked, bumped, and moaned as it waddled across the tufted-grass landscape, trying to reach up to the skies. Alcock, conscious that they were quickly running out of runway, checked the throttle again to make sure it was on full. The engines labored at their highest RPM, and the chassis strained under the stress.

As the plane accelerated, Jack's heart was in his stomach. The plane was grossly overloaded with fuel. In essence, it was a flying bomb. As the runway sped past and the plane's speed over ground increased exponentially within seconds, Jack wondered if he would ever set foot on dry land again— alive anyway.

With less than a hundred yards to go, Alcock pulled back, and slowly, inch by inch, the Vickers's nose started to pull upward. Like a bird on its first flight, it bumped and flew, bumped and flew. With no room left on the runway, Alcock pulled full back, and the Vickers lurched into its first motions of flight, rising slowly, clipping the tops of the overgrown undergrowth on its belly as it found air and lift and took them skyward on their way. At last, they were off.

"Up, up, and away!" Alcock shouted above the noise of the engines and amid the smell of fuel and oil as he turned the plane away from the shore and headed out to the Atlantic.

"Thank God for that!" he shouted across to Brown with obvious relief. They were in the air.

Brown sent a radio message: "We are off and on our way!"

Brown was navigating. A sextant and a drift-bearing plate were his tools. Under normal conditions, he would have been able to determine their position as they flew, but the weather quickly closed in around them. In the thick fog, which was like pea soup, he lost sight of all reference points and was blinded from navigating their precise position.

They were both nervous. They had discussed the perils of this situation during their preparation for the flight. Although not a navigator, Jack understood the principles and knew that to get the triangular hat, they needed at least three clear shots of three separate stars. The conditions had blinded them to even one clear shot.

"We need to get above the clouds to get a shot on Polaris!" Brown shouted through the wind, rain, fog, and fumes.

Jack looked over at him, acutely aware of their situation, as Brown pointed upward. The problem with dead reckoning was that they could easily and quickly get blown off course and might never hit land before running out of fuel in the drink, never to be seen again. He could not even entertain that thought, never mind utter it.

"Up we go, old boy." He pulled the joystick and started climbing through the thick, sickly clouds.

Jack knew that due to the tailwinds, they were tracking much faster than they had planned. They were averaging 106 miles per hour, which was good for fuel consumption, and if they kept on track within a seven-hundred-mile window, they would inevitably hit somewhere in Europe, but Ireland was their prize.

Brown raised two thumbs up to Alcock. "Good on you, Jack! I knew there was a good reason I brought you along on the ride!" he said, beaming, always with his spirits up, never thinking about disaster or defeat.

Brown poured two mugs of tea from the flask to celebrate. Alcock reached inside his thick pilot's jacket, pulled out another type of flask with his gloved hand, and poured what he estimated to be a good two fingers of rum into each mug.

"Cheers, old boy," Jack said, and they toasted to the night and their record-breaking adventure together. "To the king!" They smashed their mugs together in salute.

Alcock had dreamed of this moment when he was a prisoner of war held by the Turks. He'd had plenty of time to dream and to plan, and this was his moment—their moment. They were about to make history, unless the two thousand miles in front of them got in the way. He focused on the mesmerizing fog in front of them as they climbed, with his eyes loosely tracking the altimeter amid the thick, disorientating yellow-white blanket, trusting the instruments he had to keep him on course.

Their moment of celebration was short-lived. Within twenty minutes, with the tea and rum long gone, the weather worsened, and the rain turned to snow as they made their way east. Ice coated the Vickers, and Brown had to repeatedly stand up in the open cockpit to clear the ice from the instrument sensors. The instruments were failing in the extreme cold.

With the cold and zero visibility, Jack could feel his head start to spin and his eyes roll from the combination of the wall of fog, the cold, and the deafening sound of the engines as they were exposed to the elements. "Why the hell didn't we choose a bird with a proper cockpit?" he shouted into the wind. Brown looked nervous beside him, desperate to get above the clouds and see starlight.

Alcock became disorientated and lost control of the Vickers. The air-intake outlets were all frozen, the Rolls-Royce engines stalled, and the Vickers entered a tailspin. Brown stared down at the instruments with a look of fear in his eyes. Jack followed his gaze and could see the dials spinning around like whirling dervishes. They were descending quickly—too quickly. They were crashing toward the cold, deadly ocean below.

"Pull her up, Jack!" Brown shouted the obvious.

"I am, old boy! What the bloody hell do you think I'm doing?" Jack grappled with the controls as though his physical strength might alter their course, as opposed to his well-honed and experienced piloting skills.

Brown scrambled around the aircraft, doing what he could to resuscitate the air intakes, and as they descended, hitting the warmer air, the intakes unfroze sufficiently to breathe and to allow Alcock to restart the engines.

Jack's heart was in his mouth as he heard the two Rolls-Royce engines sputter and toil at the spark of life and eventually, with big gasps of breath, slowly crescendo into the familiar but strained sound as the smell of fuel filled the cockpit.

"Thank God for that," Brown said, slapping Alcock on the back with his big icicle-covered glove.

They broke through the bottom of the clouds and could see the ocean around five hundred feet below. Alcock wrestled with the joystick to get them pointed at least parallel or, preferably, sky bound once more.

"Pull her up!" screamed Brown to his friend. "Pull her up, Jack!" The ocean was now less than one hundred feet, perilously close. "For God's sake, man, pull her up!" Brown shouted again.

Alcock was deaf to the pleas, with all his concentration on the task at hand: saving their chance of success and their lives.

A few minutes later, as they were back into relative safety, their heartbeats settled close to normal. Alcock said, "Bloody hell, old boy, that was close."

"You're not kidding. That was too bloody close. Come on. Let's get to Ireland. No more rum for you, old boy!" Teddie Brown teased his friend. "Let's wait for that pint of Guinness, eh?"

Alcock chose not to respond.

Then, miraculously, less than thirty minutes later, Brown spotted land. "By George, I think we've bloody made it!" he said, pointing at the land mass ahead of them. "By the luck of God, I think that might be Ireland!"

"I think you might be right, my dear friend," Jack Alcock said, beaming.

It was eight thirty in the morning local time. Alcock headed for a smooth-looking field to land the plane on. They glided in smoothly, and the wheels hit the ground. Immediately, they knew something was wrong, as the wheels sank into the bog that had looked like a field from altitude. The wheels stuck in, the nose flipped forward, and they unceremoniously ground to a halt. "Oh bugger!"

They landed with just a gentle crash, with no one injured. It was 8:40 a.m., and they had completed the first nonstop transatlantic flight. After sixteen hours of flight time and traveling 1,890 miles at an average speed of nearly 120 miles per hour, they had made it with a lot of luck and, as it turned out, very little judgment. They had quickly realized early into the flight that the radio had given up the ghost in the conditions, and if they hadn't hit land, they would have had no way of alerting any potential rescuers. They had been lucky, and Jack Alcock knew that but wasn't going to let that get in the way of a fine celebration and the coveted and well-deserved prize. No one else needed to know.

"We did it!" shouted Jack as the Vickers came to a standstill and the propellers went to sleep, flaying in the mud and the bulrushes. "We went and bloody did it!"

They were welcomed to the town of Clifden like a pair of celebrities and, that night, hosted by the d'Arcy family at Abbeyglen Castle, where a barrel of Guinness was specially bought in to welcome the guests of honor, Jack Alcock and Arthur Brown.

They would pick up their prize money from no other than Winston Churchill himself and later be knighted by King George V.

Mary Beattie sat in her chair, staring into space. She had been like that for six months now, detached from the world, from her children, and from the family she once had known. She wasn't sure how she had gotten there, but the drugs had gotten her to a place where she no longer cared, where her mind had been dancing around in gardens as a child and in the sadness of her own upbringing. She had landed well, getting married and having three children, but the infidelities of her husband right before her eyes had been the catalyst that tipped her over the edge and into the chasm. It was a dark and deep place.

They had taken away her freedom. Since her attempt to end it all, they had taken away her right to make her own decisions. She was okay with that; she did not want to make decisions anyway.

She had not seen her children since. It was better that way. She was alone, lonely, and ashamed, but the drugs took the edge off those feelings too.

Her days were a monotonous repetition. She got out of bed, ready for the doctor's round in the morning, but his words were just a blur. At breakfast, she sat in her chair, looking out at the grounds of High Royds, thinking about what has passed and what could have been. Then came a morning walk around the gardens, lunch, and afternoon, and then, at night, came the nightmares that haunted her each and every night.

This morning, Wednesday, July 9, 1919, was not much different until midmorning, around ten thirty, when a doctor came to her ward with the news of her husband's suicide in Paris.

Mary's husband, William—a dashing man who had once swept her off her feet, a successful man, the father of their three children, a philanderer—had sat in a hotel in Paris just the day before.

He had left the family just a couple of days after Mary's internment. He'd packed his bags; left the children and Miss Boswell; and, on his own, gone forth.

Mary loved him. She always had. She'd loved his charm, his kindness, and his love, at least initially. However, his indiscretions had torn her apart and ripped everything from beneath her, often right in front of her face.

What have I done to deserve this? she had once thought. She'd believed things would get better over time, but like a cancer, the demons had grown inside her, and she could not take it anymore.

At one point, she had cared, but during the diminishing times when her husband chose to be home, he rarely slept in the same bed, making excuses instead and sleeping elsewhere.

She recalled the time she had walked downstairs and found him fornicating on the sofa downstairs—not any sofa but one she had selected for their new home as newlyweds. At one time, Mary had felt the pain, but she no longer did; the pain was gone. She was left only with this lonely prison, four walls around her and her mind.

Sitting alone in his hotel room off the Champs-Élysées, William Beattie, with a bottle of his favorite Liddesdale whisky, pondered the conclusion that he had already come to. He stared down at his army-issued Webley Mark IV in front of him on the desk. He touched the grip as he sipped on his whisky, remembering all the things he could have done and probably should have done differently.

Listening to the hustle and bustle of the Parisian night outside, he decided to head out one last time. He wandered the streets from bar to bar and eventually returned to the hotel at two o'clock in the morning.

At 2:11 a.m., a shot was heard ringing through the hotel and the night, and when the night manager dashed into his room, there was William Baxter Beattie, slumped in his chair at his desk with a half-empty bottle of whisky, a note to his children, and his brains spoiling the pretty fleur-de-lis wallpaper behind.

7

LONDON BOUND

July 9, 1928
London

NIKKI AND AMY BOARDED THE train at York Station
for the next chapter of their journey together. Amy's father
had secured them both employment as secretaries to a
William Charles Crocker, Esq., a prominent London solicitor
and lawyer. They were on their way to a new life, a new
adventure, a new beginning.

Both had graduated from Sheffield University the
previous November. They had both been home for
Christmas, Amy in Kingston upon Hull and Nikki in Ilkley.
The Johnson family included the parents, the grandparents,
and Amy's three sisters, while Nikki had only Miss Boswell
and her brothers, Walter and John, with both parents now
fully absent.

It was seven fifteen in the morning as they got to platform number one with their cases packed and ready to go for their new life down south.

Amy's parents had driven her over in their latest model, a 1928 New Phantom. In contrast, Nikki had taken the train from Ilkley to Leeds and on to York.

Nikki greeted Mr. and Mrs. Johnson. They treated her as if she were their own daughter. Nikki felt a little uncomfortable at their politeness in not asking too many questions and in avoiding a harsh reminder for Nikki of happier times long gone back at Lair Close, Kirk Ella.

The train pulled into the station—the Flying Scotsman route originating from Edinburgh. The porters helped with their cases as they boarded the first-class carriage and went to their reserved compartment.

Nikki and Amy settled in, stowed their bags and coats, and made themselves comfortable. It was an oblong compartment on the left-hand side of the train, with the corridor running down the side and with glass windows looking on and blinds to pull down for privacy or sleep.

Six plush upholstered armchairs sat around a folded-out table set for breakfast with white linens and silverware embossed with *LNER*.

The girls waved at the Johnsons out their window on the platform side, and Amy stood up, shouting her goodbyes to her parents and three sisters. Nikki waved politely, silent in her sadness. She missed her own family terribly.

As the train pulled away from the station, after the last wave to her family, Amy sat down, looked at her friend, and smiled.

Together they looked out the window as the train wove its way through the outskirts of the walled city and quickly made it into the lush green Yorkshire countryside on their journey south.

The steward, dressed in a blue-gray tailcoat, arrived at the door with a linen-bedecked trolley with tea and refreshments and knocked politely. "Good morning, ladies. Tea this morning?" he said with his big waiter's smile.

"Oh yes, please," they chorused, looking at each other, full of excitement for the journey, new life, and opportunity. "Earl Grey?" they asked together, giggling at the fact that they knew each other so well.

The steward placed the silver teapot on the table and inserted the infuser with the selected tea leaves. "Taylors Tea, of course," he said, placing a small jug of fresh milk and sugar, and then he took their breakfast orders: two Yorkshire breakfasts with all the trimmings, they both quickly decided. The breakfast included dry-cured bacon, Yorkshire sausage, scrambled eggs, tomato, mushrooms, and toast. It was a Bettys Tea Room staple.

They both loved Bettys. The pair would meet up in the spa town of Harrogate and go to their café on Parliament Street for a Yorkshire breakfast, for afternoon tea, or just for their fat rascals—all were delicious.

They would stay at the Old Swan Hotel, take in the spas, stroll the Stray, and plan their future dreams together.

They were young, just twenty-six, and had made it through university. They were bright, intelligent, full of beans, and ready for their new adventure.

They were both lean and fit; well dressed and appointed; well spoken, at least for Yorkshire lasses; daring; vivacious; and incredibly attractive propositions to any suitors of the male variety. They were both conscious of that, and although neither, at that point, had full-on relationships with boys, Nikki was still in touch with her young man William, and Amy had hosted Nikki's brother Walter several times while they were at university.

They were like a pair of free birds, finally spreading their wings and fleeing their cages to their new lives in London.

The journey to King's Cross would be just under four and a half hours. They could feel the power and the rush of the steam train as it reached full power. It was 202 miles from York to London.

They sipped their Earl Grey. Soon after, their breakfasts arrived, courtesy of the steward: porcelain plates with the same *LNER* and silver plate domes whisked away in synchrony, revealing the delights beneath. They started to eat.

"How was Christmas, dear Nikki?" Amy asked.

Nikki looked back over the table at her friend, sensing her pain. "It's been seven years but still very painful."

Amy nodded, understanding.

After the news of Nikki's father, just two weeks later, Mrs. Beattie had been found dead in her ward, hung around the throat with a length of gardener's wire, which she had found in the potting shed at High Royds. Unlike her father, her mother had left no letter. There was little or no closure, and the tragedy hung thick like fog on Nikki's mind.

"Walter and John seem to be doing well." Amy brightened the conversation.

After their parents had left, the brothers had finished school early and turned their hand to their calling as engineers and entrepreneurs and, at just seventeen, had set up a car sales, gasoline, and repair shop in Ilkley, servicing all the wealthy folks' cars. They had grown up in the business; it was in their blood. They were two fine young men living their passion and making good money at it too.

"The Beattie brothers. They are doing pretty well. If it was not for Walter, though, I am not sure how well John would do under his own steam," Nikki said, and Amy nodded, attentively listening. "He didn't take it too well. Worse than all of us."

Miss Boswell, the family nanny, had been left her father's estate and was custodian and executor of his will. Each month, she would sign the allowance checks for the three, and she was reinvesting some of the funds in property in Ilkley.

Although it was uncertain, there was a growing suspicion that her relationship with their father had been more than that of an employer and his employee. The three did not know what to make of that, and even if true, it was a taboo subject they had all subconsciously decided to park away in the depths of their minds. It was too painful, and besides, the double suicide of their parents, the philandering of their father, and the internment of their mother was all embarrassing and shameful enough.

Besides, Miss Boswell had been their rock for so long. They would have surely perished a long time ago if not for her efforts to support the children now grown.

"Has she married yet?" asked Amy.

Nikki just shook her head, and her silence was enough to move the conversation forward. It was a technique she had learned from Miss Esme Boswell herself.

The steward cleared their plates, and the girls looked out the window at the passing countryside, chatting now and then about university, William, Walter, girlfriends, the weather, news, and their plans for London.

"Did you read about the American girl Amelia Earhart?" Amy asked, interrupting Nikki's thoughts and the silence only friends were comfortable with.

Nikki recollected the name. "You mean the pilot?"

"She broke a world record. An altitude of fourteen thousand feet."

"Women's record," Nikki said, remembering reading the story in the *Yorkshire Post*. "In a bright yellow Kinner Airster. She called it *Canary*!"

"Now, that's what I call pioneering!" exclaimed Amy with a big grin.

At university, Amy had been a rule breaker. Engineering was regarded as only for men, and although the university did not allow women to study the subject, she had insisted she and Nikki could attend the class if they so wished. Much to the consternation of the faculty, the professors, and the men, they had been granted access and had attended the class.

"She cut her hair short and slept in that pilot's jacket for three days to blend in." Nikki remembered the photograph of the good-looking woman with cropped blonde hair and a waistline leather jacket and fur collar standing in front of her bright yellow biplane. "Miss Earhart is becoming somewhat of a superstar over there."

"You see, Nikki? We can do what we want. The world is our oyster. Why should we let them hold us back? Amelia became the sixteenth female pilot in the United States but also the most famous. Nikki, let us be the Flying Foxtrots—not just for us but for the empire!"

They broke into laughter together. Nikki looked at her friend, who had enthusiasm and courage written all over her pretty face. Her fearlessness was one of the many things she loved about her friend.

Nikki looked out the window as they traversed from the green of the countryside to the density of buildings as they made their way through London and into King's Cross Station.

"Anything is possible. Even for a woman. This is our time," said Amy. "Flying Foxtrots!"

Amelia was at work when she received the call.

"Millie, there's a gentleman on the line for you. He says his name is Captain Hilton Railey." Her coworker looked at her, raised her eyebrows, and crinkled her nose at Millie as if to say, "Aren't you the lucky one today?"

Denison House, founded thirty-five years earlier, was a woman-run settlement house in the South Cove neighborhood of Boston that supplied social and educational support, mainly to immigrant women.

In addition to her work at Denison House, her main job, Millie kept her love for aviation and was a member of the Boston chapter of the American Aeronautical Society. She flew in her spare time and as she could afford it. A year earlier, she had been the first person to fly out of, and the first official flight from, nearby Dennison Airport.

In addition, she had a freelance sales role for the plane manufacturer Kinner and was a freelance writer for several publications, including the local newspaper. Her topics focused on promoting flying and the advancement of women.

Amelia "Millie" Earhart's local celebrity status was growing, and she was quickly becoming the face of women in aviation and in the United States.

She walked over to the telephone, picked it up, and cleared her throat. "Good morning, Captain Railey. How may I be of assistance today?" she said in her Sunday-best voice.

The man on the other end of the line told her someone called Amy Phipps Guest, the daughter of some wealthy American family, had originally been sponsored for an opportunity by her family, but they had ruled out the trip as being too perilous.

"We are now actively seeking a replacement," said the man with a New York accent. "This is really a dandy deal, and well, your name came up as a potential candidate. What do you think, Miss Earhart?"

Amelia stood there in the booth, looked out the window onto the street, and wrinkled her nose, thinking she might have missed something. She paused for a moment and then said, "Captain Railey, I'm not sure I quite understand. A replacement for what exactly?"

The man on the telephone chuckled. "Yes, sorry. I was getting carried away with myself. I should have explained further." He cleared his throat. "To be the first woman to fly across the Atlantic."

Millie's head went into a spin like one of the tornadoes from her hometown of Atchison. She caught herself. "I am sorry, Captain Railey. Can you repeat that, please?"

The man cleared his throat once more and said with a little bit less patience in his voice, "Miss Earhart, do you want to be the first woman to fly across the Atlantic Ocean?"

She gathered her senses, realizing this was her big opportunity and certainly no time for hesitation, or she was in danger to lose the opportunity. "Why, Captain Railey, I would love to be the first woman to fly across the Atlantic. When do I start?"

They made arrangements for Amelia to travel to New York the following day, and the day after, she would meet with the captain and Mrs. Phipps Guest to confirm her suitability to fit the bill of "an American girl of the right type," whatever that meant.

Millie hung up, excited, and she made her excuses, went straight home to nearby Medford, and began her preparations for the next day and New York. She would leave on the early morning train to travel the five hours to New York.

She was born to fly, and this was her big chance. She was flying high!

Just four years earlier, the London Aeroplane Club had opened its doors for business as a private club, opened by Sir Philip Sassoon, a politician, art collector, and socialite.

The airfield had been a training facility during the World War I. The airplane maker de Havilland had set up shop conveniently close by. In North London, it was the perfect location to attract its target clientele: those who had sufficient disposable income in the pursuit of aviation for sport and adventure and to push the boundaries and possibilities of flight.

That day, Nikki Beattie and Amy Johnson were to be awarded their licenses. It was a cause for celebration, as they had achieved a first: not only attaining their pilot's A license but also being the first British women in history to be awarded the ground engineer's C license. It was a big deal and not just for them and for publicity for the club but also, most importantly to Amy and Nikki, for women across the nation and around the world.

Shortly after arriving in London just a year earlier, they had visited the club and met with Mrs. Elliot Lynn, and it had not taken much persuasion for them to embark upon the journey of flight—in fact, quite the opposite. Nikki and Amy had always dreamed of doing something different with their lives, and being aviators was near the top of that list of possibilities. There were additional compelling factors.

Mary Elliot Lynn was one of only six founding female members of the club. She was an Irishwoman, an aviator, and one of the most well-known women of the day. She was keen to grow female membership of the club, and she was bright-eyed at the prospect of signing up the young ladies from up north. Amy and Nikki both agreed and at once took to Mrs. Elliot Lynn, and they were confident the feeling was mutual.

The introduction of their prospective tutor did nothing to harm their recruitment efforts either. Beyond the romance of his name, Captain Valentine Baker, was a tall, good-looking war hero brimming with charisma and charm.

The combination of the above was more than sufficient for them to seal the deal. Nikki and Amy both gladly and excitedly signed up that day, and the following weekend, they started their training in earnest.

Amy's father had bought an apartment in Hampstead Heath, midway between William Crocker's law firm in the city and Edgware, where the airplane club was. Equidistant at just under seven miles in each direction, it was convenient.

The morning of the awards ceremony, Captain Valentine, known as Bakes to his friends, picked them up in his 1925 British racing-green Bentley, whose three-liter engine grunted and rattled as a signal that he had arrived.

Originally from Wales, Bakes had served in all three of Her Majesty's services, and between 1914 and 1921, he had picked up the Military Cross and the Air Force Cross for his service. He was a good-looking man with a big, warm smile, and since his military days, he'd been known as the Teacher of Dukes due to his extensive list of students in the upper ranks of society.

That day, he was crowning his two princesses of the skies as queens of the air, as he had often joked throughout their training—a great elevation from their first day of training, when he'd eyed them in their brand-new, starched, and stiff coveralls, teased them, and nicknamed them the Hampstead Harriers.

Nikki and Amy trotted out down the pathway to the road, greeted by Valentine, who opened the door, which had *Racing 9* painted on the door. He held out a hand and helped Nikki into the back, helped Amy into the front, and then sped off north up Bishops Avenue between the golf clubs and toward the Great North Way to take them to Edgware and to Stag Lane.

Like her brothers, having grown up around cars, Nikki loved the thrill of the speed but also, especially with this Bentley, the grunt of the engine, the smell of oil and petrol fumes, and the heat coming from the engine. It reminded her of her childhood and of her father. She also associated the same feeling, smells, and sensations with flight, the difference being the moment when she was airborne and soared above the clouds. For Nikki, cars came second to flying, but she had to admit, especially with Bentleys, that cars were a close second.

Twenty minutes later, they pulled into the aerodrome of the London Aeroplane Club, and Nikki remembered her first day of training like it was yesterday. The past few months had flown by.

There had been so much learning and studying to do before they even got into a plane, never mind flying one. The first phase had been the theory of flight, familiarization with the plane and its controls, navigation, and, of course, the emergency drills. After the first phase of the basics, Bakes had taken them up as passengers for familiarization for weeks before they had started taking off and landing themselves as copilots.

That had been a year earlier, and six months ago, they had both picked up their aviator certificates, numbers 8662 and 8663, and they had become the first women to certify as ground engineers. Now they were being awarded their pilot's A licenses, numbers 1979 and 1980.

The airfield was a pretty sparse affair, just a main hangar with a few sheds scattered around it. One of them housed the training room where they had spent their first few weeks; there was a main office, along with some storage sheds; and apart from the airfield itself, that was about it.

It was Saturday, and members of the club had turned out in support of the two young ladies from Yorkshire and their graduation. Sir Philip Sassoon himself awarded the certificates, with Mary Elliot Lynn and Captain Valentine Baker proudly looking on.

To signal the end of the formalities, as the celebrations began, two of the club's female members, Buffy Bateson and Micki McGuire, conducted a flyby in their Gipsy Moths, flying especially low, making the men hang on to their hats under the gust of the planes. Upon that signal, the champagne was uncorked, the reception sandwiches were unveiled, and the candles were lit on the cake. The throng of thirty or so aviators celebrated the two latest additions to their ranks, Amy Johnson and Nikki Beattie, two aviatrixes.

When the celebration was drawing to a close, they said their goodbyes, and Bakes ushered them back into the Bentley and whisked them away back to Hampstead Heath especially quickly, pushing the racer to its limits. The sun was high in the sky, the wind was in their hair, and the champagne fueled their sense of mischief and achievement.

They said farewell to Bakes, and linking arms, they trotted together back to their apartment and flopped onto the sofa.

Amy, with her big grin, asked, "What next, my dearest Nikki?"

They remembered their friend Captain Valentine Baker's famous call to action: "Tallyho!"

Aviatrix

Avidly we go in pursuit of the skies,
Valiantly soar, hope in our eyes,
Inside the box where dreams come true.
Access for many, not just the few.

Traverse the world as fast as we can go,
Roam the mountains and valleys below.
In the darkest hour, I share the moon,
X-ray focus, I'll be home soon.

—Nikki Beattie, 1929

8

TRUMPINGTON

July 11, 1929
Anstey Hall
Trumpington, Cambridge, England

ANSTEY HALL WAS ONE OF the finest houses in Trumpington and home to the Foster family. Built in 1670, it had a redbrick facade and gallery windows, with lawns to the front and a chapel to the side. Amy had planned to meet Walter in Cambridge, and thanks to an invite from her friend Helen Mary Finch Foster and her husband, Roger Parker, they were staying at Anstey Hall. It was Walter's birthday on July 9, and they wanted to celebrate. It had been a while. She had also just completed her class-A pilot's license, so a double celebration was the order of the weekend.

Since Boulevard School and Kirk Ella and even after Walter and his family had moved to Ilkley, they had remained as close as the distance would allow them to. They regularly wrote to each other with updates on their latest news. Amy would meet Nikki in Harrogate occasionally, and Walter would come along too. While at university, Walter had been a regular visitor to Sheffield, but now she was in London, and Walter was busy with his car business, so it was increasingly difficult to meet in person, and sadly, they had begun to drift apart. This weekend was an opportunity to reconnect.

It was a beautiful midsummer day in England. Amy was on the lawn with the Parkers, playing croquet. Mrs. Lambert, Anstey's housekeeper, had brought them afternoon tea: reception sandwiches, strawberry tarts, and Earl Grey tea. It was three o'clock, and Walter would be arriving soon from his two-hundred-mile trip from Ilkley.

"Mrs. Lambert! A bottle of your finest champagne! We have a visitor!" Roger Parker said as the red MG M spun around the corner through the gate, sped down the drive toward them, and crunched to a halt on the drive.

Walter had a big grin on his face. "Bloody fantastic!" he said.

Amy and the Parkers strode over to meet him, and Roger reached out to shake his hand and slap him on the shoulder. "Great to see you, old boy, and a happy birthday to you too!"

Walter stepped over to Helen, held her by her shoulders, and kissed her cheek. "The ever-beautiful and serene Mrs. Parker." He looked over her shoulder. "And the as-beautiful and gorgeous Yorkshire lassie, pilot, and adventuress Miss

Amy Johnson!" Walter Beattie was a charmer. Amy loved that about him.

"Nice car, Walt! The MG Midget. I saw the launch at the motor show in October," Roger Parker said proudly. "She's a beauty!"

Walter, still embracing Amy, walked them over to the car. Walter scooped up Mrs. Parker and put his arms around the women's waists. "Who? The car or these two beauties, old boy?" He grinned with his big, infectious smile.

"You silly old bugger. The bloody car!" Parker slapped the hot bonnet.

"Sorry I am late. Took me a little longer than I thought."

Mrs. Lambert arrived with a silver tray holding a white linen napkin, four champagne flutes, and a bottle of Veuve Clicquot.

"Perfect timing, Mrs. Lambert." Roger Parker grabbed the bottle, popped the cork with little regard for the spray of bubbles, and poured them all a glass. "Cheers!" he announced.

They all clinked their glasses and chorused, "Happy birthday, Walter!"

Parker added, "Welcome to Trumpington, old boy!" He turned to Amy. "And to our new fully qualified aviator!" He guffawed, and the group raised their glasses once more.

Amy recounted the awards ceremony at the aero club the week before, and Walter went on to explain the reason for his tardiness: "You see, Mrs. Ogden is a client of mine, and she asked if I would drive her old banger down to Cowley and pick up this little beauty." He pointed to the cherry-red MG Midget two-seater sports car. "No other than the M-Type." He looked at his blank-faced audience. "You know! The one and only beauty that won the gold medal at the Land's End Trial this year!"

Roger Parker nodded with some knowledge of the trial of speed and endurance turned joy ride. "Plenty under the bonnet then?"

"Oh yes, sir! Had plenty of fun on the way over from Cowley!"

"All the cause for more champagne!" Parker topped up their glasses and emptied the bottle.

Those were halcyon days indeed. Helen was an heir of the Foster family, wealthy mill owners and bankers. Her grandfather had sold the bank to Lloyds. Walter was a young, vibrant, and charismatic businessman in the growing car trade. Amy was an adventurer, pilot, and aviatrix.

"Come on, gang. Let's head down to the Blue Ball Inn for some fun before dinner!" Parker announced. "Let me grab the Bentley! A proper car!" He slapped Walter on the back with a grin. "I'll race you!"

The fun and the banter continued throughout the afternoon, and by their return to Anstey, they were all hungry and a little tipsy.

After they finished the three courses Mrs. Lambert had cooked up, Amy and Walter announced they were going to stroll it off, made their excuses, and headed out to walk the grounds together.

"Jolly good, old chap!" Parker said as he popped another bottle of the Veuve Clicquot. "Bloody fine glass of bubbly!"

His wife rolled her eyes over toward Amy and Walter. "I'm heading up to bed, dear, and I think you should too, given the amount you have drunk today."

With a cigar hanging out of his mouth, he had the bottle in hand and another full glass of bubbly. "Right, oh dearest. I'll be up shortly, madam!" he said, obviously not meaning a word of it.

Amy and Walter laughed at their host. "You are too funny, Mr. Roger Parker," Amy said.

It was a fine summer evening; the heat of the day had subsided as the birds sang their final tunes before nightfall. The smell of newly mown grass and flowers was in the air as they strolled across the lawns to the front of the house and the village beyond. They sat on the wall together at the bottom of the garden and had some time to catch up.

As nightfall crept in, they headed to Saint Mary and Saint Michael's. Its windows flickered from the outside as the evening candles burned their scent and welcoming glow.

Hand in hand, they walked through the big, arched wooden door into the church. Its white stone arches and white brick aisle drew them on farther to the altar beneath the arched window and display of candles.

Both were silent. It was too beautiful a moment for words. There was an air of nervous tension, an anticipation. *Could this be the moment?* Amy thought as her heartbeat quickened. She wondered if she was blushing, but in the soft light of the evening and the candles, she pushed away the thought. She took a moment to look across at Walter. His steel-blue eyes looked even bluer in the light, reflecting the magic of the candles and of the moment.

Slowly, intensely, Walter squeezed her hand three times in rhythm, like Morse code. She squeezed back the same but quicker and added one more squeeze.

They walked back to the hall, talking and laughing, staying on safe ground. Amy knew of the taboo subjects and did not want to go there; the pain was still raw for Nikki, and she assumed the same was true for Walter.

They talked of their weekend and their plans; they'd visit the university, the museums, and the town. They talked of country drives in the MG. They sat once more on the bench at the front of the house overlooking the lawns, underneath the stars of the summer evening in England's green and pleasant land.

They got back to the house to find Roger Parker sparko on his armchair, with a cigar still hanging out of his mouth, cuddling the Veuve Clicquot as though it were a childhood friend.

"You silly old fool. Parker, come on. Let's get you up to bed and to your lovely and patient wife."

"I say, old boy, that's a bit harsh, you know. You're not the only catch around here, you know." He hung on to Walter's shoulders as he winked at Amy with a cheeky and drunken grin, still hanging on to the champagne for dear life.

Amy went upstairs to retire as Walter did his best to wake Parker up. She could hear the rumbles, grumbles, and protestations behind her as Walter stirred their friend and host.

She smiled, listening to the struggle below, and then slowly and gently closed her bedroom door behind her, automatically touching the key in the keyhole. Then she caught herself, paused, and thought for a moment.

She thought of the scene at the church just a few moments ago and the three squeezes, and she wondered if they were reading from the same code book. She recalled her four-squeeze reply.

She gently and slowly took her hand off the key, leaving her door unlocked, and went to bed. "I love you too."

Nineteen aircraft of all shapes, sizes, and colors lined up on the airstrip with engines running, ready to go. Nineteen female pilots, pioneers, were at the starting line of a race that would take them from the west coast of California all the way to Cleveland, Ohio, nearly 2,700 miles, eight days, and eleven stops later. It was the first Women's Air Derby as part of the 1929 National Air Races.

The field was strong, featuring the best female aviators in the United States, plus Australian Jessie Miller, German Thea Rasche, and a lineup of the most famous female pilots of the day: Mary von Mach, Blanche Noyes, Ruth Elder, Miss America of Aviation Louise Thaden, and Amelia Earhart from Atchison, Kansas. They were all eager to show the world that women had their place in aviation.

Thousands of onlookers lined the field. The men wore straw boaters, the women wore floral dresses and hats, and children climbed up into the trees. Almost everyone with a car was on the airfield that day.

Amelia had long ago realized that she offered hope to the people and to women. Female pilots carried a responsibility to lift the nation, and the nation certainly got right behind them.

The nineteen women in their planes were not just pioneers but were heroes, role models, and the superstars of their age—a point certainly not missed by her recent acquaintance George Palmer Putnam, or GP, as he preferred to be called. He was an adventurer, explorer, publisher, and publicist from the East Coast. He was also a great admirer, and despite being married, he had pursued Amelia not only as a client but also as a potential love interest.

The National Air Races' first ever women's event was dubbed the Powder Puff Derby. That annoyed Amelia and many of the other pilots. It was the way of the male-dominated industries of the day, including the press. GP had downplayed it as Millie protested the headline in that morning's paper.

"Don't fret, Amelia. It's good for business," he had said.

"But they're undermining what all this stands for—what it really means to be a woman in this age," she'd responded.

"Yes, yes, I get it, Millie, but the point is, the more publicity you get, the more influence you will have to change things."

She'd understood his point. "Of course, but that is not their intent. You already know of the rumors that this might be the first and the last time. They are already talking about banning us from racing."

"If they do that, then they will only make the movement even more determined."

Millie had nodded. "Of course, you are right, George, but I still don't like it."

"And neither do I, dear, but you gotta fight them at their own game."

The array of planes in different makes and colors, all with their numbers painted on their fuselages, took off from the airfield one at a time to the cheers of the crowd and the melody of the brass band playing for the crowds waving their hats and flags and smiling in wonder and awe at the planes that took to the skies.

Millie looked out from her cockpit, scanning the crowd, and spotted him in his three-piece tweed suit, with his watch chain in his waistcoat pocket glinting in the sun, and his trilby and sunglasses. Just before starting orders, one of the stewards had handed her a bouquet of flowers, which she had stowed behind her seat.

Still idling, waiting for her signal to take off, she stood up in the cockpit and waved to her friend, her lover. Acknowledging her wave, he blew her a kiss, and they quietly sent their love telepathically across the distance.

It was Amelia's turn to join the race. Upon the signal, she pulled on full throttle and careered down the airstrip, bouncing up and down, until there was sufficient speed and uplift to take her skyward.

Millie had been engaged for a while to Sam Chapman, an engineer from Boston, but had broken it off the previous November. GP had shown a lot of attention to Millie. She liked that, but he was married. They had first met in New York after her seminal phone call with Captain Hilton Railey.

GP had published Charles Lindbergh's autobiographical account of his early life, a blockbuster selling more than 650,000 copies in less than a year. Millie was impressed, of course.

Although he was married, the marriage was not a happy one, and to be fair, his wife, Dorothy, was having a well-documented affair with a South African twenty years her junior. GP had tolerated it for too long and had filed for divorce earlier that year. He was now a free agent, and just the night before, he had proposed to Millie over dinner at the Clock Tower in Santa Monica: lobster, champagne, and diamonds. He had already asked several more times before.

Anyway, she had this serious business of flying to get on with, and at that, she put her head down: *First stop San Bernardino.*

At each stop along the way, they were greeted by the media and wined and dined by the local dignitaries as the engineers refueled and repaired the planes and the pilots got some rest.

They went from Yuma to Phoenix to Douglas, Arizona, and then through El Paso, Pecos, Midland, Abilene, and Fort Worth, Texas. Then they went on to St. Louis and then Cincinnati.

Somewhere along the way, fellow pilot Marvel Crosson crashed and died, apparently after passing out from carbon monoxide poisoning. Flying was a dangerous game and filled with gung-ho personalities, which was not often a good combination. People died at this game, especially the reckless.

Millie thought about GP and, outside his proposals of marriage, his business proposals. He saw the potential. Millie, a national hero, a superstar, could be an endorser of all sorts of products, from tobacco to booze to candy.

"I can make you a very happy, very rich woman, young lady," he had said with a smile after presenting his proposal.

She liked that confidence and go-getter attitude. *The sky's the limit!*

9

BEATTIE BROTHERS

August 30, 1929
Beattie Brothers Garage
Coutances Way, Ilkley, West
Riding of Yorkshire, England

WITH MRS. OGDEN'S CHERRY-RED MG Midget safely delivered and another happy customer, Walter sped down the road in his latest ride: a brand-new, top-of-the-range 1,087-cubic-centimeter Riley 9 Brooklands, registration number WB09 07, in midnight blue, one of only twelve made that year. Walter liked his cars. They were his passion, his love, and this latest acquisition was his pride.

The car had been delivered that morning to Riverside House. Earlier that morning, Walter had awoken to the sound of the roar and grumble of the engine and the shaking of the ground as the car crunched its way onto the gravel drive.

He often wondered at the similarities between his love and Amy's. The only difference was a pair of wings. Motorcars were raw and exciting; they were for the wealthy. They were his business.

He dashed downstairs; Esme was already on the porch, admiring Beattie Blue. Walter had already told her all about it. She was as excited as he was. She was looking forward to taking it for a spin together. Walter had already named the car weeks ago, even before he had placed the order.

Walter stood there on the step in his pajamas and combed his hair back with his fingers, speechless. "Wow, that is a thing of divine beauty," he said out loud. Esme Boswell, standing tightly next to him, agreed.

He signed the papers and got the keys, and Beattie Blue was officially his—well, she was an asset of Beattie Brothers, which was as good as his.

Excited about his latest acquisition, Walter went upstairs to change and get ready for the day. After he and Esme got dressed, they came back down and made breakfast. Esme toasted muffins and poured tea. As she went happily about making breakfast, Walter looked on with a feeling of contentment taking hold. She had played a major part in their lives since his parents had committed suicide. His dad had made Esme the executor of his will, and with the funds set aside for him and his siblings, she'd helped fund Beattie Brothers. He knew she'd also been investing her own money in properties in the town and had done quite well thus far.

Esme was still considered a beautiful woman, and she had no lack of admirers. Her olive skin had kept her looking youthful, and her dark mahogany eyes created a sense of the exotic and mystery that Walter found alluring.

They sat over breakfast, and Esme tried to make conversation, but Walter was focused wholly on filling himself up with the breakfast delights as quickly as he could. "Can't wait to crank her up and take her for a good ride!"

After breakfast, they did exactly that. Walter was careful not to overdo it, though. The engine needed proper breaking in before he could really let loose. They headed out of Ilkley and went straight toward Hollins Hill. Unable to resist, Walter gave the car more gas, and they both laughed with the wind in their hair and racing goggles on, with not a care in the world.

He dropped Esme at Riverside, and an hour and a half later, Walter pulled off Coutances Way onto the forecourt at the front of his garage. As he pulled up, his brother walked out of the workshop toward him in his blue coveralls with sleeves rolled up. *Beattie Brothers* was embroidered on the left side of the chest, and the Castrol oil logo was on the other side.

John greeted him with a smug smirk that usually meant he wasn't happy about something or other. "When did you get that then?" he asked in a monotone, signaling toward the Riley with a gesture intended to show he was underwhelmed.

"Oh, good morning, Walter! How are you today, my dearest brother? Now, that's a beautiful car you have there!" Walter attempted to avoid the question and remind John that they were brothers and that when good things happened, they should be happy for their sibling.

John was vastly different from Walter; he lacked ambition and drive and was risk averse when it came to money. Walter, the complete opposite, had invested all his savings and leveraged a loan from the bank to secure the property just outside Ilkley. It was not quite Harrogate but was not far off in terms of the wealth of the residents of the town. It was not a city of industry, as Bradford and Leeds were, but it was only sixteen, twelve, and seventeen miles from each of those cities, which meant he could pick clients up, take them for a ride, and use his Walter charm to close the sale. In many ways, he took after his father. Just like William, Walter was a risk taker, and so far, his risks had paid off and were paying off handsomely.

John was more like their mother. He was quiet, introverted, and a pessimist, while Walter was the opposite. John had dark moments of depression and tended to display jealously in preference to joy. Walter had been concerned for a long time that it might be something that ran in the family. That was why Walter did not mind supporting his brother and had named the garage as he had despite John's absence of any investment. Besides, John was a bloody good mechanic, reliable, steady, and a workhorse, so the arrangement worked for both of them.

Walter not only had leveraged financially but also had taken advantage of his father's network. As an early pioneer in the car industry, William Beattie had had a lot of senior and powerful connections, and they were even more willing to help after the news of his demise.

Walter had resisted becoming a sole and exclusive dealer of any single marque but instead had grown a stable of relationships and built a solid reputation that if one wanted a car, no matter how limited or rare, then Walter Beattie was the man to go to. He had also built up a loyal and expanding following of wealthy clients from the mills, factories, and farms of industrious Yorkshire.

Walter held his hands up. "Oh, John, I told you about this weeks ago." He grinned from ear to ear. "Don't you remember?"

John shook his head as if trying to work out if there was any recollection of the conversation.

"Come on. Let's have a cup of Yorkshire tea." Walter slapped him on the back and put his arm around his shoulders as they walked to the workshop office and the kettle.

"What's with the number twenty-one on the door panels?" John asked.

"I am going to race her at Brooklands," said Walter. "That's my racing number, old boy! Number twenty-one, Walter Beattie of Beattie Brothers, Ilkley, no less." He put on the voice of an announcer at the racetrack. "And here he comes around the final bend and onto the straight! Beattie Blue takes the checkered flag and is the winner of the 1930 Brooklands Invitational!" He made zooming and swishing sounds to add audio effects to the scene.

"That's no bloody invitational, Walt; it'll cost you a bloody fortune."

"Oh, thanks for all your encouragement, Brother!" Walter stared at him.

John looked down at the floor, at his own dirty, ragged steel-toed boots and then at his brother's suede dealer boots. "Besides, you'll need me to look her over before you go anywhere."

Walter looked puzzled and was a little annoyed at the lack of enthusiasm. "Why's that, John?"

"She'll need a Beattie Brothers special tune-up." He paused on purpose and looked up at Walter. "If you want to win, that is."

Walter took that as an endorsement, as was his brother's way.

"Free of charge, of course!"

"Silly bugger!"

John made the tea, and the two of them discussed the business of the day. They had plenty of work: car repairs, servicing, petrol, and sales. Walter left the dirty work to John. John liked that, and Walter led the sales. It was a perfect pairing and allocation of duties, Walter thought.

The long weekend in Cambridge had been a hoot, especially with Roger Parker and his gung-ho, by-the-seat-of-your-trousers antics and, of course, the demure company of his beautiful wife, Helen. However, the highlight of the weekend had been Amy. She and Walter had reconnected and, at the end, grown closer than they had ever been.

Despite Walter's confidence and charm in almost every other aspect of his life, Amy always unsettled him. He was not sure why and had often tried to work it out in his mind. He loved her for sure, and he knew she loved him too, so what held him back? Was it that they were too good of friends? Was it that she might say no? Was it that he was not sure? It was a puzzle he had yet to solve.

That day, he had an appointment with Viscount Henry Lascelles, the soon-to-be sixth earl of Harewood, who was interested in buying a Bentley and not just any old Bentley either.

"Let's meet up at the Harewood Arms for a beer later!" he shouted to his brother as he sped off in his new Riley 9 Brooklands, Beattie Blue. *Bloody marvelous!*

Walter drove his blue Riley 9 through the ornate main iron gates and down the gravel drive. In the pastures on either side of the road, Walter could see herds of deer—red, fallow, and roe. The stags stood proudly with their antlers aloft, and the does herded obediently with the fawns now two or three months old.

Walter rounded the huge fountain at the front of the house and pulled the blue racer to a halt outside. The engine ticked and grumbled as it cooled down after being tested it to its limits. It had passed all the tests so far, and Walter was pleased with it.

Walter was pleased with most everything, but especially that he was about to meet with the king's son-in-law. "Bloody hell! It doesn't get much better than that," he had told John that morning.

As he laughed to himself, in walked the viscount, a landowner, a peer, a Mason, and a decorated soldier. Walter instinctively stood up as he marched in. It was obvious he was a soldier and a man of wealth and influence; Walter could just tell. He had a presence about him, and he wanted a Bentley—and not just any Bentley, not just the Bentley Blower, but the Le Mans Bentley Boys car.

Viscount Lascelles liked Walter; Walter could tell. The viscount was the sort of man who would not waste any of his time on someone he didn't like.

"William Turner used to spend a lot of time here," the viscount said.

Walter nodded enthusiastically. "I have always admired his work, sir."

"He would pay for his lodging by painting us another." He pointed to the painting of a cathedral.

"Isn't that Ripon, sir?"

"It is indeed. Well spotted, young Beattie."

He was at least twenty years older than Walter—he was hard to age. *A combination of active duty behind the lines and living the life of an earl*, Walter thought.

"Turner would stay here and roam the countryside, often to Ripon, but also make his way across the country through Skipton, Settle, Giggleswick, Kirkby Lonsdale, and beyond on to the Lake District."

Walter thought that was a great idea; he was planning a road trip himself, and that would be a perfect little jaunt. "I like that one." Walter pointed to the almost invisible castle atop a waterfall with golden mountains above and the steam and the spray of the water meeting the river below.

"Ah yes, that is a mountain torrent in the style of Turner but actually by the hand of a woman, Helen Kemp-Welch. It's an interpretation of one of the grandmasters she witnessed surrounding the deathbed of Turner's friend Lord Gilpin before he died. Apparently, he paid for services rendered to a wide range of clients." He smiled wryly.

Walter nodded in acknowledgment, wishing to move the subject on to the matter at hand. "The Blower will cost a pretty penny, sir. That is, if I can even get it."

It was the earl's turn to nod in agreement. "Yes, I know it's a big ask, Beattie, but I was told if anyone could do it, it would be you. You have close to a blank check. In any case, I hear they might be in a position where the money might come in handy." He smiled again—a calculated smile—and winked at Walter.

Walter accepted the challenge, sweetened by the offer that Lord Harewood would give him the Kemp-Welch painting as a reward for his success. "Sounds like you have yourself a deal, sir." He shook the earl's hand.

"I'm glad to hear it," Viscount Lascelles said.

They exchanged further small talk, and then Walter left the mansion to get on with his day.

Bentley had been concentrating more on motorsport than mass production, and one drained money, while the other made money. Although they were winning races, things were challenging, and in Walter's view, a bit similar to Riley at that time, they needed to make the cars more affordable and up their production so Walter could more easily sell more cars himself. After all, although he loved cars, he was also in the business to make money, unlike some of his contemporaries, who had more money than sense.

This latest challenge was a tricky one, but Walter not only knew how to work out the angles but also had connections in high places.

Firstly, he knew Terry, the earl's chauffeur, and he had made a point of knowing him even better over drinks at the Crescent Inn, over a few pints of Tetley Bitter. It was amazing what beer and bars did in easing the sharing of information.

Sharing a drink was seemingly innocent but invaluable, and such was the case when Walter met with Terry Scott.

Upon hearing the viscount's desire for a Bentley, he thought, *Who better to connect with than the man's chauffeur?*

Walter was not just a car enthusiast or a businessman; he was a natural-born seller too. Insights led to sales, and that was true of his meeting with Terry.

Walter knew the Bentley director chap, Woolf Barnato, who might be able to help, he thought. Besides, they had just made the top three at Le Mans, they would need a new car for next year's race, and Walter's client was prepared to spend big. He already had known that before his meeting with the earl. He also knew that Lascelles did not just want any old Bentley; he wanted the Blower, and given Bentley's recent financial challenges, the earl spotted an opportunity, and so did Walter.

Even prior to the meeting, Walter got the deal. He would share with the viscount, landowner, old soldier, and brother-in-law to the king upon his return from his weekend road trip, now renamed the Turner Trail.

He was looking forward to that.

10

GIGGLESWICK

August 31, 1929
Falcon Manor Hotel
Settle, West Riding of Yorkshire, England

AMY TOUCHED THE WHEELS OF the Gipsy Moth down.

Walter grinned as he watched Amy land the Gipsy Moth at Ripon Racecourse, formerly the home of 76 Squadron of the Royal Flying Corps during World War I. He watched her taxi the plane off the runway, where she parked, jumped out of the cockpit in her pilot's outfit, and ran over for a big hug.

Walter said, "Nice ride. Where are we heading?"

She grabbed her pigskin bag engraved with her initials, *AJ*, and jumped into the passenger seat, and Walter sped off back to Boroughbridge Road and into Ripon, a market town and one of the smallest cathedral cities in England.

The sun was out, and the skies were blue as Walter sped the Riley 9 south past Ripley and its castle, turned right, continued through Burnt Yates and Birstwith to the Skipton Road, and headed west to Skipton.

To compete against the Bentley Boys and maybe even at Le Mans one day, he had to make it past Brooklands first and, with the right level of funding, take a crack at the big one. He was planning that when he presented the Blower to the viscount, which would be a perfect time to address sponsorship. At their meeting, the viscount had mentioned reliving his youth and his own missed opportunities vicariously through others.

"You see, Beattie, although I wouldn't swap the honor for anything, I, like millions of others, had to endure the horrors of the Great War, and somewhere along the way, I lost my youth."

Walter was happy for him to live as vicariously as he wanted through him, as long as he was prepared to pay for the privilege.

Henry George Charles Lascelles was an Etonian, and after Sandhurst officer training, he'd joined the Grenadier Guards and served between 1902 and 1905. Walter had not even been a glimmer in his parents' eyes at that point. In 1912, he'd joined the Yorkshire Hussars, and then he'd rejoined the Grenadiers to go to the western front and stayed on after the war and eventually retired from duty only four years previously.

Although far from a regular, the viscount sometimes was seen at the Harewood Arms, at the gateway to his estate.

Typically, on big days, he would show his presence similar to the way he had with his troops in the army. He would walk in with his walking stick, which he carried due to wounds suffered at the front; have a couple of pints of the local beer; and make sure he got the chance to say hello to as many of the men as he could and ask after wives, families, and children, showing them he cared.

On Christmas Eve, Easter Sunday, the king's birthday, and Remembrance Day, he would make the effort, and the locals appreciated it. He was a legendary figure, now even more so after marrying Princess Mary, the only daughter of King George V, at Westminster Abbey. Viscount Lascelles had earned a lot of respect, and he was the son-in-law to the king himself.

Walter related the story to Amy as they drove. They laughed and joked; they were friends together, inextricably linked by time and friendship.

Walter had thrived and moved on since the passing of his parents. John still bathed in the sadness every day, and Nikki struggled with the legacy of the circumstances and was haunted by the fact that history had a habit of repeating itself. It was a concern shared by Walter, but he was not obsessed with it, as she tended to be.

Walter steered the Riley 9 Brooklands past Skipton, topping ninety miles per hour along the straight past the town. Amy cheered, egging him on from the passenger seat. They reached the golf club; headed right onto Grassington Road; and, a couple of miles farther, took a left and then another left into the tiny hamlet of Hetton and to the Angel Inn for lunch.

Walter pulled up the blue Riley, and they both hopped out, ready for a long late lunch out at the front in the sunshine, amid the birds, the smell of the countryside, and, above all, good company.

They ordered little moneybags, delicious seafood in filo pastry wrapped in a parcel, and a bottle of Pouilly-Fuissé and settled down to eat. They also preordered the rack of lamb with seasonal vegetables to share.

"So, Amy, I was thinking we could take the Turner Trail this weekend."

"Sounds great. What is it?" she asked, smiling at Walter across the table.

"Well, we are already on it—Ripon, Harrogate, Skipton, a stopover here at the Angel. Tonight we will stay at the Falcon Manor, Settle, Giggleswick; then head up to Kirkby Lonsdale, the Snooty Fox; then to the Lakes, Windermere, Linthwaite House; and then on to Cartmel for a day at the races!"

"Wow! Somebody has been busy planning ahead."

They tucked into the delights delivered by the waiter and sipped their favorite wine in synchrony.

"Isn't the Falcon where they have a round billiard table?"

"How on earth did you know that? Johnnie, you are always full of surprises."

"And are we planning to meet Beatrix Potter?"

He just shrugged.

"No, but seriously, I would love to go to see Wordsworth's Rydal Mount if we can."

Walter nodded enthusiastically, taking the cue to recite one of his favorites:

I wandered lonely as a cloud
That floats on high o'er vales and hills,
When all at once I saw a crowd,
A host, of golden daffodils;
Beside the lake, beneath the trees,
Fluttering and dancing in the breeze.

Walter stopped there. He loved that poem. They both did, and they both knew the rest of the verses by William Wordsworth. Walter played it in his mind as they ate.

"I am planning to fly to Australia, Walter. Solo." Amy addressed her news head-on.

Walter looked up from his plate as he finished the moneybags and closed his knife and fork together, grabbed his white linen napkin, and wiped his lips before taking a sip of his wine. "Wow! That is a bolt out of the blue." He took a moment to think about it. "That's pretty ballsy. The first woman to fly to Australia, right? Or has that American woman Earhart done it already?"

Amy shook her head. "No, no, unless someone beats me to it, I plan to be the first. I also plan on beating Bert Hinkler's record."

"How long?"

"Eleven thousand miles. Sixteen days." She grinned.

"Is it dangerous?"

Amy shrugged and smiled at the same time, indicating an affirmative answer to his question.

She went on to explain her intended route, her preparations, and her father's commitment to spend the £600 to purchase the plane, on the proviso it would be called *Jason* as a means of promoting his patent and his ability to run it through his business as a marketing expense.

"When do you plan to leave?"

"Early May is the best window for weather and winds."

"You'll miss me at Brooklands." He smiled to hide his disappointment.

They polished off the rack of lamb and the Pouilly-Fuissé, jumped back into the Riley 9, and headed to Settle, to the Falcon Manor Hotel for the evening, where they caught up in the bar and played billiards on the famous round table before retiring early to bed.

The next morning, with the sun rising in the blue skies above, they took a walk across the River Ribble, over Castleberg Fields, and into Giggleswick.

The school chapel was at the top of the hill, and a game of cricket was underway. Giggleswick School was playing nearby town Wigglesworth.

"A rather satisfactory day in God's country," Walter said, and Amy agreed.

Back down the hill, they passed the Black Horse. They called in for a half of Timothy Taylor's and sat on the bench out front before completing the loop back over Tems Beck and into the old market town of Settle.

They were happy and comfortable in their own company, their own world. They were friends and soul mates, Walter thought. He watched as she walked briskly, full of confidence and swagger. He had always liked that about her, ever since they had met as children at school. Walter remembered their first meeting at the Johnsons'. Even at that tender age, he at once had been taken with her. She was tall, slender, and athletic and had a look of mischief in her eyes. They shared a connection of the spirits as much as an intellectual and physical attraction. He looked across at Amy, and all these years later, he realized he was as smitten today as he had been the first time he met her. She made Walter's heart sing, and he hoped Amy felt the same, but that was a boundary they both found difficult to cross.

They came across an old silver shop and walked in together.

In the window was a silver necklace with a miniature, delicate silver-and-gold globe hanging from it. It was the perfect gift for the moment. Walter pulled out his wallet and paid, and as Amy lifted her hair, he wrapped it around her neck, fastening the clasp behind and positioning the pendant in the middle of her chest. Then they kissed, and Walter whispered, "Safe travels and fair winds, my love."

Walter sensed something was afoot, even in far-off Ilkley, in his narrow perspective of luxury cars in the time of the Roaring Twenties. In his mind, the decade's nickname was less about what was happening and more about the mood at the time.

In the ten years since the end of the Great War, those lucky enough to escape alive had entered the decade with a level of enthusiasm and optimism like never before. There was a mood of the victorious on each side of the Atlantic, and as with the Bentley Boys and Riley, the focus was on the business of fun and not necessarily the business of making money. It was a time of both wealth and excess.

The euphoria followed in the stock exchanges around the world, including in London and New York. People flocked to the major cities in the pursuit of further wealth and prosperity. People from every walk of life were now investing in the stock exchange, and in some cases, they had seen their investments grow by the value of tenfold. But the markets were seriously overheated. The underlying signals were of warnings, as easy credit made borrowing easy. In some sectors, such as agriculture, there were cases of overproduction and stockpiles building up, and in some cases, there was negligence in favor of fun or, in the worst case, fraud.

But the herd continued as the bull market and the year-on-year rise for the past ten years led people to believe the streak would continue forever.

Earlier, in September, British investor Clarence Hatry and many of his associates had been jailed for fraud. Hatry, although a Londoner, had been a client of Walter's. As a provincial dealer with connections, Walter had been able to get a hold of one of the latest Rolls-Royces, jumping the queue, thanks to his late father's connections with the firm. Hatry had paid Walter handsomely for his efforts.

The news from London rattled Wall Street. Roger Babson's prediction that "A crash is coming, and it may be terrific" worried the markets enough to stimulate what most hoped was a healthy correction, but by October 24, Black Thursday, the market lost 11 percent of its value, and then, just four days later, on Black Monday, Wall

Street posted a record loss of nearly 13 percent. The slide of 24 percent over less than a week stimulated panic sell-offs and a crash that would lead into a global recession, a depression like no other experienced, especially in terms of the contrast between the Roaring Twenties and families being forced into destitution for being too heavily reliant upon credit.

Walter read the *Yorkshire Post* and the *London Times* every day and kept himself abreast of the news. He also used the papers as a valuable sales tool, gleaning insights into the rich, the famous, businessmen, and royalty and looking for opportunities to ply his trade. He was at the top end of the market for his sales business but also had built up a loyal following for his workshop, repairs, and servicing, which were less profitable but certainly good enough to keep the doors open. He concluded that Beattie Brothers was safe from the eventualities of the turbulent times.

Amy was also making the papers. He had read an interview in which she had hinted at the solo flight to Australia. He looked out the window of his sales office, and the thought of the distance between them made him sad.

On Turner's Trail and their jaunt around Yorkshire and the Lake District, they'd had a hoot. They had reconnected and had confirmed their closeness, but the announcement of the Australia trip had broken Walter's rhythm, and he'd cut short of popping the question.

He had thought about that moment long and hard, and although he still had no firm conclusion, he had made some sense of how he felt and some explanation for his hesitation— or was it an excuse? He was not entirely sure.

He did know that he did not want to get in the way of Amy's ambitions and aspirations. He loved that most about her. She dreamed big, and so did he. There was no time in life to be held back. He also believed she was not ready yet for marriage either. They both had things to get out of their systems before settling down. After all, Amy, at just twenty-six, and Walter, at twenty-three, were still young and had plenty of petrol in the tank.

Then there was the worrisome legacy of his parents. Although Walter locked it away better than John did and marginally better than Nikki did, it was still an issue for him but perhaps in different ways.

He had never worked out if it was his father's fault for being how he was or if his mother had made his father that way. Or, in reverse, had his father driven his mother to her state of mind? Or had they both been at fault, just a bad pairing, a mismatch, a tragic mistake?

Walter could not work it out, but one thing he knew for sure: he did not want to make the same mistakes. He remembered his own father's teachings: "A wise man learns from the mistakes of others, not his own" and "It is easy to solve others' problems; it is your own that are the most difficult to solve."

Walter's father had been a wise but impulsive man, and those two teachings were on target. He believed that when the time was right for Amy and him, they would both know, and he was sure that day would eventually come.

Walter was determined not to make the same mistakes.

II

BEATTIE BLUE

April 10, 1930
Brooklands Racetrack
Weybridge, Surrey, England

WALTER GRIPPED THE WHEEL OF Beattie Blue as they lined up, ready for the start, with engines running and the smell of high-octane gasoline and oil, the heat, the grumble of engines, the sensations, and the atmosphere touching every part of his body and soul. He had waited for this moment all his life.

He'd had his coveralls made in London at his favorite tailor and friends at Gieves and Hawkes—Number 1 Savile Row, no less. The coveralls were royal blue to match his Riley 9 and embroidered with the Beattie Brothers logo on the left chest and, thanks to Henry Lascelles and his connections to sponsorship, Tetley's Bitter on the right. He also wore a silk neckerchief, a pilot's leather helmet, and goggles courtesy of his love, Amy "Johnnie" Johnson, with *AJ* embossed on each.

Amy had delayed her Australia adventure, and she was with him at Brooklands. Walter was happy she had made the gesture. It meant a lot to him but added to his nervousness in his pursuit. A placing at Brooklands potentially meant a path through to Le Mans and even the Grand Prix circuit.

"Imagine what that would do for Beattie Brothers, John," he said as his brother put the finishing touches on the Riley 9. "This is our big shot." He emphasized the importance to his brother.

Many of the other boys either didn't need sponsorship or had the backing of the major motor manufacturers, such as Bentley, Austin, Talbot, and Alfa Romeo. It wasn't as if Walter didn't appreciate the earl's and Tetley's support—he did, and it was much needed—but now side by side the old Etonians and Harrovians, he felt like a distant relative, a poorer relative, and certainly not of the same stratosphere.

"Come on, John. Let's show these buggers who's boss."

John lifted his head from the engine compartment, making his final adjustments to the air mixture; shut the bonnet; secured it; and winked at Walter. "You're all set, Walt. She's purring like a dream."

Amy and the earl walked over, with Henry using his cane. They wished him good luck.

"Come on, Beattie. You can do this, old boy. I am betting on you." The earl winked at Walter.

Amy leaned over, wrapped her arms around Walter's shoulders in the cockpit of his machine, and whispered, "Go get 'em, Walter. You can do it."

Walter felt as if his head could burst. He appreciated them both, but the pressure was immense. The rival teams had crews of dozens, while the Beattie Blue had John, Amy, and the earl. It was a tough call, but as they assembled for the start, Walter was determined not to let his big chance pass by.

Hall and Benjafield, in another Bentley Blower, were long-standing prerace favorites. The other Bentley, with Birkin and Duller, was second favorite, largely due to the Bentley's recent success at Le Mans. Then there were the Austin 7 and Purdy and Cushman in the Sunbeam Cub.

Lascelles had considered letting Walter race his own new Bentley but, after discussion, agreed the Riley 9 was the better bet, and besides, the earl didn't want to totally fly in the face of his old alumni, although, after his military service and life in Yorkshire, he had more affinity to Walter and Beattie Blue.

Further down the field of favorites were the teams from Alfa Romeo, Amilcar, Delage, and Bugatti, and then there was Walter in his Riley 9 Brooklands, racing number 21, an independent entry sponsored by Tetley's Bitter, all the way from up north in the highlands of Yorkshire.

The lineup edged toward the starting line, and the starter appeared in front of them. Walter was at the back of the starting grid, in position number thirty of a total of forty racers.

The atmosphere heightened as the drivers revved their engines, and the starter warmed up the flag. *Five. Four.* The noise was deafening as the drivers pushed on full throttle. *Three. Two.* The wheels started spinning, and the rubber started burning. *One.* The checkered flag waved, and they were off!

Straight off the mark, Walter passed one of the Talbots and an Alfa Romeo, gaining two places. By the first corner, he was pressing on the Amilcar of Vernon Balls, and by the end of the first lap, with some retirements and further daring passing movements, Walter had made ground overall. It was hard to tell from the car exactly where he was placed, but as they lapped, John reached out with a board indicating his position. Walter saw the board. "Twelfth. Bloody fantastic," he said, more determined than ever.

For a split second, he thought of Amy sitting in the grandstand with the earl and sipping champagne. He hoped she was watching, and he hoped he was making her proud.

It was a long race—five hundred miles—and not just a race of speed but one of endurance and reliability too. Walter and John had spent many a night sketching out their strategy and race plan.

"Look, Walt, it's not just about how fast you drive; it's about endurance," John had said, and Walter hesitantly had agreed. "We need to make sure we have enough gasoline, obviously, but we also need to make sure we have replacement parts in case of a bump and at least one set of tires to change, probably two."

Walter was all in, but he couldn't help thinking just about the speed and the race.

They'd practiced at night after the workshop was closed and timed themselves to see how quickly they could replace the set of tires and the spark plugs, adjust the air mixture, and reset the tappets. It was just the two of them, the engineer and the driver, but they knew that beyond the big boys, they would not be alone in their two-man pursuit for victory.

The car had a 1,087-cubic-centimeter engine and fifty horsepower as standard, but John had supertuned it and made some adjustments, and they figured it got closer to fifty-five horses and maybe, on a straight with a fair wind, one hundred miles per hour.

By mile 150 into the race, Walter, in Beattie Blue, was tracking in sixth position overall, and with a couple of shrewd pit stops, tune-ups, and a full tire change at mile three hundred, Walter was in second, pushing the race leaders, March and Davis, in their Austin 7.

That was another disadvantage: all the other teams had two drivers, while Beattie Brothers had only one: Walter. He was doing fine, and by the four-hundred-mile point, Beattie Blue scorched into the lead.

Walter's dream was coming true.

Double-clutching the gear changes around every corner and maintaining speed, with sheer concentration and now devoid of nerves, Walter pushed the Riley 9 to its limit of both speed and endurance. He was in the lead, but he was fearful of the competition behind; he was determined to push Beattie Blue as hard as he could.

Four hundred ten miles into the race, with just ninety miles to go, as Walter rounded the bend to the pits, the engine of the Riley 9 burst, sending hot oil splashing onto Walter's visor. He was blinded temporarily by spatters of thick, hot oil. The engine was done, forcing him to pull into the pit stop, and the damage resulted in Beattie Blue's retirement from the race.

March and Davis, in their Austin 7, flew past Walter, beeping their horn and waving, followed by Hall and

Benjafield in the Bentley Blower, who did the same. They went on to take first and second place in the race.

Walter's dream was over. "Oh bugger, damn, and blast!"

By then, Millie was an icon, esteemed for her writing, her poems, and her passion for the advancement of women and of aviation. She was two years into one of her many roles as guest social worker at Greenwich House, a shelter for women. She was also now the aviation editor for *Cosmopolitan* magazine. As a result, she was spending more time in New York, in Greenwich Village.

Millie had designed and created a pilot's suit, which *Vogue* had publicized in a multipage feature, launching her fashion line. Marketed as "practical apparel for active women," it included zipper jackets; a new range of female-friendly polo-style shirts; and, flying in the face of tradition at the time, comfortable trousers for women.

Amelia Earhart, much like her Ninety-Nines contemporaries, was a trailblazer, and now that she was president of that organization, her profile and influence were rising with the passing of each day.

She had a lot to be thankful for, including the efforts, passion, and focus of GP. He was already a wealthy, successful promoter, ad man, and man-about-town and was a vice president of the Explorers Club. Just like his explorer brethren, he was relentless and persistent and would not take no for an answer. Prior to, during, and since his divorce, he had asked her to marry him no fewer than six times. Some said he'd divorced his wife to clear the way. She had hesitated each time and eventually agreed but on her terms.

She wrote her prenuptials the night before the wedding and insisted they should not abide by or agree to commit to what she termed a "medieval code of faithfulness." The word *obey* was removed from the civil ceremony service.

Millie liked Greenwich. Although she was a country girl in New York, Greenwich Village was exactly that: a village in a huge metropolis. "One could get lost in the labyrinth of streets yet still feel at home," she said of the place.

She would hang out with the long-term residents of the neighborhoods and eat, drink, and connect with libertarians, bohemians, authors, writers, hell-raisers, and musicians of the time, often talking about her love of poetry. One of her favorites at the time was Edna St. Vincent Millay, another leading shining light to lift the dark and repressive veil of sexism and create opportunity for all women everywhere.

Noank, a village in the town of Groton, Connecticut, a dense community of historic homes and local businesses, sat on a small, steep peninsula at the mouth of the Mystic River and had a long tradition of fishing, lobstering, and boatbuilding. That was where Millie and GP agreed to marry, secure from the eyes of the millions who acclaimed her as America's most famous aviatrix.

On February 7, 1931, the press covered the story on many of their front pages.

Miss Amelia Earhart, slender blonde social service worker, who has been the only woman to fly the

Atlantic in an airplane, was married to George Palmer Putnam, publisher, author and explorer, of New York in his mother's home overlooking Long Island Sound.

The ceremony lasted but five minutes and was presided over by a probate judge. The only witnesses included GP's mother and uncle, Judge Arthur Anderson's son, Robert, and a pair of twin black cats.

> "There was no fuss, no religious ceremony, no demonstration," said Mrs. Putnam, pointing out that the house contained no flowers and that no one in the neighborhood had been informed. Brown shoes and stockings and a close-fitting brown hat were worn by Miss Earhart in addition to a brown traveling suit.
> "Brown seems to be her favorite color," said Mrs. Putnam.

They were a perfect and complementary pairing. Millie was an explorer in her own right, an aviatrix, a challenger of the status quo, and she had a national following and knew she had the opportunity to influence—a rare opportunity in those days as a woman. Now, as an emerging fashionista, she had the chance to actually influence and make a difference. She wanted to do that more than anything; it was more important to her than any of her activities and roles. It was a bigger-picture play for Amelia Earhart.

The newspaper article continued.

> As Mr. Putnam slipped a plain platinum ring on Miss Earhart's finger the cats, coal black and playful,

rubbed arched backs against his ankles. Then, while Miss Earhart, who has been said to resemble Colonel Lindbergh, put on a brown fur coat over a brown suit and light brown blouse, Mr. Putnam telephoned his secretary, Miss Josephine Herger, in New York, announcing the wedding.

Immediate afterward he and Mrs. Putnam bade the others goodbye and drove down the winding lane leading from the cream-colored, two-story house to the main Connecticut highway and the outside world.

Millie wrote to various newspapers and publications shortly after the articles to remind them that under no circumstances should they refer to her as Mrs. Putnam. She was Miss Amelia Earhart.

They were both back to work that Monday.

12

FLYING SCOTSMAN

August 30, 1931
Moscow, Russia

AMY TOUCHED THE WHEELS OF the Moth down onto the Russian airstrip. She and her copilot, Jack Humphreys, were the first two to ever have made the flight from London to Moscow in one day: 1,760 miles and twenty-one hours in the air.

The next leg of their journey would be to fly across Siberia and then head to Tokyo to set a new record time from Great Britain to Japan, but Amy's mind was on other matters right now.

She had recently taken a flight with a Glaswegian pilot named James Mollison, who was known as the Flying Prince and was a charmer for sure.

During the eight-hour flight together, they had laughed and giggled, and he had told stories of his escapades in the

Royal Air Force. His posting had been in Waziristan, and at that time, he had been the youngest serving officer in the service at eighteen years old. He told of his time in Australia, and he had just set the record time of eight days and nineteen hours from Australia to England.

The Flying Prince also had a reputation for being a bit of a playboy. That made Amy nervous, but she did like him. They had an immediate spark. There was an energy between them, and there was almost a sense of rivalry, which, in Amy's view, meant he must have thought their skills almost equal, which was the best a woman could get in those days. A man and woman on equal footing? Amy liked that idea.

He proposed to her at the end of those eight hours together in the air. In the moment, she accepted. The immediate response weighed on her mind and went against every instinct in her body, but once she accepted, there was no going back. She had to remain true to her word. Her Yorkshire word was her bond, just as her father had taught her.

Of course, she was flattered, and her heart fluttered, but at the same time, she was flustered, not knowing how she should respond. Her response was reactionary, not measured. She did not have any time to consider the wider implications of her acceptance, including the effect on her childhood sweetheart, Walter.

It had been two years since Amy and Walter had gone on their grand tour, their Turner's Trail of Yorkshire and the Lakes. She had half expected Walter to step up then, but he hadn't. There had been a moment at the silversmith's shop in Settle when Amy's heart fluttered, but alas, the gift had been a necklace and not a ring.

As she thought through her dilemma, she checked herself and realized she had the silver-and-gold globe in the tips of her fingers, as she often did in times of her deepest thought.

Amy was independent for sure. She had ambitions and dreams. She was now in pursuit of her own flight path, and it was in a different circle from Walter.

Though he'd had to retire from the race, he had competed at Brooklands, and she had been there. After the race, he had sent her a photograph: Walter, Amy, John, and the king's brother-in-law proudly standing in front of his Riley 9 Brooklands, number 21, at the start of the race—Beattie Blue, as he had named her. Amy kept the treasured photograph in the inside of her *AJ* pigskin flight bag.

Amy had thought about taking the lead and popping the question herself. That was not done at that time, but after all, she was a true-blue Yorkshire lass, and she could have if she had wanted.

Should she have? She had even plucked a flower, as the girls had done at school, and picked off the petals one by one, saying, "He loves me; he loves me not," until all the petals were gone, and the last one revealed the truth. She had done it four times, and each time, the answer was "He loves me."

But if he truly loves me, then why doesn't he do something about it?

That was the question that kept preying on her mind. On the face of it, he seemed unaffected by the loss of his parents. Compared with John, the difference was clear, but when she thought of Nikki and the mask she wore to cover her pain, she realized maybe Walter was the same way.

She knew Nikki's secrets, or at least enough of them to be concerned. Her secret unwillingness to have children. Her fear of her husband's infidelity. Her fear of having children and ultimately letting them down, as she had been let down herself. The fear of mental illness cropping up again in her bloodline.

Maybe those fears existed inside Walter too, or was it simply that he was having too good of a time, as she was?

It was no secret that some men of Walter's age shied away from commitment. It was also no secret that men of Walter's age with good looks and charm liked to play the field. She had not heard any rumors, but she wondered if that was a possibility.

She felt a tinge of guilt. But to be fair, since their grand tour, they had drifted apart again over the past couple of years. Amy had been busy flying in London, in Australia, and all over. Walter had been busy building his business in Ilkley, pursuing his dreams of racing. He still wrote her a monthly letter, and Amy always replied, but it was not quite the same. Maybe they were more like brother and sister than marriage material after all.

She wrote to her best friend. Nikki would know what to do. They planned to meet in Tokyo, and they would talk it through then. Or maybe Amy would just share her news.

She breathed a sigh of relief. She had made her decision. The Flying Scotsman was, after all, a bit of a catch!

It seemed that weddings were all the rage. Nikki met her love, a dashing Royal Air Force pilot with a promising career ahead of him.

They met at a dinner at Blenheim Palace; he was in his blues, and Nikki was in a black House of Worth cocktail dress, haute couture. The organizers of the event had paired the rich and powerful together, with politicians sharing affiliations at the same tables, a table with the most senior officers, the army together, the navy together, and then the most eligible bachelors and bachelorettes at the same tables. By luck, Nikki was seated next to Flight Lieutenant Bob Baxter.

They met at the dinner table and laughed and joked between introductions and exploratory conversations, and as the dinner drew to a close, they decided to take a stroll on the beautiful grounds of the palace in the twinkle of the clear late-autumn skies above. Nikki was shivering, and he quickly draped his blue overcoat over her shoulders.

It was getting late, 10:20 p.m., and Bob had to make his way back to the transport that would whisk him and the boys in blue back to nearby Bicester Airfield, just a short sixteen-mile hop up the road. They said their good nights, and Bob let her keep the coat.

"Until next time." He smiled at her.

"I hope so," Nikki responded coyly.

They exchanged contact details and dates. It would be the start of a whirlwind romance. Nikki watched the bus leave the gravel drive and head down through the grounds toward Oxford Road.

"Good night, Bob Baxter," she said aloud as she watched the lights fade into the distance.

Seven weeks earlier, she had met Amy in Tokyo. Amy's mind was already made up. Nikki did not have the time or the chance to plead her brother Walter's love for Amy. It was too late for that. Nikki knew her friend, and when her mind was made up, that was it. She felt sad for Walter, and she felt happy for Amy, yet she harbored concerns about the reputation of the Flying Scotsman, despite his undeniable good looks, charm, and notoriety.

Nikki did not even try to intercede; she just listened to Amy's plans of marriage, which would happen soon, the following July.

Nikki met up with Bob several times over the coming weeks, and after a Christmas together in Yorkshire, they met in London to watch *Cavalcade*, the latest piece by Noel Coward, at the Theatre Royal, Drury Lane. They enjoyed predinner cocktails at the Bow Street Tavern, followed by the show and then dinner afterward at the Waldorf Hotel on Aldwych. Nikki needed to borrow his overcoat again as they strolled the London streets while reviewing the show and building upon their flourishing acquaintance.

They talked about the Schneider Trophy seaplane race at Calshot Spit and about Flight Lieutenant John Boothman, in his Supermarine S.6B, breaking the world speed record by going 340 miles an hour. Just two weeks later, Flight Lieutenant George Stainforth had topped it with 407 miles an hour. Bob knew both the men, and the idea of speed thrilled both Bob and Nikki, both aviators. The pace of progress was astonishing.

Ramsay MacDonald had just retained Number 10 as prime minister in a crushing landslide victory for the National Party. From that topic, Bob and Nikki moved on to the tragic death of a Celtic goalkeeper who'd fractured his skull in a football game against the Glasgow Rangers in the Old Firm derby. Bob was a Scotsman, and Nikki liked that parallel to Amy's suitor.

Amy's plans for her wedding were being completed. It would be held at Saint George's Church in Hanover Square in London. Nikki was in charge of organizing the reception afterward. Bob's and her dinner venue that night was on her shortlist of reception venues.

As they walked back toward the Waldorf, Bob paused for a moment and guided Nikki to face him. Nikki knew this was serious, and her heart fluttered like never before. She was a pilot and accepted the risk and the nerves each time she flew, but this was different. Although he was always confident, she could tell he was nervous too, but they were both helped by the earlier cocktails and postdinner drinks.

"Nikki, will you marry me?" He had a ring box in his hand and opened it to reveal the finest diamond ring Nikki had ever seen, from Ogden's of Harrogate, no less.

"Why, Robert Baxter, you sneak. When did you do that?" she said, knowing full well he must have bought it while they were in Yorkshire after Christmas, while she and Amy sat in Betty's across the road, having afternoon tea. She was impressed.

They'd had a wonderful Christmas together. They had stayed at their friends the Radcliffes' house at Rudding Park, with all its beauty and splendor. They'd had Christmas Eve service in the chapel, Christmas Day feast, and Boxing Day at Wetherby Races, and the following day, she'd gone into Harrogate and to Betty's with Amy.

They'd had a wonderful time together. She knew Bob was her man, and Amy approved too.

She had not gone to Riverside that Christmas, as the memories were too painful, and her relationship with Miss Boswell had deteriorated. She did not approve of what appeared to be going on. She did not approve at all.

She looked into Bob's eyes; he was still nervous. Her moment of thought and pause was adding to the traditional drama associated with a proposal of marriage. Nikki was aware, but at the same time, saying yes too quickly, or too slowly, could have negative consequences. As with flying, she knew that timing was everything.

She held out her hand with her engagement finger. "There is nothing I would like more in the world, my darling Robert," she said, and he slipped the diamond ring onto her finger. They kissed under the streetlamp outside the Waldorf and went inside arm in arm.

Scotty

You bonny wee Scot,
appeared from the blue, why not?
Your wit, your charm, your old overcoat,
the cheek, you charm, that wee little note.

Think I was once destined alone.
Now with hope, we together atone.

Happiness in life and sadness too.
I think of our blessing, and my, I will, I do.

Promise me it will forever be.
Much in the past I did not wish to see.
I hope for us that it will be true.
In exchange, all I have, I will give to you.

—Nikki Beattie, 1931

On April 16, 1932, Nikki and Bob returned to Rudding Park and were married in the Radcliffes' family chapel.

They had a small gathering. Bob's family came down from Edinburgh: his mother and father and his two brothers and their wives. Amy and Jim came, of course, as did the Johnsons and their daughters; Bob's friends from the air force, including the record breakers Boothman and Stainforth; the Radcliffes; and Nikki's brother John. Walter sent his apologies that he was away somewhere or other.

Nikki knew it would have been too painful for him to see Amy and Jim together and engaged. She knew that would have pushed him further on the path he was seemingly taking, a path of potentially poor choices in his life. That saddened her greatly, but she pushed the thought to one side. She tried not to think about it too much. It was too painful.

The wedding came and went. Later, in July, Amy was to marry Jim in London.

On the other side of the Atlantic, after much hesitation and several proposals, Amelia Earhart had married publisher and publicist George P. Putnam, who would launch Amelia's career and make her one of the most famous women in America, in aviation, and possibly in the world.

Meanwhile, in Ilkley, at the register office, Walter Beattie and Miss Esmerelda Boswell married. Apart from Walter's friend chauffeur Terry Scott and his wife as witnesses, there were no other attendees. There was no reception, no pomp and circumstance, just a quiet, private affair.

For richer or for poorer.

13

FRIENDSHIP

May 20, 1932
Harbour Grace, Newfoundland,
Labrador, Canada

AMELIA WAS DISAPPOINTED, AS HER first flight over the Atlantic was not what she had hoped for. It turned out the "right kind of girl" Captain Railey had been looking for was intended to simply sit in the back of the Fokker VIIb as a passenger with pilot Wilmer Stultz and engineer Louis Gordon at the helm. On June 17, 1928, they landed at Pwll, near Burry Port, South Wales, twenty hours and forty minutes later. Amelia said of the flight to the waiting press, "Stultz did all the flying. I was just baggage, like a sack of potatoes. Maybe someday I'll try it alone." She smiled at the camera.

Despite her disappointment, by then, she was already a star. Her husband, GP, had put her on the map, and when they returned stateside, they were greeted with a ticker-tape parade along the Canyon of Heroes in Manhattan and then onto Washington, DC. Although Millie met the president himself, Herbert Clark Hoover, she still felt like a passenger and the token woman in the proceedings. That wasn't good enough for Millie; she felt cheated of the opportunity to make a real impact, a real difference.

Now it was her turn; she would fly the Atlantic solo, and she would take center stage alone on her own, without reliance on the male of the species. She would do it not for the stardom but for women everywhere.

The equality of women in a man's world had always fascinated her, even from an early age. Why should she wear a floral dress rather than more comfortable, practical bloomers? Why should she sit inside the house, doing needlework, while the boys played outside with their contraptions, fun, and games? Why should men control glorious pursuits, such as the pursuit of flight?

She had watched her dutiful mother suffer the alcoholism of her father. She had seen the women at Denison House— the poverty, the sadness, and the desperation to survive, never mind thrive. She remembered her work at the hospital in Toronto—the nurses, the death, the sadness. She even thought of her sister and her perfect subservient wife life in Chicago.

She knew that none of those were options for her, and she was determined to fly the flag for women to have a say, influence, and choice.

This was not just for her; this was for everyone, she thought as the engine of her Lockheed Vega 5B gurgled, whirred, and hummed to life.

As she got ready to taxi, journalist Stuart Trueman from the *Telegraph-Journal* handed her a copy of the day's newspaper as confirmation of the date of her departure. Her intention was to fly to Paris to emulate the journey of famous American aviator Charles Lindbergh five years earlier.

As her Lockheed bounced across the Newfoundland field at the edge of the ocean, she gathered speed and, at the right moment, pulled back the joystick, and she was airborne. "Up, up, and away!" she shouted down in the vain hope that GP could hear her above the noise of the engines.

They had been married for fifteen months now, and she was pleased that he embraced her liberal views of marriage at the time. She believed in equality, and they both pursued their careers separately; however, he used his connections and skills to attract the notoriety and fame that in turn led to greater and more lucrative endorsement fees for a wide range of products.

Millie felt a level of imposter syndrome. She was, in reality, an okay pilot. She lacked many of the deeper, more academic, practical skills of navigation, for example, relying on landmarks as her guides.

Although she was apparently, according to the press, easy to look at—some said beautiful—she downplayed her womanhood and could easily be mistaken, especially in her pilot gear, for a boy with short-cropped blonde hair. She even wore men's underwear, as it made for easier access to attend to calls of nature while in the cockpit.

In an article after the *Friendship* voyage across the Atlantic last time, she had said, "Today I have been receiving offers to go on the stage, appear in the movies and to accept gifts ranging from an automobile to a husband ... I will be happier when the pressure of life in the public eye diminishes."

The endorsements were too attractive and included gyroplanes, Mobil oil, Whitney planes, and Wasp engines, which she felt okay with, as they were related to her core pursuit: aviation. But then came others, such as Horlicks, tomato juice, and chewing gum, all under the premise that she used their products while making her often long flights. She was sort of okay with that.

Although a nonsmoker, with her carefully created image, GP persuaded her to endorse Lucky Strike, but the outcry forced her to donate the $1,500 fee to Admiral Byrd's second Antarctic expedition. She had known all along instinctively that it was a bad decision, and from that point, she watched more carefully and pushed back more in being selective on the endorsements she would or wouldn't sign up to. Besides, they did not really need the money anymore.

The Orenstein Trunk Company approached her about creating her own range of travel cases, which she thought was an excellent idea. It prompted her to create and launch her own fashion line. Millie was taking control.

She said, "I hate ruffles. Good lines and good materials for women who lead active lives."

She would use interesting and aviation-related materials, such as parachute silk and the tightly woven Grenfell cotton.

"Different-size tops and bottoms and tails for tucking."

As she flew over the ocean, she could imagine the designs and the garments in her mind. Millie did a lot of her thinking while in the air; it was an escape and the only real place she felt complete in the world.

"Flying may not be all plain sailing," she mused, "but the fun of it is worth the price."

She flew into the night, the fog, the ice, and the cold.

Amelia and GP had a good arrangement between them. He worked the money, and she did the flying. She also liked writing and promoting both aviation and women's right to have equal footing in the world.

During the many long and sometimes lonely periods of flight above the clouds, she would write poetry in her secret journal. She was an accomplished writer and an editor at *Cosmo* and would share her stories of her aviatrix life.

Since a child, she had always had a deep love for poetry. As girls, Amelia and her sister would play with words and even invented a prose of communication in their secret world of the Dee-Jays.

She had taken to submitting her works to various publications under various noms de plume, including Emil A. Harte. Despite her notoriety and her public profile, Millie was an extremely private person.

The night before she and GP had married, she'd penned, on her soon-to-be mother-in-law's personal stationery, the prenuptials in what would be their premarital agreement. GP had reluctantly agreed to her terms of an open marriage, including her "right to leave if she was not happy in the first year." Millie also said, "Please let us not interfere with the other's work or play, nor let the world see our private joys or disagreements."

Millie, the girl from Kansas, was making her impact in her own way the best she could and for the things she was impassioned about.

The flight was uneventful. There were a couple of mechanical issues. The strong northwesterly winds had thwarted her hope of matching Lindy's record to Paris.

Fourteen hours later, she spotted land ahead—not the beaches of the northern French coast but the craggy but beautiful shores of the Emerald Isle.

As Millie brought the plane to land in a pasture in Culmore, Derry, Northern Ireland, a farmhand asked her, "Have you flown far?" He shouted as the engine of the Lockheed wound its way down.

Millie shouted back with a big, gratified smile, "From America!"

Nikki was excited as she readied herself that morning. They were heading to a luncheon reception at the aero club and would get to meet the famous Amelia Earhart after her solo flight across the Atlantic and her arrival in Ireland the previous week.

It had been a busy schedule for Miss Earhart: an Institute of Journalists luncheon in the afternoon the day before, shopping in London, and an interview with journalists. Nikki read the article in the newspaper with fervent interest.

Over tea at the American embassy, Amelia had told the ambassador's daughter that she had added little to aviation: "Because after all, the Atlantic has been crossed many times. The trip was merely a personal satisfaction to me."

Nikki and her now husband, Bob Baxter, read the article together at the breakfast table, drinking Earl Grey, of course. It went on to quote her as saying, "I had made up my mind to fly alone, because if there is a man in the machine you can bet your life that he wants to take control."

Nikki elbowed her husband in the ribs as she read the line out aloud. She remembered Amelia's disappointment at being the passenger in her earlier transatlantic flight a few years earlier and her reference to being a sack of potatoes.

According to the article, Amelia had said, "Well, I had already flown the Atlantic with men in control, and I was determined that if I did it again, then I was the one going to control the machine."

Nikki continued to read out loud. Millie had expressed the opinion that women had a greater capacity for physical endurance than men and that airplanes had developed into such a state of efficiency that many of them plunged in where a man would hesitate.

"I love this woman." Nikki looked up from the newspaper and kissed her husband.

It was hard to disagree, even for Bob, a man and an aviator himself. "This woman has balls," he said. His response was a sign of respect.

"Well, my darling husband, we get to meet the lady herself this afternoon." She winked and labored over her use of words. She was enjoying being married and having a husband.

They left the Hampstead Heath apartment and headed to the luncheon. Amy and her soon-to-be husband would be there as well.

It was the first time women were to be allowed into the club. "What a treat!" Nikki joked sarcastically with her husband as they arrived.

Apparently, the club committee had made the decision on the basis "As an air record has been created in the skies, then one should also be set on the land!"

"Damned right!" Nikki agreed wholeheartedly. "You men!" She nudged Bob again.

The Beattie-Baxters pulled up outside 119 Piccadilly in their 4.5-liter Invicta S-Type and stepped out as the valet went to park the car. It was not the racing Bentley Nikki had ridden in with Captain Valentine, but there had been far more risks associated with that car and that man. Bob was not quite to that extreme; he was focused, reliable, and not likely to stray too far. That was what Nikki liked about her husband: he was a much safer bet.

After the luncheon, Lord Gorell led the question-and-answer session and introduced the guest of honor, Miss Amelia Earhart—or Mrs. GP Putnam, her married name, which she had chosen not to adopt. The audience listened in intently.

"My altimeter stopped working almost as soon as we left Harbour Grace," Amelia told the audience. "By the time we got near the Irish coast, I was unable to gauge my height accurately. I was flying through very thick thunderstorm weather, and I could hardly see in front of my nose."

The audience was transfixed. Nikki looked at the woman before her. She was tall, athletic, toned, slender, and good looking—a natural beauty but with cropped blonde hair and square edges, not round. She had the look of a tomboy, but there was something about her that drew attention, a magnetism. It was no wonder she was an international star.

"I tracked up the coast and found clearer weather and a railway line, which I assumed would take me to a town or a city and maybe even an airfield. Of course, I am an American and expected to find one. Every town has an airport, right?"

Everyone in the room laughed at her joke with a round of polite applause.

Nikki looked over at Amy across the table with her Flying Scotsman. Although she was also famous and had notched up equal, if not greater, achievement, she was not at the stratospheric level of Amelia Earhart. Nikki looked at Amy's soon-to-be husband and compared him to Amelia's, GP, an adventurer, publisher, publicist, and businessman, and Nikki worked out the differentiation and the distinction between the two.

"I didn't find one and flew around the town below me, Londonderry, until I found a suitable field and plopped the Vega right down and back to earth."

The room burst into a round of applause. Nikki glanced around the room and noted that some of the aviatrixes in attendance, including Lady Baillie, Winifred Spooner, and her beloved Amy, clapped more slowly and a little less enthusiastically than their male counterparts, who were clearly struck by the blonde Kansas beauty from across the pond.

"I was flying blind in a confusion of winds blowing to the north and then to the south. Eleven thirty till dawn, I only had my directional gyro and my two magnetic compasses. When I saw the lush green fields of Ireland, I knew that I had made it and I was in a new home."

The room erupted into rapturous applause again and, led by the men in the audience, a standing ovation. The ladies in the audience were the slowest and most reluctant to take the bow.

They were all in this together, but it was a time of highly competitive people, particularly women wishing to make their own mark on the world. Icons like Amelia were making an excellent job of attaching the vision, the dream, to notoriety, celebrity, and wealth. Nikki sensed a tinge of jealousy from some parts of the room.

"Maybe the limelight is more important than the mission itself," Nikki said. Bob did not quite hear, and Nikki thought it fruitless to pursue the discussion, at least for now. *Onward!*

14

HIGHFLYERS

July 29, 1932
Saint George's Church
Hanover Square, London, England

THEY WERE ON THEIR FINAL approach along Regent Street. Nikki and Amy were in the back of her husband's Invicta. Amy was the bride that day, and Nikki, newly married to Bob, was the maid of honor for the proceedings. They had been lifelong friends, and that day was another important day in their journey.

Bob Baxter was a steady bet for Nikki, and she was happy with her choice, while Jim Mollison had more glamour attached but a lot more risk too. His playboy reputation preceded him, and his proposal of marriage after just eight hours on a flight together worried both Amy and Nikki; nevertheless, that day was the big day.

It would be a low-key affair at the church with a reception afterward, just a small group of guests at each.

Bob steered the Invicta and made the turn onto Maddox Street, and Nikki saw the throng of well-wishers, reporters, and photographers lining the street on either side to get a glimpse of the prince and princess of British aviation tying the knot.

"Don't they have someone better to chase around the streets?" Amy asked, her irritation plain in her tone of voice.

Nikki knew it wasn't really a question. Amy often underestimated the level of her own notoriety. She loved the flying but missed her own peace and quiet and the normality of life. She found a bizarre contrast between the solitude of flight and the almost claustrophobic pressure on terra firma.

Nikki glanced over at Amy, who was dressed in a simple black dress, black fur shawl, and black bonnet. The only white garments were her gloves and her clutch bag. The outfit was understated yet stylish and not the traditional white wedding affair Nikki and Amy detested.

Bob parked the car. Nikki ushered her friend through the crowd and to the steps of the church, and once inside, they made their way to the altar, where James Mollison was sitting in his double-breasted gray suit. He stood up from where he was patiently waiting and turned to greet his bride with his charming signature smile. Nikki spotted the smile and turned up her nose.

The service was short, and afterward, the wedding party dashed through the crowd, pausing for a few moments to give the photographers their prize and their story, and then were whisked away to the reception. Mr. and Mrs. Mollison would become known as the Flying Mollisons or, as the redtops called them the next morning, the Flying Sweethearts.

The after-dinner speeches came from the Scotsman himself and, unusually for the day, from Amy too. She was insistent that their marriage be on equal terms. "Why shouldn't I do a speech as well?" she had asked Nikki in the car on the way to the church.

After the proceedings were over, Amy was quickly back to her business of flying. She went on to set a solo record while flying from London to Cape Town in her Puss Moth G-ACAB, *Desert Cloud*, breaking her new husband's record.

"Now that's what I call equality," she said as she met Nikki on the runway.

Next up was planning the next flight. By then, Amelia Earhart had stolen the hearts of the world, and thanks to her husband, she was one of the most famous women of the time. It was not that Amy wanted the fame—not at all—but she was competitive, and she wanted fair credit for her own contributions to aviation and for women.

Even early on in Jim and Amy's marriage, there were rumors about her husband's dalliances, and Amy decided to lock them away, dismissing them as idle, and likely jealous, gossip.

The couple planned to take the mantle of her American rival. The Flying Mollisons would fly together from Great Britain to New York—another first and another record.

In July the following year, the Flying Mollisons boarded a de Havilland DH.84 Dragon G-ACCV named *Seafarer* at Pendine Sands, South Wales. This would be their first leg, followed by a world-record attempt for the longest nonstop flight from New York to Baghdad.

For more than two weeks, thousands of people had poured into Pendine in anticipation of the Flying Sweethearts' next venture across the Atlantic and beyond. On the day of takeoff, a crowd gathered on the beach as the black Dragon Rapide taxied with the Mollisons as joint pilots. *Seafarer* was scrolled in big white letters like a signature on the black fuselage.

Pendine Sands was just spitting distance across the bay from Burry Port. Four years earlier, in June 1928, Amelia Earhart had landed as the passenger on *Friendship* with Stultz and Gordon, the pilot and engineer, as they made the journey in reverse across the Atlantic. Despite not taking an active part in the flight, Earhart had become the first woman to do so, as a passenger, not as pilot.

The Mollisons were competitive, even in marriage. Up until the night before, the couple had argued about who would be pilot and copilot. In the end, over dinner with the Beattie-Baxters, Bob had suggested a flip of a coin should decide to break the stalemate. Bob, seen as the most neutral of the four, had tossed the coin, it had landed on tails, and the Flying Scotsman had won the toss, much to Nikki's and Amy's disgust. The couples had retired to their rooms with little conversation.

The next day, Amy and her husband boarded the plane for the flight. Amy had the controls; she had obviously won the argument overnight, and she would take off and be in charge. They had compromised that he would land the *Seafarer* in New York.

Amy steered the *Seafarer* carefully through the throng around the plane and onto the golden white sands of Pendine; opened the throttle; and began their takeoff, gaining speed. Then came uplift with the joystick back, and they were airborne.

Nikki watched the plane fade into a black dot and then disappear into the clouds. She turned to Bob and said, "Good on her. She got her way." She looked over at her husband. "Happy wife, happy life, my dear," she snapped with a look of disapproval as they continued the drive. "What do you make of Captain Jim?"

Bob Baxter thought for a moment, "He's all right, I guess. Why?"

"I'm not sure." She paused. "Never have been."

They both knew of his reputation, and they had both heard the recent rumors. Everyone had; they were all around.

"He drinks too much," she said.

"Don't we all?"

"No, I mean he drinks too much. Like last night, downing the brandies before such a big flight."

"Well, that's how a lot of those pilots survived the war. Those who did survive."

"And I think he's smug." Nikki cut back to her point.

They drove through Carmarthen and took a right onto the main thoroughfare that would take them past Cardiff, Newport, and Bristol, where they would stop over for the night before making the rest of the 230-mile journey home.

Since both the girls were now married, Bob had moved into the apartment with Nikki and made it their marital home as Amy moved out to her new home. It was pleasant enough—at least until they had a family, Bob had said several times. That concerned Nikki, who was not sure she wanted children.

As they drove onward, Nikki looked out the window, thinking about her childhood in Skelton and then in Kirk Ella. *Happy times for the most part*, she thought to herself. She had often tried to work out what had gone wrong. They'd had everything they needed. Her father's business had been going well. The children all had been bright, fit, and healthy. Why had her mother never been happy? Had she been the reason Father never was around? Or had it been Father's fault that Mother was so unhappy? Had he made her that way?

She saw the face of Miss Boswell, once the rock of the family, in the window. Nikki gritted her teeth, hiding her anger from her husband. Nikki had never told him. In fact, she had not even told her best friend, Amy. How could she? *Was the woman in his study that night Mrs. Johnson, or was it Miss Boswell?*

She now knew for sure that her father had been having an affair with the nanny, but she also knew that he and Mrs. Johnson had been close too. She had watched them together and noticed their coincidental absences. She also knew there had been others.

Nikki thought of the last time she had seen her mother, as Mary had been carted off in the ambulance to High Royds. She thought of the news of her parents' suicides within days of each other, one in Yorkshire and the other in France, both lonely, a million miles apart.

She thought of her brothers and of Walter in particular. *What was he thinking in marrying Miss Boswell? What the hell was she thinking?* For how long had it been going on?

The thought made her feel nauseated. That was why she kept it locked away, in addition to the worry of it getting into the society gossip mill. *Heaven forbid!*

"They won't last, you know," Nikki said into the silence.

Bob looked at her with concern. "Are you still thinking about that? Maybe we should move on and think about happier things." He paused for a moment. They would be in Bristol by eight o'clock, in time for dinner and then bed. "Maybe starting a family? Maybe starting tonight?"

Nikki turned and slapped him on his knee. "You are a naughty boy." She would welcome the comfort and the physical pleasure, but she didn't have the nerve to tell him she didn't want babies or to go into the reasons why.

Nikki realized that *gypsy moth* had multiple definitions.

Gypsy Moth

Why, why, oh Gipsy Moth?
I see you; I hear your wrath.
Engines roar, memory lingers,
anger spreads from head to fingers.

Why, why, oh gypsy moth,
do you do the things you doth?

Think I loved and trusted you more;
now it feels like you keep the score.

Why, why, oh gypsy moth,
was it all right to take the cloth?
So young and impressionable too,
too early to be married to you.

I fly in your namesake above the clouds,
my escape away from the crowds.
On my own, just me and my mind,
thinking it best just to leave you behind.

Lymantria dispar is your natural name,
Latin; destroy and invade is your game.
I thank my sanctuary, the real Gipsy Moth.
Listen to his engines as take me south he doth.

—Nikki Beattie, date not known

15

SHADOWS

July 31, 1933
Riverside House
Ilkley in Wharfedale, West Riding
of Yorkshire, England

ESME BOSWELL SAT ALONE AT the dining table with a big black ledger in front of her. With her deep brown eyes, dark hair, and olive complexion, Esme knew she was still considered a good-looking woman, but now into her half century, the years had started to take their toll. She looked into the window at her reflection from the darkness outside and stared into her own eyes filled with memories past.

The dining table had not moved since they moved in fifteen years ago. It was still in the bay window overlooking the river and the riverside walk.

She had finished her work for the evening. She had written the checks. She had placed Nikki's in an envelope addressed to Hampstead Heath, London, with no note.

She knew Hampstead Heath well. She had grown up in London but not in that swanky part of the town. She had grown up with the Pearly Kings and Queens. Her family had been tinkers and gypsies, travelers from Ireland, and had fit in with the culture and the people of East London. They'd had no schooling, little education, and no money. Esme had taught herself as a child, stealing books from the local library and bookshops, and had been responsible for passing on her knowledge to her brothers. From eight years old, she had been teaching in some form or another.

She continued to stare at the window, at her reflection.

She had made her break when she was barely twenty years old, when a fine gentleman had picked her up off the streets and taken her back to his hotel in Mayfair. He had just had a baby daughter and complained that he was not getting the marital attention he deserved. That night, Esme had obliged and filled that void. A month later, she'd arrived in Skelton, Yorkshire, and become the nanny to the Beattie family. That had been thirty years ago now.

She opened the black ledger before her and placed Nikki's envelope beside the two checks for John and Walter. She would deliver John's in the morning and Walter's when she went to bed later that night.

She glanced across at the day's *Yorkshire Post* and the photograph of Amy and her new husband, Jim, in New York on the front page. They had crashed the *Seafarer* into a field in Connecticut after running out of fuel.

From a distance, Esme had kept a close eye on Nikki and her friend and their exploits in the air. She had also seen pictures of their weddings in the papers a couple of years earlier. Of course, she had not been invited to either. That made her sad and angry. After all, she was a victim as much as Nikki or any of them, having been picked up on the streets as a vulnerable teenager and trapped in a marriage as a concubine looking after her lover's children.

"Hardly bloody sunshine and roses," she said to herself in the window with her cockney accent. "Who else would've bloody put up with that apart from you, Esme?" she asked her reflection.

Esme had been in love with William Beattie. She never had been sure if that love was reciprocal, as she had witnessed his dalliances with the wives of his clients and customers. She remembered the conversation with Nikki, who had seen him with a woman she thought was Mrs. Johnson. Only years later had Nikki realized it was Esme. Amy's mother and Esme shared many common features. Both were pretty, with brown eyes, brown hair, and olive skin. Esme understood the mistaken identity and had managed to suppress that conversation for many a year.

The night before William had left, she had been worried about his state of mind. His wife had been committed to a mental health system that, in reality, few ever returned from.

They had known about her issues for many a year, and Mary's finding out about William and Esme's affair had tipped her over the edge. They all had tolerated the arrangement for a few years, as people simply did not get divorced back then—stiff upper lip and all that—and there had been no way in hell Esme was going back to live in the squalor of the East End of London.

That night, he'd handed her an envelope and explained the contents. "This is my will and testament, Esme. If anything happens to me, I want you to be in charge."

To her protestations, he had gone through the instructions of selling the garage in Hull and selling Lair Close. With the cash in the bank, the bonds, and investments in various clients' companies, there was plenty of liquidity to take care of the children and Esme.

She looked into the window and remembered his sad smile, his eyes, and the gentle kiss on the lips. They had not made love that night, their last night together; it had not felt right for either of them.

Esme was now the executor of the will, and part of the deal was for her to distribute the checks to the children each month.

Over the past decade and a half, she had placed smart investments, including the purchase of several properties in the town in her own name. By now, she was wealthy in her own right.

Still staring into the window, deep into her soul, she wasn't sure if Nikki was right that she was the devil incarnate or if, like Esme thought, she was also a victim, of falling in love with William and being betrayed only for him to leave, go kill himself, and leave her on her own, apart from a big pot of money, which, of course, helped.

That was how she had justified it in her mind. The money helped. There was no way she was going back to poverty, and that was her recompense for the sacrifices she'd made more than thirty years previously. That was her conclusion, and maybe she actually was a victim in this sad, tragic, and awful affair.

She turned to the front door as Walter came in. He had been working on his latest project in the garage. She kissed him on the cheek, made him a hot cocoa, and poured him a Liddesdale.

Esme had been looking after Walter in some shape or form for the past twenty-six years. Gypsy moth.

One hundred seventeen pilots, all the American female pilots of that time, had been invited to the first ever meeting of what would become known as the Ninety-Nines. The purpose of the meeting was to gather to establish mutual and collective support via a single registry of all the female pilots in the land and an organization founded for the advancement of women in aviation.

Louise Thaden from Arkansas presided as secretary of their inaugural and historic meeting. She was an aviator. She had taken a job in San Francisco in sales in 1926, and as part of her salary negotiation, she had secured free flying lessons as a perk. In 1928, she'd secured her pilot's license and become the first female pilot licensed in the state of Ohio.

By the time of the meeting, she had already established her name as one of the leading female pilots in America, setting several flying records and winning numerous flying events and races.

Earlier that year, she had become the first pilot to hold the women's altitude, endurance, and speed records simultaneously. She also had set the women's altitude record of more than twenty thousand feet in December a year earlier. That March, she had set the women's endurance record with a flight lasting precisely twenty-two hours, three minutes, and twelve seconds.

She was a legend, but then again, there were many legendary aviatrixes at that time, and most of them were in the room that day, including Pancho Barnes, Opal Kunz, and Blanche Noyes, all well recognized on the 1920s aviatrix circuit of the day.

At the hangar at Curtis Field, the group of women gathered from around the country with an eclectic mix of accents from across the nation. Some wore their Sunday best of dresses, skirts, clutches, and gloves, and others wore the more practical attire of overalls, skullcaps, and goggles.

Louise and Millie were great friends and rivals. Louise had beaten Earhart in the Powder Puff Derby just a few months prior, in which Amelia had come in third place.

The women sat around in a half circle and listened to Louise and Amelia talk about the importance of the Ninety-Nines and how, under the threat of sexism, they had to stick together to ensure that their voice was heard and that they could continue to exercise their right to take to the air.

They all knew there was resistance. The men at the top of the aviation echelons did not want their man's world interrupted.

For many, the first Women's Air Derby earlier in the year had been the last straw; it had been labeled the Powder

Puff Derby, an assault that belittled their efforts in the sky. Thaden made the connection during her speech.

"It is women like you and Millie here"—she pointed to Earhart, who stood by her right side as they addressed their audience—"who are pushing the limits in the skies, and by publicizing our endeavors, at some point, we will overwhelm these ridiculous and sexist protestations."

The hangar broke into applause. There was a movement to ban women from the air races, and there was also a great resistance to that move.

"We must stick together, be strong, and not stand for these morons to keep us from the skies." Millie added to the momentum. "Women must try to do things as men have tried. When they fail, their failure must be but a challenge to others."

"And that is you, ladies—every single one of you." Thaden pointed around the room, taking time to engage eye to eye and nodding as the crowd applauded and muttered words of agreement and encouragement.

In 1930, women were banned from competitive flying in one of the biggest crimes of blatant sexism of the era. In 1931, Amelia Earhart became president of the Ninety-Nines, with Thaden as treasurer. In 1935, after much demonstration, lobbying, and persuasion, women finally would be let back onto the flying circuit.

The Ninety-Nines were born that day and continued from that day on. The following was their song:

> In the air, everywhere,
> it's the song of the Ninety-Nines.

Wings in flight, day and night,
with the song of the Ninety-Nines.
On the line, fliers fine,
ships and spirits tuned in rhyme.
Keep that formation over the nation,
with the song of the Ninety-Nines.

They were pioneers, leaders, and aviatrixes, one and all.

Dark clouds were gathering in Europe once more. By November of the previous year, the Nazi Party had won most of the seats in the Reichstag, but they did not yet hold the majority in the German parliament. They were unable to form a coalition and therefore unable to support a candidate for chancellor.

The former chancellor, Franz von Papen, persuaded the then president, Paul von Hindenburg, to appoint Adolf Hitler as chancellor on January 30, 1933. The appointment led the way to the Enabling Act of 1933 and the beginning of the process of transformation of Germany from the Weimar Republic into Nazi Germany, one party with a totalitarian, autocratic ideology: National Socialism.

Hitler's aim was to eliminate Jews from the nation and to establish a New Order following what he saw as post–World War I injustice and the domination of Europe by Great Britain and France. His plan was to steer the nation out of the Great Depression and accelerate economic recovery for Germany.

His policies were winning popular support across the nation.

In April, Hermann Goring, a German World War I flying ace, was appointed to set up the Luftwaffe, Hitler's air force. In breach of the Treaty of Versailles, German pilots started training in secret at Lipetsk Air Base in the Soviet Union.

The might and fury of Germany were on the rise.

Hanna Reitsch, born in Hirschberg, was just twenty-one years old and a full-time glider pilot and instructor. Glamorous and committed to the cause, she soon became a target for Hitler and his new Luftwaffe and a valuable asset of propaganda. A woman in his ranks, a daring stunt pilot, endurance flyer, and record breaker, she would become a test pilot for his latest weapons of war from the air.

After his Fascist coup d'état ten years previously, Benito Mussolini, prime minster of Italy, was pushing his Fascist agenda for others, such as Hitler, Salazar in Portugal, and Franco in Spain, to follow his lead.

Bedriye Tahir Gökmen became the first woman in Turkey to earn her pilot's license. Lotfia Elnadi was the first Arab African woman in Egypt to do so. Maryse Hilsz from France was breaking records, as was Carola Lorenzini from Argentina, and Aline Rhonie flew solo from New York to Mexico City. These women all were leading the way for others to follow in their flight paths.

The times were changing and not necessarily for the better.

Thirteen-year-old Dorothy Pierson ran to the front door to greet the mailman with anticipation. It had been three weeks since she had written to her hero, and she knew that surely she would reply. She shuffled through the letters, and there it was. It popped out in front of her, a typed envelope addressed to Miss Pierson.

She went to grab a butter knife from the kitchen and carefully slit open the envelope. She held the paper up to her nose and took a deep breath, trying to sense the person, the perfume, or some other clue from the sender.

Dorothy had written to her for advice about fulfilling her dream of one day becoming a pilot. She had read the articles about her adventures and those of the other women in the skies, but Amelia was her favorite. Dorothy was her number-one fan.

She ran up the balustrade staircase to her bedroom to read the letter undisturbed. She closed the door behind her, sat on her bed, opened up the folded letter, and laid it on the bed in front of her as if it were a rare artifact like those she had seen in the Smithsonian.

She read each word slowly out loud.

> Miss Pierson
> Locust Avenue
> Rye, New York
> August 14, 1933
>
> Dear Miss Pierson:
>
> It is very hard for me to advise you about taking up aviation as a vocation inasmuch as I do not know you. However, if you are really determined to fly and

are willing to make the sacrifice necessary, I should certainly not discourage you from the attempt.

Dorothy gulped with a sense of anxiety. This was certainly not the overwhelming yes she had been expecting. She had shared with Miss Earhart her wish, her dream, and her aspiration, and she had also included in her letter that it was with her parents' blessing. Dorothy would lie on the lawn of their house or on the nearby beaches in the summer, looking up into the sky and watching the seagulls float on the wind, wondering what it must be like to fly.

The letter went on.

Of course, the first step to becoming a pilot is to have a physical examination by a Department of Commerce physician. You can find the name of the examiner in your district by writing to the Department of Commerce in Washington, Aeronautics Branch, or calling the local airport. He can tell you whether or not you are physically able to fly. If you can, the second step is to find means of taking lessons; and if you cannot, I assume you would still wish to enter some other part of the industry.

Her father, a banker in the city had a client named George Putnam, also from Rye, who happened to be the husband of Amelia Earhart herself. He had agreed to pass on Dorothy's letter and request for advice.

Dorothy was fit and healthy. She played tennis at the nearby Westchester Country Club and rode her horse, Krafty, who was stabled at a nearby barn. She did not have any concerns about her fitness. She made a note in her journal to call the Aeronautics Branch in Washington.

> There are many positions in aviation open to women, not only in the clerical field but in the factories. There are air hostesses and a number of specialized jobs. Perhaps one of the best ways of getting in is to perfect yourself in secretarial work and obtain a position on the fringes, relying on your ability and desire in order to succeed.

Dorothy could feel her cheeks redden as she read the words on the page. "On the fringes" was exactly the phrase her mother had used when Dorothy expressed her desire. Had she or her father coached Amelia on how best to respond?

> As far as women's opportunities in flying go, I think they will improve, as they have in all industries. Just now, there are no pilots on the regular scheduled airlines. Someday I expect there will be. However, women do earn their living by teaching, by joy-hopping, by ferrying airplanes from factory to purchaser, etc.

Dorothy's mood lightened. Perhaps there was some hope after all. The letter concluded.

> I think you are fortunate to have the full support of your parents. If there are any questions you would like to ask me, I shall be glad to attempt to answer them.
>
> Sincerely yours.

After reaching the end of the letter, Dorothy sat on her bed with letter in hand, gazing out the window at the birds in the trees and in the skies above.

She would write a follow-up letter of thanks, of course, and ask more questions, and she would make a telephone call to the Department of Commerce to get the criteria of qualification to become a pilot, at least one day. The clouds opened up above.

16

BLACK MAGIC

August 1, 1933
Broadway, from the Battery to City Hall
New York, United States

MORE THAN TWO HUNDRED THOUSAND people lined Heroes Way as the Flying Mollisons sat high above the seats, on the back of a black Cadillac, with ticker tape streaming from the high-rise buildings above. Both had cuts and bruises still visible, but Jim Mollison looked the worse for wear of the two, with a white bandage on the side of his face.

Just a week earlier, the *Seafarer* had crashed. They had been hazardously low on fuel while flying over Connecticut, when they'd spotted the lights of Bridgeport Municipal Airport below. Mollison had taken the precaution of circling five times, but then they'd run out of fuel, and to Amy's dismay, Mollison had unceremoniously crashed the *Seafarer* into the ground, throwing the Mollisons from the wreckage.

"Next time, James—that is, if there is a next time—if I take off, I will land the bloody thing as well," she'd said. It was not a question.

Despite that, they were the first couple to have made the journey across the Atlantic, and they were getting "quite the welcome," as Amy described it.

They were heading to City Hall, where Mayor O'Brien would welcome them to the city of New York and present them with a gold medal each for being "the first couple to ever make the trip from the old country in such a manner."

That morning, the *New York Times* had carried the story.

City Welcomes Flying Mollisons

Parade from Battery, Welcome by O'Brien and Presentation of Medals on Program. Flying Pair Enjoy Sirens. Amy Johnson Thinks That Ours Are Louder and More "Lovely" Than Those in England.

"I am not quite sure I said it exactly like that," she'd huffed as she read the morning paper over breakfast at the hotel. "But I have to say, these Americans have been very warm and welcoming," she'd added.

Jim had agreed while taking a mouthful of pancake. "Never had these for breakfast before," he'd said, "but they are pretty bloody good." He'd nodded, pointing at the jug of sweet brown syrup that had come with his order. "Damn fine."

Their intended onward trip and attempted record to Baghdad was off the table now, as the *Seafarer* was too badly damaged and beyond repair. After the parade, they would return to England and plan their next adventure, either as a couple or not.

"If we do the India trip next year, I insist that I am in the lead," she'd said that morning.

Jim had continued with the crossword and let out a grimace. "Yes, dear."

"We made ourselves look bloody fools out there." She'd pointed at the paper and the photograph of the *Seafarer* smashed up in the field and the couple's undignified evacuation.

After much deliberation between them, the Mollisons took their next trip in the following year, setting a record time from Britain to India in the de Havilland DH.88 G-ACSP *Black Magic*. It was part of the MacRobertson Air Race between Britain and Australia, but when they got to Allahabad, they were forced to retire due to engine trouble.

Nikki had been spending more time at home now that both she and Amy were married. Amy was flying the world with Captain Jim, as Nikki called him, and Nikki and Bob were enjoying their newlywed life.

Bob was by then a squadron leader and often was at various stations, including Bicester, near where he'd been when they first met. Nikki would meet him at the aero club as he flew in from wherever he had been that week, and occasionally, Nikki would take out her Gipsy Moth to go see him for the weekend.

They were two pilots having a nice life. Nikki still worked at William Charles Crocker's law firm, and Bob Baxter was still in the Royal Air Force.

She had managed to avoid the conversation about starting a family, although they enjoyed a healthy love life fueled by their frequent separation.

Nikki was not ready for babies and knew deep down inside that she never would be. It was a conscious decision. She did not want children; she just had not found the courage or the right time to share this with her husband. She quietly hoped she never would have to; rather, she would just let the issue slip away. Besides, they were enjoying a good life. They had two salaries and a nice apartment in a nice part of town and enjoyed flying the skies when possible.

They weren't quite the Flying Baxters, but they were both content with leaving that to Amy and her husband.

Nikki kept an avid eye on the Mollisons' progress and always made an effort to see Amy when she was back in England. They normally just met up as two Yorkshire lasses, with her excuse that Bob was out of town, but the reality was that Nikki had no time for Amy's husband. Amy knew that, and her own patience in the marriage was wearing thin.

In May 1936, Amy broke another record, regaining her record from England to Cape Town in her Percival Gull G-ADZO, and they met up at the awards dinner during which the Royal Aero Club presented Amy with the Gold

Medal for having made the round trip in just seven days, twenty-three hours, and forty-six minutes. Nikki had read the news in the paper.

Britain's Sky Queen

Britain's leading aviatrix today made a clean sweep of her task of recapturing her records for flights between London and Cape Town and return. She landed at Croydon this morning to set a new mark of four days, seventeen hours, and seventeen minutes from the Cape after making the trip south earlier this month in the record time of three days, six hours, and twenty-nine minutes.

Nikki was proud of her friend, and although the fame and the pressure were not something she would have chosen, she often found herself living vicariously through her best friend's adventures and achievements.

Nikki often thought of music in her head as a way to make sense of all that surrounded her and of the memories of her mother and her father.

I'm taking a ride with my best friend.
I hope she never lets me down again.
She knows where she's taking me.
Taking me where I want to be.
We're flying high; we're watching the world pass us by.
Never want to come down.
Never want to put my feet back down on the ground.

Nikki knew that she had a mental closet and that skeletons and worse lived inside. It was a dark place where she locked things away.

She was good at keeping the door shut, but every now and then, something would creep out: a smell, a thought, or a memory that would trigger the pain. She had kept it away from Amy, at least for the most part. It was something she dealt with when alone. Nikki and Bob's lifestyle, with Bob often away at least three or four nights a week, was a good enough dark blanket to shield and keep her secrets out of plain view.

Nikki and Amy, although best friends, were different people with dissimilar needs. Their chosen lives suited them just fine; however, Nikki and Bob were in a happy marriage, and Amy was not.

"What on earth should I do?" Amy asked Nikki of the situation one day over lunch. "They're only rumors, but there's no smoke without fire," she added, justifying her position.

Nikki did not respond yet. She just kept quiet and let her friend talk it through out loud. Clearly, this had been weighing on her mind, and frankly, why wouldn't it have been?

"I mean, proposing after just eight hours? Why didn't I see that as a warning sign? And why the bloody hell did I accept? With all his fame, I wonder how many other bloody women he has worked his magic with. I mean, I might not mind if he was having an affair with Marlene Dietrich or Joan Crawford or even Millie Earhart, but have you seen these bloody women he's messing around with?"

Nikki just shook her head, letting her get it all out.

"Mrs. Beryl bloody Markham, of all the people! Jim would need a bloody stepladder to get up there," she said.

Nikki blurted out an uncontrollable snigger. "And she looks like a bloody Afghan hound!" They both found the comedy in the moment.

"Nikki, although you never said it to me straight, I know you never liked him." She looked at Nikki knowingly. "Come on. I've known you most of my life." She smiled.

Nikki did not object; she just shrugged and smiled back.

The next day, October 21, 1936, Amy announced to the press that she was separating from her husband.

Flying Mollisons Flying Solo

With a broken nose but a firm heart, Mrs. Amy Mollison announced the famous Flying Mollisons will set solo marital courses.

The article went on to say that the broken nose was from a plane crash, and her broken heart was from an alleged affair Mollison was having with another flier, Mrs. Beryl Markham.

"I've heard rumors about Jim for another month," said Johnson. "Well, Jim is going his way, and I am going mine."

That was that.

Millie's around-the-world flight had been in the planning for more than eighteen months, and she and her copilot were now well into their attempt. Financed by Purdue University, the flight would be the longest circumnavigation of the world at twenty-nine thousand miles, tracking the route around the equator for the first time.

After they had failed in their first attempt while flying in the opposite direction from Oakland, California, to Hawaii and beyond, they had decided to go the other direction and had flown from Oakland to Miami on the East Coast unannounced. In Miami, she formally announced to the press her intention to circumnavigate the globe.

Amelia and her copilot, Fred Noonan, were the last two standing, as frustrations had led former collaborators to throw in the towel.

Although Millie by then had many flying miles under her belt, she was known to be lacking in the navigational skills needed for such a flight, preferring navigation by landmarks instead. As there was a lack of such luxuries when crossing swaths of ocean, Fred Noonan was on board as navigator for the attempt.

Noonan was a licensed ship's captain and experienced in both marine and flight navigation. He had recently left Pan Am, where he had established the China Clipper seaplane routes across the Pacific. He had also overseen the training of the airline's pilots on navigation between San Francisco and Manilla.

Earhart had come under some criticism when the Electra crashed on takeoff from Hawaii during their first attempt.

Earhart blamed a blowout of the right tire, while others blamed pilot error—her error.

Amelia was renowned for her sometimes gung-ho approach or what some called, combined with her inexperience, her naivety or even recklessness. Topping their individual frailties, they both lacked almost any experience in running the aircraft's radios.

On June 1, call sign KHAQQ left Miami and headed south to various stops in South America and then across to Africa, the Indian subcontinent, and Southeast Asia. They arrived in Lae, New Guinea, on June 29. They had completed twenty-two thousand miles of the journey and had just seven thousand to go.

That was a lot of flying time together, and Amelia's overenthusiasm and Noonan's liking for alcohol were beginning to overflow, fueled by the seriousness of the most daunting and dangerous leg of their journey so far.

On July 2, the heavily loaded Lockheed Electra, with its add-on equipment specification and fully loaded fuel tanks, took off from Lae Airfield. It was midnight GMT and ten o'clock in the morning local time.

Amelia and Noonan were flying into the unknown toward their intended destination: Howland Island, a flat sliver of land only a mile long and less than a third of a mile wide standing only ten feet above sea level. It would be like finding a needle in a haystack. They would both need to be on top of their game and pray for clear weather too.

Their target destination was 2,500 miles away, and the fuel calculations were a critical element of their planning.

Total weight, RPM, and flight hours were used to calculate that 1,100 gallons of fuel were sufficient.

This leg would test the experience of Earhart as a pilot and the strength of the navigational skills Noonan possessed.

They were, however, not alone. The United States Coast Guard had arranged for the USCGC *Itasca* to be in the vicinity of Howland Island to support the endeavor, offering radio support and, in effect, a homing beacon for Earhart as she got closer to the island. In addition, they could also stoke up the ship's boilers to create smoke and a visible beacon.

Around three o'clock in the afternoon local time, Amelia reported her altitude at ten thousand feet, and by five o'clock, due to low cloud, she had dropped the Electra down to 7,500 feet and a speed of 150 knots. Their position was close to the Nukumanu Islands, eight hundred miles into the flight.

The crew on the *Itasca* received further routine calls providing updates on position and weather reports.

Earhart reported her position at two hundred miles out and requested that *Itasca* switch on its direction finder. That was when the crew realized that although they could hear Earhart's radio transmissions, evidently, she could not hear them.

A half hour passed, and they received the same request, now reported at one hundred miles, within reach. Again, the crew tried to respond to her message but with no success.

Another forty-five minutes later, the crew reported the following on their communications log:

Earhart on NW, says running out of gas, only half
hour left. Cannot hear us at all. We hear her and
sending on 3105 ES 500 same time constantly.

The coast guard crew were frantic and helpless. Either
the Electra's radio equipment was not working, or Earhart
had it on the wrong reception frequency. There was nothing
they could do. The captain ordered the engine room to stoke
up the boilers and make smoke.

Just a couple of minutes later, they received the following
message:

Call sign KHAQQ calling *Itasca*. We must be on you
but cannot see you, but gas is running low. Been
unable to reach you by radio. We are flying at one
thousand feet.

The coast guard managed to send a location message via
Morse code that Earhart confirmed she received, but they
could not get a bearing on the signal.

The radio on the *Itasca* broke its silence one final time:

We are running online north and south.

The crew interpreted that as Earhart and Noonan
believing they had reached Howland Island, yet they were
nowhere to be seen. The coast guard proposed many reasons
in speculating why that would have been.

The *Itasca* continued to smoke up the boilers and send
up flares and signals in the hope that Noonan and Earhart
might spot them from wherever they were.

The Electra, Noonan, and Amelia Earhart were never seen again.

Lonely as a Cloud

All my attention, all my love.
My heart sings when I rise above.
Even in my darkest hours,
looking out at our field of flowers.

I remember the day you called,
and since, my world has cannonballed.
Early morning whistling our tune
as the sun rises across the dune.

Revving up my little yellow bird,
hearing your voice in the silence, absurd.
All this day, I think of you,
remembering all the things we said we would do

To you, with love, I will remember you.

17

WAR

September 4, 1939
Hampstead Heath, London, England

NIKKI READ THE HEADLINE OF the *London Times*: "War!" The storm had been brewing for a while. Although without a formal declaration, Japan had, in effect, been at war with the Chinese for the past couple of years in their pursuit to dominate Asia. In Europe, Hitler had been tightening his grip and control in Germany, building his weaponry, his armies, and his military, a dictator state with uniforms, swastikas, and strange salutes.

World War I had radically altered the political map of Europe and in its wake left a vacuum. The victors had split up the assets and power of the Central Powers and, in some cases, their territories, causing a rise in nationalism.

During the 1919 Paris Peace Conference, the League of Nations had been formed in an effort to prevent future armed conflicts through collective security among nations and disarmament of militaries and navies of potential warring factions.

Nationalistic sentiments arose especially in Germany because of the significant territorial, colonial, and financial losses due to the Treaty of Versailles. Germany had lost 13 percent of its territory and all its overseas possessions.

Nikki had likened it to the humiliation of a prizefighter in a public defeat, with the victor forcing them to apologize and then taking their gloves, binding their arms, and making them vow never to fight again. It did not make sense to her.

As long ago as 1923, Hitler had made an attempt to overthrow the government, and ten years later, as chancellor, he'd abolished democracy and created his own New World Order.

"Was that not a loud enough signal to the rest of Europe?" she asked aloud.

Hitler had been rearming the nation in defiance of the rest of Europe and the world, and as Russia, now the Soviet Union, formed protective alliances with the likes of France, Germany was creating its own Axis of power with the likes of Italy and Japan, who were in support of General Francisco Franco's Nationalist rebels in Spain.

The Olympic Games in Berlin three years earlier had been a big two fingers to the Allied powers of Europe, a show of Germany's strength and might and a show of the growing anti-Semitism and racism in the country.

Many had feared the warning signs, but with a combination of widespread pacifism and hope coupled with the distractions of the moment, the world turned a blind eye to the buildup and, as a result, somewhat emboldened the rise of the Nazi war machine.

Now, with that war machine mobilized and Hitler's invasion of Poland, the only alternative left for Britain was to declare war.

The hairs on Nikki's neck stood up as she read the article. It was Monday. Bob had taken a long weekend and was home with her at the apartment. They were having a late breakfast together following a refreshing and much-needed sleep-in.

"This has been brewing for years," Nikki said. It was hard to disagree. "Why on earth didn't we do something about it early rather than letting it get so far?" It was a question on everyone's mind.

"Question is, how far will he go?" Bob said. "If he sticks to just Poland, then I think we can see through that, but if he goes farther, then who knows? This thing could get really messy." He showed a strained smile and slow nod, meaning he thought it was really serious.

"And the size of his armies," Nikki added. "And not just the size but the technology. His armies are not only the biggest but the most technologically advanced in the history of the world."

"If we are not careful, we will all be speaking German." The statement was Bob's attempt at humor but had a profoundly serious and concerning potential reality to it.

"You don't really think so, do you?" she asked.

He just shrugged, ate his last piece of toast, and took a sip of his tea.

As they both had a day off, they had planned to head into London that afternoon and take in a show in the West End, but since the news, there had been rumors that all the theaters were closing down in fear of London's being bombed.

"Is it really that serious?" she asked Bob.

"My dearest Nikki, we are now officially at war."

She gulped for a second as the seriousness of the situation sank in. They canceled their plans and took a walk on Hampstead Heath instead.

This must be serious, she thought. *Very serious indeed.*

In May 1939, the Military Training Act meant that every single male between the ages of twenty and twenty-two was required to undertake six months' military training. This was Neville Chamberlain's British government response of preparedness to Hitler's chest beating in Berlin and getting ready for a potential war. Many thought it was too late. Some 240,000 registered.

Four months later, the same day Britain declared war on Germany, Parliament passed the National Service Act, which meant every male between eighteen and forty-one, single or not, was to be conscripted into the military. The only exceptions were the medically unfit and professions classified as essential, such as banking, farming, medicine, and engineering.

Conscientious objectors had to appear before a tribunal to argue their reasons for refusing to join up. If their cases were not dismissed, they were granted one of several categories of exemption and were given noncombatant jobs instead.

Although conscription of women was yet to be passed in Parliament, it was probably inevitable, and many women did sign up to support the cause of the nation and the distinct and scary threat at their door.

There was a real feeling of fear at the time. Great Britain was simply not prepared for war, especially a war with a nation as militarily advanced as Germany. There was a great feeling that Chamberlain and his predecessors had been asleep at the wheel and had done nothing in the face of the most glaring and obvious signals coming from Germany.

Not long after that fateful day when a state of war was declared between Britain and Germany, Nikki and Amy were enjoying some leisure time together in Hampstead Heath. Bob had been called away back in September, so it was just the two of them. They were debating the situation and the right response for them under the circumstances. They were both qualified and experienced pilots, and they both wanted to make contributions to the war effort and to defeat the evil of Adolf Hitler.

"The elections are coming. We need a strong leader to take us through this," Nikki said.

"It looks like Churchill is the frontrunner, and that's the sort of spirit we need," responded Amy.

"As far as Chamberlain, he should be charged with treason." Nikki was referring to his famous visit to Germany the previous year when trying to broker a deal of peace with Hitler. Amy agreed.

Over the weekend, they had deliberated back and forth, but with their minds now made up, they agreed to sign up for the Air Transport Auxiliary. They would be the first among fewer than a dozen female pilots to sign up for the war efforts. This was their contribution.

"Why should war just be a man thing anyway?" Amy said.

"Damn right!" Nikki was on board and in full agreement.

It was a daunting prospect in light of the memories and stories from World War I, the losses, and Hitler's military, which was visibly more powerful and mightier than that of Great Britain. Any prospect of a potential conflict with such a military force was frightening, to say the least.

"We need to pull up our socks. We need to engage our best and brightest minds, our designers, and our engineers, and we need to build ourselves a defense and the capability to fight back and win this bloody thing," Amy said, sounding like Churchill himself.

Nikki recalled her father's contributions in Hull and Bovington and his absence from her childhood. She visualized her father in his khaki uniform with three pips and a crown. How much she'd loved him, and how she missed him dearly.

"And don't forget the best pilots," Nikki added as they walked arm in arm toward the enlistment office.

They both were aware of the enormity of what they were about to do, but they also both held a huge national pride and deep sense of duty.

For king and country!

18

DOUBLE CROSS

January 1940
Wormwood Scrubs
Du Cane Road, London, England

THE BRITISH SECURITY SERVICE, THE MI5, were
on the move. Given the rapid expansion of their activities
and service, the MI5 needed a new home and moved into
the infamous Victorian prison Wormwood Scrubs in the
West of London. It seemed an unlikely location for such an
organization, but the creation of decoys was the mastery of
the agency.

There were rumors of German spies in Britain, from
hairdressers in Glasgow to infiltrators in the military,
air force, and navy; engineers in factories; bankers; and
businesspeople, including prized personalities.

Hitler had some compelling methods of persuading his spies, whether or not they originally had German roots. Through belief in his mantra, by fear, or through greed, he managed to amass a small army of willing operatives on Britain's shores and across mainland Europe.

Propaganda campaigns abounded across Britain and the empire, warning of the dangers of inadvertently letting out secrets, telling too much, or even just being overheard in casual conversation. The mood of the time was claustrophobic; people never knew who was listening in, who was watching, and who was friend or foe.

The network of German spies would send their snippets, however seemingly harmless, to Berlin for them to piece the intelligence together to make sense out of the chaos.

They saying "Loose lips sink ships" was born.

The MI5 staged operations to find the spies; capture them; and, even more beneficial to their efforts, turn them, the principle of which had been around for some time.

The operations were overseen by the Twenty Committee, which in turn lent its two Roman numerals, *XX*, to what would be termed Double Cross, a system that turned Nazi spies to the allegiance of the Allies, at which point the spies continued to operate, feeding false and misleading information back to Berlin.

The origins of Double Cross went back to an adventurous MI5 double agent in the mid-1930s, World War I fighter ace Christopher "Mad Major" Draper, who flew under fifteen of London's eighteen bridges in 1931—a feat that impressed Hitler, among others, leading him to be recruited. He did little for Hitler but did relate back to the MI5 how Germany managed their network of agents—enormously useful intelligence for the Double Cross initiative.

The Mad Major's intelligence led to MI5's discovery of a Welsh-born electrical engineer spying for the Germans, whom MI5 codenamed Snow and who became the first in a series of 120 wartime German agents turned by MI5 into double agents.

Their new home at Wormwood Scrubs was temporary, as it was bombed during the Blitz in September 1940, after which most staff transferred to Blenheim, near Oxford. The director and some other senior officers and counterespionage operations officers stayed in London at a former MGM building on St. James's Street. Its identity was camouflaged by a large To Let sign outside.

The enemy is among us.

Walter Beattie sat in his Nissen hut with his friend Jules Constantine, the son of a wealthy Greek shipping tycoon, playing cards by the oil-burning stove to keep warm in the pervasive cold of Iceland. They had been there since mid-May, taking over from the invading force of the Royal Marines and Colonel Sturges, releasing the Marines to invade somewhere else.

The British had been concerned about Iceland for some time and had placed a naval blockade around the island to prevent profitable shipments to Germany. The Nazis were also showing increasing interest in the island as a potential strategic naval base commanding the North Atlantic but within reach of North American shores, if they decided to invade North America at some point in their plan of domination.

On May 10, 1940, 746 of Sturges's Marines had invaded the Nordic island nation, which previously had been of neutral status and in a union with Denmark. It had been a relatively quick and clean incursion, making way for the occupation of two British Army brigades.

Walter and Jules had been there since as a shrinking part of the British contingent as Z Force arrived from Canada to relieve the British to return to the defense of their own islands. They themselves would be leaving back to Britain early in the New Year, by the end of January latest, in a matter of days or of weeks at worst.

The Icelandic men despised the occupiers with a venom. Not only had they cut off lucrative trade with the Germans, but with the influx of males who were opposite the stereotypical Icelandic men, the British and Canadian alternatives were proving popular to the Icelandic women.

Fraternization with the occupying force was on the rise, as were prostitution and pregnancies. The large-scale occurrence came to be known as *ástandið*, meaning "the condition" or "the situation" in Icelandic. Those pregnant and who had children as a result would be named Hansson, meaning "child of his" or "child of the unknown."

Walter and Jules were looking forward to getting off the island. Walter laid down his hand on the makeshift card table between them. "Running flush," he said, revealing a ten, queen, and jack of spades with a big smile at his friend opposite.

Jules, with a cigar hanging out of his mouth, grinned back. "As good as that is, my friend, what about this little beauty?" He laid down his own flush but one consisting of the jack, queen, and king of hearts. "How's about that, Wally?"

"You bugger!"

They had already seen enough of this place. Beyond the weather and the tremendous gales, a four-tonner full of troops had gotten swept up by the wind and taken out to sea as if a ragdoll cast into the ocean, with no survivors.

Then there were the U-boats circling the island like a pack of hungry sharks, picking off the ships one by one.

A pair of British squaddies had popped pills to damage their bodies so much that they would qualify to be unfit for duty. It had worked: they had been so unfit that they'd had drug-induced heart attacks and died. They had been only in their late twenties, and their bodies had been buried in the loneliness of the Commonwealth war graves on the island.

It was Christmas Day, and they had been to the mess for the sorry excuse for a Christmas dinner, the only solace being that Jules had managed to get himself a flask of brandy in an otherwise dry land.

They leaned back in their chairs with the cards exhausted and sat in front of the stove, warming their hands and sipping the brandy from their army-issue mugs.

"Did you hear back from your lady friend?" Jules asked.

Walter shook his head. "Nope."

Jules knew all about Walter's own ástandið situation.

Walter had, for the first time, shared his inner secrets with his new friend. He had somehow felt it easier to share with someone outside his immediate circle. Jules, once a stranger but now a friend, brought a new perspective. They'd been thrown together in the same uniform, with no more identity as the son of a millionaire for Jules and no Beattie Blue for Walter. They were just two men in a Nissen hut in Iceland, sharing a flask of brandy and the heat of a stove.

"You will, Wally. You will." Jules slapped him on his knee in encouragement. "You both know that Scotsman was a mistake; she basically told you that in her last letter."

"I know, but what about my mistake?"

Jules looked as his friend, pursed his lips, and breathed in. "Well, old boy, that's where it gets a little tricky," he said, smiling but as though in pain and not in humor.

Walter knew he had messed up. He lived with it every day. When he'd heard of Amy's engagement, he'd sought comfort, and Esme had taken advantage of the situation.

He kicked himself. He recalled the Turner Trail, his intention, and all the opportunities he'd had to pop the question—but he had not gone through with it. Instead of the ring he had intended, he had bought her a necklace. Then, after Rydal Mount, Beatrix Potter's house, their winning streak at the races, the trip back to her Gipsy Moth, and a long wave goodbye, he'd returned home to Ilkley, to his own gypsy moth of an altogether different type.

He had adopted his brother to his unit, and John was also in Iceland with him, but John had no idea of the situation. He was oblivious and caught up in his own misery. Walter was not even sure what he had to be miserable about. John had married Betty just before they enlisted. Many couples got married before the husbands' enlistment at the time.

"Betty is a good Ilkley lass and would make a good wife and a mother someday," Walter had told John.

Walter now said to Jules, "Marry before you leave to war! What a bloody clever idea that was!"

Jules just laughed. "Have another sip of brandy, my friend, and stop beating yourself up. Don't worry; you will hear back from your aviatrix friend. I promise you."

Walter shrugged and nodded. Unlike his brother, Walter was ever the optimist and saw the bright side of most situations. "Come on. Let's double or quits." Walter dealt the cards for another round of three-card brag.

Life was like a game of cards.

First Officer Amy Johnson sat in the cockpit of the Airspeed Oxford AS10 on the tarmac of the airfield. She would head the 135 miles south to Blackpool and then 150 miles onto RAF Kidlington, Oxford. Her trip, three hundred miles in total, was a straightforward ninety-minute flight. It was a routine trip: shepherding planes, packages, and sometimes secret cargo in preparation and readiness for the war effort. She had made similar sorties many times before.

Amy and Nikki had both joined up with the ATA in May the previous year, just a few months after Great Britain declared war on Germany.

In an astonishingly brief spell of time, Hitler had built the most powerful military known to man, including the latest technology and equipment of land, sea, and air and a reported eighteen million military personnel as part of the Wehrmacht's combined forces, which was just under half the total population of Great Britain at the time. Germany had the fastest tanks, the biggest and most powerful armaments, the navy, the U-boats, and the fastest airplanes. Great Britain was truly on its back foot, and they were playing catch up as best as they could. These were incredibly scary times.

As Amy waited for the engine to finish warming up, she reflected on her dinner with Nikki at the officers' mess the previous evening. Amy was taking the Airspeed Oxford to Kidlington, and Nikki was taking her Avro Anson with a passenger list of engineers to her new home airfield of RAF Uxbridge. She was meeting up with her beloved Bob, who was now stationed at Bomber Command.

Between bites of her mutton casserole, Amy had said, "We'll be done by Christmas," with a level of sarcasm.

Nikki had just looked at her. "I've heard that one before."

Amy had remembered the service at Saint Matthew's all that time ago. "Less than twenty-five years on, you would have thought we had learned something by now."

"This is different, Amy. Very different."

Amy had looked puzzled. "How?"

"This is evil. Pure evil." Nikki had nodded at her friend and sipped from her glass. "I'm not sure how we can win without the help of the Americans," Nikki had added, drawing from what limited insights her husband could share from his role in the effort.

Amy had wanted to change the conversation back to less uncomfortable ground. They, like everyone else at the time, were aware of who knew what, who did not, and who was listening in on casual conversations that potentially could reveal a lot. *Walls have ears.*

She'd wanted to keep the conversation on safer ground, but Amy found it ironic that the longer they knew each other and the more they went through, with more water under the bridge, the less safe ground they had to cover.

Amy knew Nikki did not like talking about childhood, Boulevard, and Kirk Ella. It was painful to watch her face if those subjects were ever brought up. Amy had no interest in talking about her "little Scottish mistake," as she referred to her ex-husband, who now also was serving in the ATA.

"I just hope I don't bloody well bump into him" had been Nikki's only comment on that matter. Nikki had disliked him from the beginning.

"I should have listened to your instinct." Amy had smiled at her friend.

Moving swiftly on, they'd talked about the apartment in Hampstead, Bob, and his new job but not in detail. "Loose lips and all that," Nikki had said, smiling across the table. Amy had sent a simple smile back across the table.

These were serious times, and there were reports of Nazi spies everywhere, especially in Scotland, apparently taking advantage of the remote and sparsely populated coastline to make land and have an easier point of entry. It was also rumored that Hitler was prepared to pay big money to recruit sometimes high-profile people who otherwise would have been beyond suspicion.

"They spotted a U-boat up in Sutherland just last week," Nikki had said, "sailing up the Kyle of Tongue."

Amy had shaken her head and moved the conversation on again, thinking she would tentatively probe sacred ground. "I heard from Walter."

Nikki had slowed her chewing. "Oh yes? What did he have to say?"

"He joined the Royal Electrical and Mechanical Engineers. He adopted John so they could be in the same unit, so they would be together during the war."

"Oh good." Nikki had looked happy that her brothers would be together through whatever was to come.

"They're in Iceland." Amy had considered her friend's face. "He sends his love."

"To you or to me, Amy?"

"You, you silly sausage!" The conversation had been over.

Now, the next morning, they were lined up side by side with ground crew at the ready. At the order to start the engines, the two planes jittered and spluttered to life, warmed up, and settled down into the British-engineered hum, a sound they both loved—a strangely comforting sound that throbbed and touched every part of the body, every nerve, every sensation. The only moment better was when the plane was airborne and glided up into the clouds and beyond.

The two women saluted each other. Nikki took off first in her Avro, and then, three minutes later, Amy prepared to take off in her Airspeed, heading out on a very different flight path.

"Goodbye, my darling!" Amy shouted after Nikki as she flew out of sight. "Until next time, my love." For some unknown reason, she had a waver in her voice, and she had to take a deep breath to hold back the emotion.

Amy taxied to the runway, sped down the tarmac, and pulled back the throttle, and she was up. The first stop was Blackpool. She would touch down in less than an hour, pick up her payload, and then be off again on her mission.

In addition to a courier, the Airspeed Oxford was a twin-engine monoplane and a medium-sized bomber. With a normal combat crew of three, it was thirty-four feet in length, had a fifty-three-foot wingspan, and was eleven feet in height. It could carry 7,500 pounds fully laden and had a fuel capacity of more than 150 imperial gallons. Its two Armstrong Siddeley Cheetah engines pumped out 350 horsepower each, and it had a top speed of 192 miles per hour.

The Airspeed was capable of a range of up to five and a half hours of flight time or more than one thousand miles, which was sufficient to fly to Amy's hometown of Kingston upon Hull; to France; to Reykjavik, Iceland; or even to Cologne, Germany, and back.

That day, Amy was distracted. There was something else on her mind. She turned her thoughts to Nikki and the sadness in her heart. Amy knew her better than anyone, yet she did not really know her at all. Nikki had been through a lot, with her mother, her father, and the whole nanny affair.

When they first had met, on the face of it, the Beatties had seemed a happy family. *But then again, looks can be deceiving.* Amy knew that about her own failed marriage. *Why the bloody hell did I say yes? Why didn't I just go and see Walter instead?*

She felt guilty about the Walter situation. He had been smitten from day one and finally had admitted it to Amy after her sixteenth birthday party. She already had known, of course, and by that time, he had been in Ilkley. There had not been much they could do about it at that tender age. Amy had loved Walter too. They had been more like childhood friends, but she'd loved him nevertheless.

Amy felt almost guilty for some of Nikki's sadness. She could have been a better friend, asked more questions, and been there for her more than she had been. She knew of Nikki's reluctance to have children, and she knew Bob desperately wanted a family. She knew Nikki was concerned that Bob, like her own father, would stray if she did not give him what he wanted. She balanced that with her concern that her mother's mental health issues might be hereditary.

Amy knew she could have been a better friend, and she also knew that things might have been different if Walter ever had followed up with his proposal to marry one day. She never mentioned it to Nikki. Amy had no idea if she knew or not, but they never talked about it. It was another taboo topic on their conversation list.

Amy mused as she looked out the windshield of the Airspeed. They both had a lot of secrets. They both kept them locked away safely deep inside.

There was heavy cloud cover as she headed into Blackpool. With icy rain coming down, she steered the Airspeed down the coast, ducked under the clouds, spotted the familiar landmark of Blackpool Tower, and turned inland toward Stanley Park and the north edge of the golf course and then on to Newton Drive and her sister's house.

She steered the Airspeed lower and flew overhead—low enough to rattle the windows, she thought. She giggled to herself as she pictured her brother-in-law feeling the house shake and thinking the world was coming to an end.

Amy circled and came in for another flyby, and sure enough, her sister Molly and her husband, Trevor, were in the backyard. Molly was waving, and Trevor was scratching his head. The sight made Amy laugh even harder to herself. She saluted on her final flyover and touched down at the Squires Gate airfield ten minutes later.

Her mood sank again as she spotted the flight of brand-new Supermarine Spitfires heading north, likely to 602 Squadron in Scotland. Her ex-husband was among the dozen pilots delivering the new toys straight from the Supermarine factory in Woolston.

"Why the bloody hell does he get to fly Spitfires?" she mumbled to herself. She was experiencing seven emotions in one that day.

She regretted ever saying yes to the Flying Scotsman. It had been a big mistake and against the advice and the blessing of her father, who was not starstruck with Mollison, the Flying Prince of the air.

When she first had told him, in his typical Yorkshire way, he had looked her in the eye with genuine concern and said, "Are you sure he isn't homosexual, my dear?"

Amy burst into laughter at the memory. Her father always said how he saw things, never too concerned about the optics. That was why Yorkshire folks sometimes were seen as being rude or insensitive, a common misconception. In reality, Yorkshire folks were just honest and told the truth.

"I bloody well wish Glaswegians were as honest." She stared out the cockpit at the flight of Spitfires, still thinking of her father's words and, despite her husband's reputation, thinking her father might have been right after all.

The weather was quickly closing in on the airfield with thick fog and freezing rain. Traffic control closed flight operations. Amy hung around, out of sight of her ex-husband, and eventually decided to stay over for the night. She headed to her sister's home on Newton Drive. Amy did not mind that at all. It was always nice to see her sister.

Amy had a long-standing connection to the town. Back in 1931, she had flown in the Blackpool Air Pageant, along with several Schneider Cup aces, including Winifred Brown, winner of the 1930 King's Cup. She had returned later that year for a lecture on her solo flight to Australia and then again on her way back from her honeymoon in Scotland. That memory prompted her to quickly move on.

Molly had moved to Blackpool seven years ago when her husband, Trevor Jones, secured a job as the town clerk. Amy loved Molly, but she was lukewarm about her husband. There was not anything wrong with him; he just was not Amy's cup of tea. She thought he carried the world on his shoulders and was not the optimistic type of personality she was drawn to. Nevertheless, it would be nice to have dinner with them and, more importantly, be as far away as possible from the danger of bumping into her ex-husband and his merry band of Brylcreem boys.

The next morning, she was anxious to get out of Blackpool. Her Airspeed Oxford was ready, and the weather conditions had improved sufficiently to press on. Amy had a job to do.

She picked up her payload, per her orders, and twenty-five minutes later, she was back in the air, heading farther south. Her flight path took her between Liverpool and Manchester, over Stoke-on-Trent and Birmingham, and on to her destination.

As she made it through the thick, freezing fog and soared into the cover of the clouds in the wind and the freezing rain, the Airspeed buffeted around in the air.

Amy was an experienced pilot who had traversed much of the world, so she was not concerned about a spot of nasty English weather.

It was a normal day with typical January weather, a routine flight.

Everything was tip-top and tickety-boo.

Seaman Bruce Parker stood on the bridge of the HMS *Haslemere* with his hands lightly gripping the helm. He glanced down at the binnacle and squinted at the compass. Pleased that he was keeping the ship on course in spite of the heavy weather, he returned his attention to the roiled waters of Herne Bay. The Thames Estuary was gray and cold and sporting steep waves topped with white crests. The tide was running foul, and the snow blew almost horizontally as the vessel battled its way home. It was just a few days into 1941, yet Parker felt the year was already long in the tooth. It had been a nervy day. En route from Portsmouth, they had come under attack from both the Luftwaffe from the air and Hitler's navy gunships, but now they had made it to relative safety in the estuary.

The captain had ordered the ship to remain on its highest level of alert, despite its being almost home to safe harbor. All remained routine as Parker continued steering the ship up the bay. Suddenly, the lookouts sounded the warning. They'd spotted an unidentified plane coming toward them. It was the size of a midrange bomber, and although it was a single plane, Parker knew from experience that usually meant more to come.

The captain coolly instructed the gunners to be at the ready and his signaler to make contact with the unidentified threat. It had been a long day for the crew of the *Haslemere*, and they were weary-eyed in the freezing and miserable conditions. Parker continued on course as he listened to the radioman in the adjacent wireless room.

"This is the Royal Naval ship HMS *Haslemere* calling unidentified aircraft. Identify yourself."

The radio crackled silent.

"This is the Royal Naval ship HMS *Haslemere* calling unidentified aircraft. Identify yourself."

Each time, the urgency in the radio operator's voice heightened.

"I repeat: this is the Royal Naval ship HMS *Haslemere* calling unidentified aircraft. Please identify yourself."

The radio came to life with a muffled response from the flier.

"Please confirm your identity and the day's signal. I repeat: please identify yourself and the day's signal."

Again, a muffled response came over the radio; the operator was just able to make out the words. Parker gripped the wheel tighter. The pilot had just answered with the wrong code word. That meant the plane might be an enemy bomber on some kind of secret mission.

"Ask them again," the captain said as he stood in the door of the wireless room. "Tell the pilot that this is his final warning."

"That signal is incorrect. I repeat: that signal is incorrect. Please provide the correct color signal of the day, or prepare to be engaged."

The atmosphere on the bridge was tense. Was this an attack or a wayward flier? Parker wasn't sure, but he knew his captain was prepared to give the order to fire on the plane.

"Please confirm your identity and the day's signal. I repeat: please identify yourself and the day's signal."

There was another muffled response.

"Seaman Parker?"

"Aye, sir!"

"Take evasive measures. Hard to starboard! All ahead flank speed!"

"Aye aye, Captain!" Parker said, turning the wheel hard right.

The ship heeled into the turn as the engine room dialed up the speed. The captain ordered the gunners to fire at will. The antiaircraft cannons boomed into action, spewing rounds skyward, with dull green tracers marking the path of the gunfire. The plane banked hard left, dove, and pulled briefly up before the tail blew off in a bright flare of deep orange fire as an explosion engulfed the aircraft. Parker had seen such death scenes before, and he never relished the deaths of other human beings, not even the enemy. To him, the war was a sad tragedy perpetrated on the world by a trio of madmen.

Parker turned the ship hard left. He saw a figure parachuting down as the plane went into a sharp nosedive. Then a second chute popped. The plane burst into flames as it flew straight into the bay, exploding on impact.

"All ahead slow," the captain said.

"All ahead slow, aye," Parker said, and he signaled the engine room accordingly.

"Come round to fifteen degrees," the captain said.

"Fifteen degrees, aye," Parker said, easing the helm to put the bow on a bearing to bring the ship to the last point of visual contact. Both pilots had gotten out of the plane before it crashed, but their location was obscured in the heavy weather.

"Ease her off!" the captain yelled. "All back slow!"

Parker realized that in a moment of lost concentration, he inadvertently had steered the ship into a shoal. The engines backed off in slow reverse, and he felt the bow slide off the sandbar.

"All back slow," the captain said, his voice revealing the tension of the moment.

"Casualties two points off the port bow!" one of the lookouts shouted.

The captain ordered Parker to make for the crash site. The light was fading fast. Parker knew if they were ever to stand a chance at recovering the pilots, it was now or never. In another few minutes, the darkness would close visibility down to zero. It was already hard for him to navigate to the crash site.

"We've got wreckage!" one of the lookouts shouted. "But I've lost the pilots!"

"Bring her beam to the wind," the captain said.

Parker turned the ship so the wind blew off the right side, creating a lee on the left side for the lifeboat that the captain sent to rescue the downed pilots. The search came up with nothing but one wing of the Airspeed Oxford and then two items of luggage, one with the initials *AJ* and the other with Amy's full name. Parker quickly heard the scuttlebutt that the captain had found a photograph of a small group of people standing proudly in front of a blue Riley 9 with number 21 on the side and a logbook, leaving no doubt to the downed pilot's identity. The identity of the second pilot remained a mystery.

The government covered the incident up, saying Amy Johnson had overshot her destination, run out of fuel, and crashed somewhere in the lower Thames. For those who knew what really had happened, the main question focused on what Johnson had been doing in the area. She had been more than one hundred nautical miles from the flight path she had filed before taking off, and no one knew why or how such an experienced pilot could make such a big mistake.

For Parker, the incident was just one of many bad ones thus far in what was turning out to be a bloody war indeed. Still, like millions of others, he wondered what the real story was behind Amy Johnson and her mysterious appearance in a location where she should not have been on that fateful January 5, 1941.

EPILOGUE

AFTER MY DAD'S FUNERAL, I learned more about his secret life. I found some of the answers in my father's treasure chest. I leafed through his old identity and pay book from World War II. He had carried it in his top left chest pocket since the day he enlisted and through Iceland, the Normandy landings, North Africa, Germany, and then Palestine before he was demobilized.

As I did so, an old piece of handwritten paper fell out and wafted to the floor. I did not need to read the signature; I recognized his writing. I also had a good guess whom the poem was about.

> Where do you go to, my lovely,
> when alone in the sky?
> What are the thoughts that surround you
> and for the reasons why?

What were you thinking, my lovely,
when you tied the knot?
Were you not thinking of me?
Just like that forget-me-not.

I remember us in the village
where we both once grew up.
I recall our trip to Cambridge,
the church we would one day walk up.

Where did you go to, my lovely?
You went and left too soon.
Where are you now, my lovely?
I will see you in Brigadoon.

—Walter Beattie, June 6, 1944

That was the same day my father boarded the troop ship in London and headed to the French coast, to Gold Beach, during the Normandy landings. He was just one of the 160,000 brave Allied airborne and ground troops sent as part of Operation Overlord to defeat Hitler's Nazi Germany.

The poem told me whom he was thinking of in his darkest hour and what those old plane prints he left me, given to him by his love, meant to him. The poem was just another small piece of a puzzle that remained unfinished.

As I contemplated the story, my uncle Tommy told me about those early days of flight and my aunt Nikki's part in making aviation history, and I wondered if my aunt could fill in some additional gaps. I booked a flight to Gloucestershire, England, and drove to her home.

I hadn't seen Aunt Nikki in many years. We'd fallen out of touch so long ago that she represented a mere fragment of memory from my boyhood. The family had never been close. After I'd joined the Special Air Service fresh out of high school, I really never had looked back on those times. My troubled youth had led to a troubled adulthood that the army had helped to put right but not entirely. I didn't have the time or the inclination to dwell too much on the past.

I was nervous on the drive north as I circumnavigated the M25 and then got on the M40 in my rental car. I'd felt like splashing out and rented a BMW M5. I had owned one for a bit while living in Yorkshire, and I liked the car and the connection to my reason for visiting.

German manufacturer Bayerische Motoren Werke originally had made aircraft engines and then diversified into motorcycles and cars. The aviation connection interested me, as did the irony that the Germans were still probably the best engineers on the planet. It had always puzzled me how a country could start two world wars yet be left with assets like BMW, Mercedes-Benz, Porsche, Siemens, and many more, all contributors to the Nazi war machine that had been so devastating to many millions of people.

My father also had been a massive BMW fan, and his pride and joy had been a 633 CSi, his last car before sadly giving up the wheel. It had been terrible to see someone with a lifelong love of cars and driving realize he was too old and too dangerous to be behind the wheel. I remembered the day when, with me as a passenger, instead of stopping at a crossroad, he'd shifted down the gears, going straight across, and a car almost had taken us out completely. Not generally known for having bad nerves, even I had been shaken up.

A few months had passed with several similar incidents, and he had made the decision to hang up his boots on his own for the safety of the general public. It had been a heart-wrenching decision for my father to make.

As a gesture, I had purchased my first BMW to make up for the loss in the family—a gesture not lost on my father at the time.

At Oxford, I pulled onto the A40 through Witney and Burford and then on toward Stow-on-the-Wold on the A424 as memories of my last trip flooded back to me.

Many questions rang in my ears. I got to the crossroads and took a right onto the B4081 and continued on into my destination: Chipping Camden.

Earlier that day, I had stopped off at Fortnum and Mason in the terminal and grabbed a nice little hamper and a confection equivalent to Betty's fat rascals. I was armed with my notepad and pen and some of the items from my father's possessions. I also had plenty of questions.

I checked my Bremont. It was just after three o'clock. The watch had been a treat I bought for myself on the release of my last book, *Cold Courage*. Everything Bremont did reminded me of the quality of the past with the technology of the future. I often found the amount of connections that existed between my writings and reality almost eerie. I recalled the story of how the two English brothers had named their company.

They were flying across France in their 1930s biplane, the weather was closing in, the engine was misfiring, and they were forced to make an emergency landing in a farmer's field. The farmer invited them into his home, and it happened he was a former pilot who'd served during World War II and, evidently, a gifted engineer, as his home was filled with half-restored clocks and engine parts. He extended his hospitality, and the brothers, appreciative, named their company after that farmer, Antoine Bremont.

My uncle Tommy was right that I liked stories, but then again, as time had gone by, I had come to realize that stories liked me.

I pulled up outside the stone cottage on the corner of Back Ends Lane and Aston Road, got out of the BMW, took a deep breath, paused for a moment, and rang the doorbell. It was as if I were going back in time to unearth an old treasure chest. I remembered the same bell ring from what must have been at least twenty-five years earlier.

I waited for a few moments, and I could see through the door pane that someone was coming. The door opened, and a young lady in a nurse's care uniform answered. Her accent was Polish, I guessed.

"Good afternoon. How can I help you?"

I explained that I was there to see my aunt Nikki and had flown all the way from California to come see her.

She stepped to one side, let me in, and led me through the cottage to the same room I had sat in with my father and Nikki all those years earlier. The fire was roaring, and I looked at the eclectic mix of oddments and decorations from world travels, the stag and the antlers, the hunting trophies, and the tiger-skin rug still in front of the fire.

I also spotted the photographs around the room of her and her husband, Bob Baxter, in various parts of the world. I saw their wedding photo outside Rudding Park, a picture of my father with Beattie Blue, a photograph of Nikki and Amy with *Jason* in Darwin, and the picture I remembered from childhood, which I now knew was of Aunt Nikki, my father, and Amy Johnson together.

I sat down on the sofa, and Aunt Nikki sat in her chair with a blanket over her knees and the fire twinkling in her steel-blue eyes, which were the same as my father's eyes and, I realized at that moment, the same as my own.

She looked at me without any sign of recognition.

"Hello, Aunt Nikki. It's me—William," I said. Nothing. "Walter's son. Your brother's son, William. We spoke after the funeral."

Her eyes slowly lit up with realization. "Of course. William, how are you?"

I gave her a quick rundown of myself and my life over the last twenty-five years: my marriage; my own son, William; Australia; my divorce; and my father's passing. I knew she'd been told of his death and had been unable to attend the funeral because of her fragile mental state. I reminded her anyway, hoping her long-term memory might kick in enough for her to answer some of my questions. I wondered if she knew the real story behind Amy Johnson's death.

She sat there slowly shaking her head. At the memory of her brother and of her best friend, she suddenly turned from a look of delight to one of sadness. I shared with her the hamper and the fat rascals, which seemed to cheer her up a little, just as the nurse brought us a pot of tea with two cups and saucers. I checked with Aunt Nikki—it was Earl Grey, of course.

Taking some time out to finish my latest book, I decided to head to one of my favorite places on the planet: La Playa Carmel Hotel in Carmel-by-the-Sea. I loved the romance of that old jewel in the town nestled on the beach, with its eclectic mix of shops, restaurants, and the occasional bar. The town was nothing wild—in fact, quite the opposite. It was conservative and quiet but comfortable and relaxed and an ideal place to complete the final draft of my latest book.

La Playa, overlooking Carmel and Pebble Beach, had a rich history. Originally built by artist Christian Jorgensen, it had been a gift to his wife, Angela, daughter of the famous Ghirardelli chocolate family of San Francisco. Back then, it had been the first property in the town with its own swimming pool.

By 1917, the home had been turned into a hotel, the Strand, and by the 1940s, it had become a place to visit, be seen, and relax. In 1983, Steve Jobs had launched the Macintosh computer to his development team at the hotel. Over the decades, La Playa had earned its reputation as the Grand Dame of Carmel.

It was five thirty, and I sat on the Pacific Terrace, looking down on the manicured garden below. It had been a long day. I had taken the day off from writing and hiked around seventeen miles past the mansions, the golf courses, and the beautiful views of the ocean. For February, it had been a lovely day; the sun had shone through, giving a respite to the winter rainstorms over the past few days.

Having showered and changed, I was ready for a predinner beer or two and picked up my copy of the *Guardian* newly arrived from London courtesy of British Airways. There was a two-day lag, but that was fine; it was better than American newspapers for sure.

I ordered a pint of Anchor Steam, took a swig, told the waiter I would be ready for another in short order, and opened my paper. There wasn't much going on, but it was always good to connect with the homeland, wherever I was in the world.

I flipped to the sports pages to catch up on the Premier League results over the past week and was pleased to see that my team, United, had beaten Charlton Athletic 4–1, with Dwight York putting away two.

I saw extracts from Monica Lewinsky's videotaped deposition in the Bill Clinton scandal. Britney Spears's "Hit Me, Baby, One More Time" was making its way up the charts, Former heavyweight boxing champion Mike Tyson was jailed for twelve months for assaulting two motorists following a traffic accident. Bill and Melinda Gates had given $3.3 billion to their foundation.

My second Anchor Steam arrived as I flicked through the paper. Two sets of young couples had arrived on the terrace, romancing their way to dinner, and another couple in their Californian seventies reminisced about decades long gone. I had always found it interesting that in California, you did not see old people in the same way you saw old people in Glasgow, for example. There was something about the Californian spirit that kept people young.

I got toward the back of the newspaper before getting into the horoscopes and problem pages, and then I stared aghast at the article popping out in front of me.

I Shot Down Amy Johnson's Plane

Sarah Hall on an Old Soldier's Solution to a 1941 Mystery

My writing journey had often taken twists and turns, and I'd experienced eerie coincidences throughout. All my novels, fiction based on fact, had a personal story to tell, and they often related to me and my own experiences and those of my friends and family.

I had often found connections that I had not known existed, but this one was the most profound of all.

I continued to read the article.

> Rumours have circulated that Britain's most famous female pilot ran out of fuel, was blighted by bad weather, or struck by barrage balloons as she flew a wartime aircraft to RAF Kidlington above the Thames Estuary on January 5, 1941. She baled out, and her body was never found.

I was, of course, familiar with the story. I recalled the conversation with my uncle Tommy at my father's funeral and my conversation with my aunt Nikki. The book was already on my roster of future titles. I would include the revelations about my grandmother and her tragic demise; my grandfather's suicide in Paris out of guilt from the demise of his wife and his multiple affairs, including one with the family nanny; and my father's first love, Amy Johnson, and his decision, out of some sort of revenge, to marry Miss Boswell, who was twice his age and once had been his own father's lover, after Amy married someone else.

I would write of the alienation of a once happy and prosperous family and the bitterness that existed beneath and my father's lack of willingness to swap his monthly allowance for a divorce while masquerading as husband of my mother.

I would write of Amy's love for the Gipsy Moth and of the name's two meanings. The Gipsy Moth was a pioneering biplane of the golden era of aviation and was the plane that made Amy's name and launched her as a national hero and aviatrix. However, a gypsy moth also was one of the despicable creatures on the World's 100 Worst Invasive Alien Species list. Its Latin name, *Lymantria dispar,* was composed of two words: *lymantria* meant "to destroy," and *dispar* meant "to separate."

As I thought about my future project, I wasn't sure if the story was about a plane, an aviatrix, a tragedy, a love, a mystery, or Esmeralda Boswell, a Pearly, a Pikey, and a gypsy moth by the Latin definition.

The article went on. I was transfixed. This was an even more complex twist to the already complex tale.

But yesterday an alternative explanation was offered for the loss of the feminist pioneer and wartime heroine when an old sailor claimed he shot down her aircraft because she failed correctly to signal she was flying a British plane.

My mind raced. I had heard the stories of conspiracy surrounding her mysterious disappearance, but this was a new one I had not expected.

Tom Mitchell, an eighty-three-year-old retired gardener, said he served as an antiaircraft gunner aboard the patrol vessel HMS *Haslemere* in 1941. Mitchell said the weather was awful on that fateful late afternoon on January 5. The ship was steaming up Herne Bay when an unidentified aircraft appeared out of nowhere. After giving the pilot a chance to provide the code word of the day, the pilot provided the wrong code. The captain ordered the gunners to take the plane out. Luggage retrieved from the wreckage clearly identified the pilot as Amy Johnson. Mitchell said the government hushed up the incident, hoping to avoid a public outcry. Mitchell said the crew was sworn to secrecy and that he had kept the secret from that day on.

Was this sailor my uncle Tommy? I doubted that could be, but I remembered what he'd said at the wake at my father's funeral: "There are plenty of us Mitchells out there, you know, Willy."

The article went on and quoted the old sailor in question, Tom Mitchell of Crowborough, East Sussex.

"We felt absolutely terrible," Mitchell said yesterday. "We all thought it was an enemy plane until we recovered the luggage at the crash site. Of course, we were upset, but it was wartime; we were doing our jobs, and we got on with it. But it's not something I've wanted to talk about until now. I don't want to die without telling the world the truth about how Amy Johnson was brought down with friendly fire."

The article mentioned other claims that Johnson had been shot down and had not run out of fuel, as the official line had always stipulated. Aviation historian David Luff believed she had been fired at by a naval convoy, and the tragedy had been hushed up by a government anxious to avoid damaging morale.

According to the version of events by the Air Transport Auxiliary, which had employed her as a professional pilot from 1939, Johnson had run out of fuel after overshooting her destination by a hundred miles. But that explanation, which would have seen her dramatically misjudge the distance from Blackpool to Oxford, seemed implausible, given that she had successfully flown to Australia in 1930, Japan in 1931, and Cape Town in 1932.

The article then noted that various official lines shared in their denial of the claim. *Why would they admit the lie now, fifty years later?*

Sitting back, I laid the paper on the table before me and ordered a Liddesdale. The drink was a tradition in my family. Liddesdale was a place in Scotland where my father's roots had been planted through history, a reminder of our ancestry, including my own grandfather and his last hours in Paris before taking his own life.

From the terrace, I could hear the people below now dining, with the soft murmur of conversation, glasses clinking, and the symphony of plates and silverware. I was now alone on the terrace. I looked out across the gardens amid the distant sound of the waves crashing onto the beach and the twinkle of lights across that fairy-tale town in California a million miles away from where the story had all begun.

I reflected on my father telling me, "Don't join the army. Join the navy or air force instead; it's cleaner, more comfortable, and far more gratifying." I remembered my own journey. I had ended up in the army and not the other two. I remembered the Air Training Corps: donning the uniform; attending the parades and the summer camps; and, most memorably, piloting the gliders and copiloting the Chipmunks and the Bulldogs and doing barrel rolls and loop-the-loops in the former.

I toasted my grandmother Mary Beattie, my grandfather William Beattie, my aunt Nikki, my uncle Tommy, my mother, and my father. *God bless his soul.*

I thought about the Gipsy Moth, my father's collection of prints gifted by his first love, and his sadness as she married another. I thought of Esmerelda Boswell trying to work out if it was her fault, if she was a gypsy moth or, in a way, a victim of the circumstances too.

I thought of the picture of my father, Aunt Nikki, and Amy with her own Gipsy Moth behind them—a scene of a different age, of happiness and adventure. They'd been three pioneers: two aviatrixes and my father, a hero to many, especially to me.

At that moment, I decided I would move that book to the top of my to-do list and tell the tale that deserved to be told after all those years: the tale of my aunt Nikki, Amy Johnson, my father, and the pioneers and aviatrixes during a golden age.

One question remained: *Who was the mystery passenger on Amy's plane the night of January 5, 1941?*

Secrets

Secrets exist; they appear like devils in the mist.
They lie dormant for sometimes years without a sound.
When they do sneak out, then like thunder abound.

Secrets exist with the tightening of a fist.
The passing of time, their existence reveals,
mostly with sadness, lacking fairness of misdeals.

Secrets exist, maybe a lover's tryst.
There is often good reason they live so long;
usually, someone somewhere has done something wrong.

Secrets exist; my family clearly cannot resist.
Through the generations, the mysteries have grown.
I have learned from them I want to limit my own.

Then secrets will exist no more.

TIME LINE

THERE WAS MUCH GOING ON in the unprecedented times described in this novel. World War I raged on to World War II just twenty years later. Innovation was careening at a pace never seen before—sadly, fueled by the two conflicts— especially in the fields of automotives and aviation.

The following time line is out of respect for the people who played their parts—the aviators, the heroes, and, especially, the women who were committed to challenging the status quo like never before and gaining equal footing in what was predominantly a man's world and during extraordinary times.

1784	
June 4	Marie Élisabeth Thible of France becomes the first woman to fly in a hot-air balloon.

1799	
October 12	Labrosse becomes the first woman to parachute jump.

1803

	Hayden Wischet designs the first car powered by the de Rivaz engine, an internal combustion engine fueled by hydrogen.

1810

August 15	Sophie Blanchard makes her ascent in Milan to mark the forty-second birthday of Napoleon Bonaparte and later that year becomes his chief of air service.

1811

April 16	Wilhelmine Reichard is the first German woman to make a solo flight in a balloon.

1870

	Siegfried Marcus builds his first combustion-engine-powered pushcart, followed by four progressively more sophisticated combustion-engine cars over a ten- to fifteen-year span that influences later cars.

1880

	Karl Benz develops a gasoline-powered mobile auto. This is considered to be the first production vehicle, as Karl makes several other identical copies. The automobile is powered by a single-cylinder four-stroke engine.

1882

	Enrico Bernardi from France creates the first petrol-powered vehicle, a tricycle for his son Louis. He drives it through the streets of Paris, a village near the city of Verona.

1886

	Mary Myers of the United States sets an altitude record with a balloon: four miles.

1888

	Teresa Martinez y Perez is issued a British patent for navigable balloons.
July 24	Amelia Mary "Millie" Earhart is born in Atchison, Kansas, to Amelia "Amy" Otis, the granddaughter of a federal judge, and lawyer Samuel "Edwin" Stanton Earhart.

1903

July 1	Amy Johnson is born in Kingston upon Hull in the East Riding of Yorkshire to Amy Hodge, the granddaughter of a former mayor of the city, and John William Johnson from a family of fish merchants.
December 17	Brothers Orville and Wilbur Wright succeed in flying the first free, controlled flight of a power-driven heavier-than-air plane. Wilbur flies the plane for fifty-nine seconds at a height of 852 feet. This first flight takes place at Kill Devil Hills, North Carolina, four miles south of Kitty Hawk.
	Aida de Acosta of the United States is the first woman to pilot a motorized aircraft solo in a dirigible.

1904

	Queen Margherita of Italy creates the Roman Aero Club for ballooning.
	Charles Rolls and Henry Royce cofound Rolls-Royce, a car and aircraft engine manufacturer, in Manchester, England.

1908

May to June	Mademoiselle P. Van Pottelsberghe de la Poterie of Belgium flies with Henri Farman on several short flights at an air show in Ghent, Belgium, becoming the first female passenger on an airplane.
September	Thérèse Peltier of France makes the first solo flight by a woman in an airplane in Turin, Italy, flying around two hundred meters in a straight line about two and a half meters off the ground.
October 7	Edith Berg, business manager in Europe for the Wright brothers, becomes the first American woman to fly as a passenger.

1909

February 23	John McCurdy, a Canadian, makes the first powered flight in the British Empire in the *Silver Dart* at Baddeck, Nova Scotia. The flight lasts for less than half a mile and lands safely on the ice.
June 16	La Stella, the first aero club for women, opens in Saint-Cloud, near Paris.
	Katharine Wright, sister of Wilbur and Orville Wright, is instrumental in advancing her brothers' aviation business. She is the first woman invited to a meeting of the Aéro-Club de France and is awarded the Légion d'honneur in recognition for her contributions to early aviation.
	Marie Marvingt of France is the first woman to fly over the North Sea.
	Madame La Baronne Raymonde de Laroche of France is the first woman to pilot a solo flight in an airplane.
	Prior to this year, no two airplanes of identical design exist in America.

1910

March 8	Madame La Baronne Raymonde de Laroche from France becomes the world's first woman to earn a pilot's license from the Aéro-Club de France.
June	Charles W. Hamilton makes the first night flight in America at Camp Dickinson, Knoxville, Tennessee.
August 29	Marthe Niel of France becomes the world's second woman to earn a pilot's license.
September 2	Blanche Stuart Scott becomes the first unofficial American woman to fly solo.
September 3	Hélène Dutrieu of Belgium is the first woman in the world to fly with a passenger.
September 10	Bessie Raiche of the United States is credited with the first official solo airplane flight by a woman in the United States.
November 8	Marie Marvingt of France becomes the world's third woman to earn a pilot's license.
November 25	Hélène Dutrieu becomes the first Belgian woman and the fourth woman worldwide to earn a pilot's license.
December 7	Jeanne Herveu of France becomes the world's fifth woman to earn a pilot's license.
	Hilda Hewlett of England is the first woman to be a cofounder of a flight school.

1911

May	Jules Vedrine of France is the only competitor to finish the cross-country race from Paris to Madrid.
June 15	Marie-Louise Driancourt of France becomes the world's sixth woman to earn a pilot's license.
August 1	Harriet Quimby becomes the first American woman and the world's seventh woman to earn a pilot's license.
August 10	Lydia Zvereva is the first Russian woman and the world's eighth woman to earn a pilot's license.

August 29	Hilda Hewlett becomes the first English woman to earn a pilot's license. She later becomes the first woman to teach her child to fly in the same year.
September 13	Amelie Beese becomes the first German woman and the world's ninth woman with a pilot's license.
September 29	Walter Brookins sets an American record by flying 192 miles from Chicago to Springfield, Illinois, making two stops.
October 6	Beatrix de Rijk is the first Dutch woman and the world's tenth woman to earn a pilot's license.
October 10	Božena Laglerová is the first Czech woman to earn her pilot's license.
November 19	Lyubov Golanchikova becomes the first Estonian woman to earn a pilot's license.
December 10	Cal Rodgers completes the first transcontinental flight in the Wright EX *Vin Fiz* from Long Island, New York, to Pasadena, California.
	Hélène Dutrieu, a Belgian cycling world champion, stunt cyclist, stunt motorcyclist, automobile racer, stunt driver, pioneer aviator, wartime ambulance driver, and director of a military hospital is the first woman to win an air race.
	The Ford Model T, created by the Ford Motor Company seven years prior, becomes the first automobile to be mass-produced on a moving assembly line. By 1927, Ford produces more than fifteen million Model N mobile autos.

1912

April 16	Harriet Quimby is the first woman to fly across the English Channel.
August 15	Lilly Steinschneider becomes the first Hungarian woman to earn a pilot's license.
	Amelie Beese of Germany is the first woman to patent an aircraft design.

	Hélène Dutrieu is the first woman to pilot a seaplane.
	Hilda Hewlett is the first woman to cofound an aircraft factory.
	Rayna Kasabova becomes the first woman to participate in a military flight.

1913

January 3	Rosina Ferrario is the first Italian woman to earn her pilot's license.
June 21	Georgia "Tiny" Broadwick is the first woman to jump from an aircraft, dropping from two thousand feet in Los Angeles.
July 17	Alys McKey Bryant becomes the first woman to pilot a plane in Canada.
September 23	Roland Garros makes the first crossing of the Mediterranean Sea.
December 1	Lyubov Golanchikova becomes the first test pilot.
	Ruth Law is the first woman to fly at night.
	Katherine Stinson and her mother start the Stinson Aviation Company. Stinson also becomes the first commissioned female airmail pilot and the first woman to do night skywriting in the same year.
	Ann Maria Bocciarelli of South Africa is the first woman in Africa to earn a recreational pilot's license.
	Katharina Paulus develops the first modern parachute that fits inside a pocket or bag.

1914

February 6	Elena Caragiani-Stoenescu becomes the first Romanian woman to earn a pilot's license.
May 11	Else Haugk is the first Swiss woman to earn a pilot's license.
June 6	The first flight occurs out of sight of land, from Scotland to Norway.

June 24	Igor Sikosky sets an unofficial world distance record by flying a 1,590-mile round-trip flight from Saint Petersburg to Kiev, Russia, in an Ilya Muromets aircraft.
June 28	Archduke Franz Ferdinand and his wife, Sophie, are assassinated in Sarajevo, sparking events that lead to World War I.
August 4	Britain declares war on Germany after the Germans invade Belgium and declare war on France, triggering World War I.
August 8	Sir Ernest Shackleton's ship the *Endurance* sets sail from Plymouth, England, on its Imperial Trans-Antarctic Expedition.
October 1	Amalia Celia Figueredo becomes the first woman in Argentina to earn a pilot's license.
	Eugenie Shakhovskaya is the first woman to become a military pilot when she flies reconnaissance missions for the czar.
	Lydia Zvereva is the first woman to perform an aerobatic maneuver (a loop).

1915

	Marie Marvingt of France is the first woman to fly in combat.

1916

September 2	Direct radio in-flight communications are used for the first time.
	Zhang Xiahun becomes China's first female pilot.

1918

April 21	Baron von Richthofen, otherwise known as the Red Baron, the German war fighter pilot credited with eighty air combat victories, is shot down and killed near Vaux-sur-Somme, France.

November 11	Germany surrenders, and all nations agree to stop fighting while the terms of peace are negotiated. On June 28, 1919, Germany and the Allied nations (including Britain, France, Italy, and Russia) sign the Treaty of Versailles, formally ending World War I.
November	Orville Wright notes to a friend as World War I comes to an end, "The Aeroplane has made war so terrible that I do not believe any country will again care to start a war."
	Amelia Earhart enlists with the Red Cross in Toronto and becomes a nurse's aide at Spadina Military Hospital, treating wounded soldiers from World War I and victims of Spanish flu.

1919

June 15	Alcock and Brown make the first nonstop flight across the Atlantic Ocean, from Newfoundland to Ireland, in their Vickers Vimy plane.
December 10	Vickers Vimy G-EAOU lands in Darwin, Northern Australia, completing a 135-hour journey from England to Australia.
	Bentley Motors Limited is founded by W. O. Bentley in 1919 in Cricklewood, North London, and becomes widely known for winning the 24 Hours of Le Mans in 1924, 1927, 1928, 1929, and 1930.

1920

February 22	The first US transcontinental mail service arrives in New York from San Francisco. The trip takes thirty-three hours and twenty minutes—three days faster than rail service.
December 28	Amelia Earhart takes her first flight in Long Beach, California, with pilot Frank Hawks, a ten-dollar, ten-minute ride paid for by her father and the start of a passion for flight.

May	Carmela Combre is the first woman to pilot a plane in Peru, though she never attains a license.
June 15	Bessie Coleman becomes the first African American woman to receive a Fédération Aéronautic Internationale (FAI) pilot's license.
October	Violet Guirola de Avila of El Salvador completes a flight in Guatemala, becoming the first Salvadoran female pilot.
	Amelia Earhart saves $1,000 to pay for flying lessons at Kinner Field, Long Beach, with teacher Anita "Neta" Snook.
	Adrienne Bolland becomes the first woman to fly over the Andes.

1922

March 15	Amalia Villa de la Tapia from Bolivia is the first female pilot licensed in Peru.
April 8	Thereza Di Marzo is the first Brazilian woman to earn a pilot's license.
October 22	Amelia Earhart takes the *Canary*, which she terms *Yellow Peril*, to an altitude of fourteen thousand feet, breaking the world record for a female pilot.
	Tadashi Hyōdō becomes the first Japanese woman to earn a pilot's license.
	Anesia Pinheiro Machado earns the Aero Club of Brazil Brevet No. 77 for her solo flight. She becomes the first female pilot in Brazil to carry passengers.

1923

May 3	Lieutenants Oakley Kelly and John Macready complete the first nonstop coast-to-coast airplane flight, from New York to San Diego, in twenty-six hours and fifty minutes.

May 15	Amelia Earhart becomes the sixteenth woman in the United States to be issued a pilot's license, number 6017.
August 23	Lieutenants Lowell Smith and John Richter of the US Army Corps set an endurance record of thirty-seven hours with the aid of in-flight refueling.

1924

July 1	The US Post Office Department opens regular day-and-night airmail service between New York and San Francisco.
November 24	María Bernaldo de Quirós is the first Spanish woman to receive a pilot's license.

1925

June 12	Daniel Guggenheim donates $500,000 toward the establishment of a School of Aeronautics at New York University.
October 31	Amy Johnson and her friend Nikki Beattie graduate from the University of Sheffield, having studied Latin and French and earned degrees in economics.
	Kwon Ki-ok is the first Korean woman to earn a pilot's license.
	Gladys Sandford becomes the first woman in New Zealand to earn her pilot's license.

1926

March 20	USS *Langley* is commissioned and becomes the first American aircraft carrier.
May 9	Commander Richard E. Byrd and pilot Floyd Bennett complete the first flight over the North Pole.
September 3	Lieutenant James H. Doolittle, showing Curtiss airplanes in South America, flies over the Andes Mountains.

	Millicent Bryant is the first Australian woman to earn a pilot's license.

1927

May 20	Charles Lindbergh takes off from Roosevelt Field, Long Island, New York, and, thirty-three and a half hours later, lands at Le Bourget Aerodrome, seven miles northeast of Paris, at 10:22 p.m. on May 21 to a crowd estimated at more than 150,000.
June 29	Albert Hegenberger and Lester Maitland, on the *Bird of Paradise*, make the first transoceanic flight from Oakland, California, to Honolulu, Hawaii. It is the longest open-sea flight to date.
October 15	Dieudonné Costes of France and his navigator, Joseph Le Brix, make the first nonstop crossing of the South Atlantic.
	Marga von Etzdorf of Germany is the first woman to fly for an airline.
	Dagny Berger is the first Norwegian woman to receive a flying certificate.

1928

February to May	Mary, Lady Heath, an Irish woman, becomes the first aviatrix to fly from Cape Town, South Africa, to Croydon Aerodrome in London.
March to April	Mary Bailey of England is the first woman to fly solo from England to South Africa.
May 31	Charles Kingsford-Smith, along with Charles Ulm and James Warner, radio, and Harry Lyons, navigator, complete the first transpacific flight, from Oakland, California, to Brisbane, Australia.

June 16	Amelia Earhart sets off from Trepassey Harbor, Newfoundland, in a Fokker F.VIIb called *Friendship*, essentially as a passenger of pilot Wilmer Stultz and copilot Louis Gordon. Exactly twenty hours and forty minutes later, they land in Pwll, Burry Port, South Wales.
November 29	Commander Richard E. Byrd, Bert Balchen, Captain Ashley C. McKinley, and Harold I. June, flying from camp in Little America, are the first to fly over the South Pole.
	Maria de Lourdes Sá Teixeira of Portugal earns the first pilot's license for a woman in her country.
	Eileen Vollick is the first Canadian woman to earn her pilot's license.
	Janet Bragg is the first woman admitted to the Curtiss-Wright School of Aeronautics.
	Park Kyung-won becomes the first Korean woman to earn a second-class pilot's license.

1929

January 28	Amy Johnson is issued her aviator's certificate, number 8662.
March 16	Louise Thaden breaks the women's endurance record with a time of twenty-two hours and three minutes.
July 6	Amy Johnson receives her A pilot's license, number 1979, and, in the same year, is the first British woman to obtain her ground engineer's C license.
August 18	Women's Air Derby is held in the United States for the first time. Louise Thaden is the winner. The race is dubbed by the press the "Powder Puff Derby."
September 24	James H. Doolittle becomes the first to fly entirely by use of instruments and radio aids from takeoff to landing without reference to the ground.

October 29	The Wall Street Crash of 1929, also known as the Great Crash, is a major stock market crash that occurs in 1929. It starts in September and ends late in October, when share prices on the New York Stock Exchange collapse.
November 2	A group called the Ninety-Nines is founded to support and mentor women in aviation.
	Fédération Aéronautique Internationale creates a new category for records set by female pilots.
	Charles Kingsford Smith, an Australian, is the first person to circumnavigate the world. Leaving from Oakland, California, he makes the first transpacific flight to Australia in three stages—Oakland to Hawaii, Hawaii to Fiji, and Fiji to Brisbane—and then, from there, completes the circumnavigation, crossing the equator twice.
	Florence Lowe "Pancho" Barnes becomes the first stunt pilot, working in Hollywood.
	Phyllis Arnott is the first Australian woman to earn a commercial pilot's license; however, she flies only for pleasure.
	Elsie MacGill of Canada becomes the first woman to earn a master's degree in aeronautical engineering.
	Audrey Fiander becomes the first female pilot in Rhodesia, now Zimbabwe.

1930

January	Aris Emma Walder becomes Uruguay's first female pilot when she attains her license in Buenos Aires, Argentina, at the Morón Aerodrome in a Curtiss JN-4D.
March	Berta Moraleda performs in an air show. In May, having completed her training at the Escuela de Aviación Curtiss, she becomes the first female pilot in Cuba.
April 20	Charles Lindbergh and Anne Morrow set a transcontinental speed record from Los Angeles to New York in a time of fourteen hours and forty-five minutes.

May 5	Amy Johnson leaves Croydon Airport to become the first woman to fly solo from England to Australia, landing at Darwin, Northern Territory, on May 24, eleven thousand miles later.
May 15	Ellen Church convinces Boeing Air Transport to hire her and seven other women as the first flight attendants. They are required to be nurses, be unmarried, and weigh under 115 pounds.
May	Laura Ingalls, a distance and stunt pilot from New York, sets a stunt record of 980 consecutive, continuous loops in a little less than four hours at Hatbox Field in Muskogee, Oklahoma.
June 4	Lieutenant Apollo Soucek, flying a Wright Apache, an open-cockpit plane, sets a new world altitude record of more than forty-three thousand feet.
June 11	John and Kenneth Hunter's refueling endurance flight over Chicago breaks all records when they remain in the air for 533 hours, 41 minutes, and 30 seconds.
July	Graciela Cooper Godoy obtains the first license for a female pilot in Chile.
September	Maryse Bastié of France breaks the sustained flight endurance record for women, remaining aloft for thirty-eight hours.
	Elinor Smith and Evelyn Trout of the United States are the first women to refuel a plane in flight.
	Mary Riddle becomes the first Native American to earn a pilot's license. She is a member of the Clatsop and Quinault tribes.

1931

August 5	Katharina Paulus makes her final balloon flight at age sixty-three. She has more than 510 logged balloon flights and more than 150 parachute jumps to her credit.

February 7	Amelia Earhart marries businessman, publisher, and publicist George Palmer "GP" Putnam at his mother's home in Noank, New England.
April 8	Amelia Earhart, in a Pitcairn, establishes the autogyro altitude world record at more than eighteen thousand feet.
July 1	*Winnie Mae* completes the first circumnavigation of the world by a lone aircraft, piloted by Wiley Post and Harold Gatty.
July	Amy Johnson and copilot Jack Humphreys become the first people to fly from London to Moscow in one day, completing the 1,760-mile journey in twenty-one hours. They go on to Siberia and then Tokyo, beating the record from London to Japan.
October 5	Clyde Pangborn and Hugh Herndon make the first nonstop crossing of the Pacific in a Bellanca CH-400, from Japan to Wenatchee, Washington, United States.
	Anne Morrow Lindbergh becomes the first US woman to earn a glider pilot's license.
	Marga von Etzdorf is the first woman to fly over Siberia.
	The Betsy Ross Air Corps is formed in the United States to provide military support flying.

1932

May 20	Amelia Earhart takes off from Harbour Grace, Newfoundland, and, fourteen hours and fifty-six minutes later, touches down in a pasture in Culmore, north of Derry, in Northern Ireland, to be the first woman to fly the Atlantic solo.
July 29	Amy Johnson marries Scottish pilot Jim Mollison after meeting him on a flight earlier that year, during which he proposed within eight hours into the flight, and she accepted.
July	Amy Johnson beats her husband's solo record, flying from London to Cape Town in her plane *Desert Cloud*.

	Amelia Earhart is the first female pilot to fly solo across the Atlantic Ocean, in the Fokker F.VIIb-3m named *Friendship*.
	Ruthy Tu, British trained, becomes the first Chinese woman to earn a pilot's license and the first woman to join the Chinese army as a pilot.
	Maude Bonney becomes the first woman to do a round-Australia flight.
	Urmila K. Parekh becomes the first Indian woman granted a pilot's license.
	Hermelinda Urvina of Ecuador becomes the first woman in the country to earn a pilot's license.
	Emma Catalina Encinas Aguayo earns the first female pilot's license in Mexico.

1933

July	Amy Johnson and her husband, Jim Mollison, take off from Pendine Sands, South Wales, on their way to New York on their plane *Seafarer*, on their first leg of his attempt to beat the world record for flying from New York to Baghdad.
	Bedriye Tahir Gökmen is the first Turkish woman to earn her pilot's license.
	Lotfia Elnadi becomes the first Arab woman, first African woman, and first woman in Egypt to earn a pilot's license.
	Maryse Hilsz of France is the first female pilot to fly from Beijing to Paris.
	Fay Gillis Wells is the first American woman to fly a Soviet-made airplane.
	Carola Lorenzini is the first Argentine pilot certified as a flight instructor.
	Aline Rhonie is the first woman to fly solo from New York to Mexico City.

1934

October 23	Jeannette Piccard becomes the first female balloonist to reach the stratosphere.
December 31	Helen Richey becomes the first woman to pilot a commercial airliner. She later resigns because she is not allowed into the all-male pilots' union and is rarely allowed to fly.
	Amy Johnson and her husband, Jim Mollison, break the record from Britain to India on their plane *Black Magic*.
	Marie Marvingt is the first woman to run a civil air ambulance service.
	Marina Mikhailovna Raskova of Russia is the first woman to instruct at a military flight academy.
	Jean Batten of New Zealand is the first woman to do the England-to-Australia round trip.
	Maryse Hilsz of France is the first woman to do the Paris-to-Tokyo round trip.
	Maude Bonney is the first woman awarded a Most Excellent Order of the British Empire (MBE) award, for her contribution to aviation.

1935

January 1	Helen Richey becomes the first woman employed as an airline pilot at Central Airlines.
January 12	Amelia Earhart is the first woman to fly a solo round trip from Hawaii to the continental United States.
May 8	Amelia Earhart flies nonstop from Mexico City to Newark, New Jersey, in fourteen hours, eighteen minutes, and thirty seconds, becoming the first person to fly this course nonstop from south to north and the only woman to fly it either way.
July 1	Brothers Al and Fred Key land at Meridian Airport and set a world record for sustained flight through air-to-air refueling at 653 hours and 34 minutes. They set off on June 4.

	Marie Marvingt becomes the first person to practice aviation paramedicine.
	Nancy Bird Walton is the first Australian woman to hold a license to allow her to carry passengers.
	Lee Ya-Ching, a Chinese actress, becomes the first woman to be licensed by the Boeing School of Aeronautics.
	Phyllis Doreen Hooper earns the first female pilot's license in South Africa.
	Katherine Sui Fun Cheung earns the first commercial license issued to a woman of China.

1936

	Sarla Thakral becomes the first Indian woman to earn her private pilot's license.
	Beryl Markham from England is the first woman to fly solo across the Atlantic Ocean from east to west.
	Lee Ya-Ching becomes the first woman to be licensed as a pilot in China.
	Phyllis Doreen Hooper earns the first female commercial pilot license in South Africa.
	Mulumebet Emeru is the first female pilot of Ethiopia. She is a student, but her flight training is interrupted by the Italian invasion of Ethiopia.

1937

March 17	Amelia Earhart attempts her first round-the-world flight. The plane never leaves Luke Field, Hawaii, as it crashes on takeoff, and the damaged plane needs repairs.
June 1	Amelia Earhart's second around-the-world flight starts in Oakland, California. This time, she flies from west to east, from Miami to South America, Africa, the Indian subcontinent, and Southeast Asia. She makes it to Lae, New Guinea, on June 29.

July 2	Amelia Earhart leaves Lae Airfield and goes missing near Howland Island in the central Pacific Ocean. Her last known position is near the Nukumanu Islands, about eight hundred miles into the flight.
August 27	The world's first jet-propelled aircraft takes to the air.
	Willa Brown is the first African American woman to earn her pilot's license in the United States.
	Sabiha Gökçen of Turkey is the first female combat pilot.
	Hanna Reitsch of Germany is the first woman to earn a helicopter license.
	Maude Bonney is the first woman to fly solo from Australia to South Africa.
	Susana Ferrari Billinghurst is the first female commercial pilot of Argentina.

1938

	Phyllis Doreen Hooper becomes the first female flight instructor in South Africa.
	Amy Johnson and Jim Mollison divorce, and Amy reverts to her maiden name.
	Hanna Reitsch of Germany is the first person to fly a helicopter inside a building. She flies a Focke-Achgelis Fa-61 inside the Deutschlandhalle in Berlin.
	Berta Servián de Flores becomes the first Paraguayan woman to earn a pilot's license.
	Aline Rhonie becomes the first American to earn an Irish commercial pilot's license.

1939

January 5	Amelia Earhart is declared dead in absentia after numerous attempts to find her body.
May 15	A. Kondratyeva, a Soviet balloonist, sets a record flight of twenty-two hours and forty minutes from Moscow to Lukino Polie in a balloon.

September 1	Adolf Hitler invades Poland.
September 3	Britain and France declare war on Germany.
September 15	Jacqueline Cochran, flying a Seversky monoplane, sets a new international speed record of 305 miles per hour for 621 miles in Burbank, California.
November 13	María Calcaño Ruiz becomes the first Venezuelan female pilot, attaining her license in Long Island, New York. Her Venezuelan license is issued the following month.
November 17	The Women's Auxiliary Air Force of the South African Air Force is founded.
December 5	The South African Women's Aviation Association (SAWAA) is formed with 110 women as first members.
	Inés Thomann becomes the first Peruvian female pilot when she is licensed at the Escuela de Aviación de Las Palmas.

1940

January 1	The Air Transport Auxiliary (ATA) appoints its first eight female recruits. Amy Johnson joins as pilot first officer.
	Effat Tejaratchi becomes the first Iranian woman to earn her pilot's license.
	Phyllis Dunning (née Hooper) becomes the first South African woman to enter full-time military service as the commander of the South African Women's Auxiliary Air Force (SAWAAF).
	Mirta Vanni becomes the first female commercial pilot in Uruguay.

1941

January 5	Amy Johnson goes missing and is presumed dead as her plane crashes into the Thames Estuary near Herne Bay, Kent, England.

January 14	Amy Johnson's memorial service is held at the church of St. Martin-in-the-Fields, London.
July 2	The Canadian Women's Auxiliary Air Force (CWAAF) is formed.
October 8	Joseph Stalin creates three regiments of female pilots for the Soviet Union military. The 588th Regiment is later called the Night Witches.
	Jacqueline Cochran of the United States is the first woman to fly a bomber across the North Atlantic.
	Ada Rogato becomes the first certified female paratrooper in Brazil.
	Dick Ballou writes "The Song of the Ninety-Nines."

DEFINITIONS AND CLARIFICATIONS

Amelia Earhart: In 1928, Amelia Earhart became the first woman to fly across the Atlantic as a passenger. She gained fame from the flight, but it was by no means her most significant contribution to aviation. She became the first woman to fly across the Atlantic solo in 1932. In 1935, she became the first person to fly solo across the Pacific, from Honolulu to Oakland. Two years later, Amelia and her navigator, Fred Noonan, began an around-the-world flight from Miami eastward. After completing twenty-two thousand miles of their journey, they were last seen on takeoff from Lae, New Guinea, on July 2, 1937.

Amy Johnson: Amy Johnson flew her first solo in June 1929. In January 1930, she was the first woman to obtain her ground engineer's certificate. Also in 1930, Amy was the first woman to fly solo from London, England, to Australia.

Anita Snook: Mary Anita "Neta" Snook Southern was a pioneer aviator who achieved a long list of firsts. She was the first female aviator in Iowa, the first female student accepted at the Curtiss Flying School in Virginia, the first female aviator to run her own aviation business, and the first woman to run a commercial airfield.

Ann Wood-Kelly: Ann Wood-Kelly, an American from Philadelphia, was an aviator who flew with the British Air Transport Auxiliary in World War II.

Anne Morrow Lindbergh: Anne Morrow Lindbergh was the first American woman to earn a glider pilot's license. Determined to help her husband, Charles, on his pioneer routes for the airlines industry, she learned Morse code and earned a radio operator's license. In 1933, she went with her husband on a five-month, thirty-thousand-mile survey through Greenland, Iceland, Russia, England, Spain, Africa, and Brazil. In doing so, she made a world record for radio communication between plane and ground stations when she contacted Sayville, Long Island, while flying off the coast of West Africa. She was the first woman to be awarded the National Geographic Society's highest award, the Hubbard Gold Medal, for her achievements as copilot and navigator on that trip.

Air Transport Auxiliary (ATA): This British civilian organization was set up during World War II and headquartered at White Waltham Airfield. It ferried new, repaired, and damaged military aircraft between factories, assembly plants, transatlantic delivery points, maintenance units, scrapyards, and active service squadrons and airfields. It also flew service personnel on urgent duty from one place to another and performed some air ambulance work. Notably, some of its pilots were women, and from 1943, they received equal pay to their male coworkers, a first for the British government.

Beryl Markham: Beryl Markham was an English pilot who learned to fly in Kenya and planned to be the first pilot to fly nonstop from London to New York City, crossing the Atlantic from east to west in September 1936. She ran out of fuel just off the coast of Nova Scotia and made a safe water landing.

Bessie Coleman: Bessie Coleman was the first African American to earn a pilot's license, but she had to travel to France to do so, because none of the American schools would train blacks. She earned her pilot's license in France in 1921, returned to America, and took up stunt flying to earn money. She died while test flying her newly delivered aircraft in 1926, the day prior to a flying event scheduled in Florida.

Blanche Noyes: Blanche Noyes received her pilot's license in April 1929, the first woman in Ohio to do so. In 1935, she joined the Air Marking Division of the Bureau of Air Commerce.

Blanche Stuart Scott: Technically the first American woman to fly solo in 1910, when a block on her aircraft's throttle jolted out of place and she went airborne, Blanche Stuart Scott was not credited with being the first American woman to solo by the Aeronautical Society of America, because the flight was ruled an accident.

Bobbi Trout: Bobbi Trout earned her pilot's license in 1928. In 1929, she regained the women's endurance record from Elinor Smith and, at the same time, gained records for the first all-night flight by a woman, most miles covered by a sixty-horsepower engine, and heaviest fuel takeoff to date. With Elinor Smith in November 1929, she set an endurance record of 42 hours and 3.5 minutes, which was also the first refueling endurance record tried by a women's team.

Boulevard School: Boulevard was a secondary school in Kingston upon Hull attended by Amy Johnson and her friend Nikki Beattie.

Bremont: Bremont is a British watchmaker based in Henley-on-Thames, London, England. It was founded by brothers Nick and Giles English, sons of former RAF pilot Euan English, who tragically died in a flying accident in 1995. Since, Bremont has built a business crafting precision chronometers in the spirit of the golden age of aviation.

Brigadoon: According to legend, Brigadoon is a mysterious Scottish village that appears for only one day every one hundred years.

Charles Lindbergh: Charles Augustus Lindbergh was an American aviator, military officer, author, inventor, and activist. At the age of twenty-five, in 1927, he went from obscurity as a US airmail pilot to instantaneous world fame by winning the Orteig Prize for making a nonstop flight from New York to Paris.

de Havilland: The de Havilland Aircraft Company Limited was a British aviation manufacturer set up in late 1920 by Geoffrey de Havilland at Stag Lane Aerodrome in Edgware, on the outskirts of North London. Operations were later moved to Hatfield in Hertfordshire.

dirigible: An airship, or dirigible balloon, is a type of aerostat or lighter-than-air aircraft that can navigate through the air under its own power.

Elinor Smith: In 1927, at the age of just sixteen, Elinor Smith was the youngest pilot ever to receive a Fédération Aéronautique Internationale license, signed by Orville Wright. The next year, at age seventeen, she became the first and only pilot to successfully maneuver a plane under all four New York City bridges, resulting in a ten-day grounding by the mayor of New York and much publicity. In November 1929, she joined Bobbi Trout in trying for the first in-flight refueling endurance record for women, which lasted more than forty-two hours. At age nineteen, she was voted the Best Woman Pilot in the United States in 1930, the same year her hero Jimmy Doolittle was voted Best Male Pilot.

Evelyn Sharp: Evelyn Genevieve "Sharpie" Sharp was an American aviator who was born in 1919 and died in 1944 at the age of just twenty-five.

Edna Gardner Whyte: Edna Gardner Whyte got her pilot's license in 1931 and her transport license in 1932. She set up her own flight school, and in 1938, she had flown so many hours that she ranked first in flight hours on *Look* magazine's list of female American pilots. She was the tenth American woman to obtain her helicopter rating.

Fay Gillis Wells: During a test flight of an experimental airplane, Fay Gillis Wells was forced to parachute to safety, which led her to become the first female member of the Caterpillar Club. She earned her pilot's license in 1929 and then was hired by Curtiss-Wright to show and sell their planes. She combined her love of flying with her love of journalism throughout her long and inspirational career.

Flying Scotsman: The Flying Scotsman is an express passenger train service operating between Edinburgh and London, the capitals of Scotland and England, via the East Coast Main Line. The service began in 1862; the name was officially adopted in 1924.

Fred Noonan: Frederick Joseph "Fred" Noonan was an American flight navigator, sea captain, and aviation pioneer who first charted many commercial airline routes across the Pacific Ocean during the 1930s. He was also the navigator of Amelia Earhart's round-the-world attempt in 1937.

Gipsy Moth: The de Havilland DH.60 Moth was a 1920s two-seat British touring and training plane developed into a series of aircraft by the de Havilland Aircraft Company.

gypsy moth: *Lymantria dispar*, commonly known as the gypsy moth, European gypsy moth, or North American gypsy moth, is a moth in the family Erebidae that is of Eurasian origin. The meaning of the name in Latin is composed of two words: *lymantria* means "to destroy," and *dispar* means "to separate." The gypsy moth is listed as one of the World's 100 Worst Invasive Alien Species.

Harriet Quimby: In 1911, Harriet Quimby was the first American woman to earn a pilot's license, and she was the second woman in the world to do so. She was killed in a plane accident in 1912.

Hélène Boucher: From France, Hélène Boucher was the holder of the women's world speed record, when she crashed in rough weather and died. She summed up her desire to pursue aviation records with the following: "It is the only profession where courage pays off and concrete results count for success."

High Royds Hospital: High Royds Hospital was a former psychiatric hospital south of the village of Menston, West Yorkshire, England. The hospital, which opened in 1888, closed in 2003.

Jean Batten: A New Zealander, Jean Batten flew solo from England to Australia in 1934, beating Amy Johnson's record by four days. Soon after, she flew from Australia to London, becoming the first woman to fly from England to Australia and back. She later became the first woman to fly from England to Argentina.

Jessie Woods: Jessie Woods helped her barnstormer husband create the Flying Aces, the longest-running air circus. Jessie, who learned to fly in 1929, walked the wing, parachuted, flew as a stunt pilot, performed gymnastics from a rope ladder, and, at age eighty-one, rode the wing again.

Juanita Bailey: Juanita Bailey was a female pilot otherwise known as the Flying Beautician.

Katherine Cheung: Katherine Cheung was the first Asian American woman to earn a pilot's license in 1932. Three years later, she obtained an international airline license and flew as a commercial pilot. She flew aerobatics in an open-cockpit Fleet and regularly entered competitive air races. She planned to return to China in 1937 to open a flying school, but a male friend was killed while flying her airplane. Her father, who had been extraordinarily supportive of her flying, was then on his deathbed and secured a promise from Katherine to give up flying.

Katherine Stinson: Katherine Stinson was the first woman to fly the mail and the first woman in the world to own a flying school. In 1913, Katherine and her mother created Stinson Aviation Company to rent and sell airplanes. In 1917, Katherine toured Asia and was the first woman to fly in Japan or China.

Kingston upon Hull: Hull, or Kingston upon Hull, is a port city in East Yorkshire, England, where the River Hull meets the Humber Estuary.

Kirk Ella: Kirk Ella is a village on the western outskirts of Kingston upon Hull, five miles west of the city center, situated in the East Riding of Yorkshire, England.

Lady Mary Bailey: From Ireland, Lady Mary Bailey earned her pilot's license in 1926 and immediately flew the Irish Sea. She became the first woman to qualify for a blind-flying certificate. Two years later, she left London on a solo flight to Cape Town, South Africa. She returned solo via the west coast of Africa.

London Aeroplane Club: This recreational flying club for aviators in the north of London, England, opened in 1925.

Louise McPhetridge Thaden: Louise Thaden was winner of the first Women's Air Derby in 1929 and was the only woman to hold three aviation records simultaneously (altitude, endurance, and speed). She and copilot Blanche Noyes became the first female team to win the Bendix Transcontinental Air Race against male competition in 1936.

London North Eastern Railway (LNER): LNER is a British railway company that also ran several ships.

Matilde Moisant: Matilde Moisant was only the second American woman to earn a pilot's license. She also set several altitude records and was the first person of either gender to land a plane in Mexico City.

Nancy Bird Walton: Australian pilot Nancy Bird Walton earned her license in 1933 and her commercial license in

March 1935. She was one of the first two women in New South Wales to fly at night and the youngest woman in the British Empire to qualify for a commercial license. In 1949, she formed the Australian Women Pilots' Association.

New Phantom: The Rolls-Royce Phantom was Rolls-Royce's replacement for the original Silver Ghost and was introduced as the New Phantom in 1925.

Pancho Barnes: Pancho Barnes earned her first world speed record in the early 1930s, beating Amelia Earhart's record. In 1931, she and Lavelle Sweeley organized female pilots and medical personnel into the Women's Air Reserve to provide aid during national emergencies.

Phoebe Omlie: Phoebe Omlie was the first woman to earn a transport license, in 1927. In 1930, she won the Dixie Derby Air Race, and then she won the National Air Races in Cleveland in 1931, the first year women were admitted to the race.

Royal Air Force: The United Kingdom's aerial warfare force, the Royal Air Force was formed toward the end of World War I, on April 1, 1918. Following the Allied victory over the Central Powers in 1918, the RAF emerged as the largest air force in the world at the time.

Rolls-Royce: Incorporated in February 2011, Rolls-Royce Holdings PLC is a British multinational engineering company that owns Rolls-Royce, a business that was established in 1904 and today designs, manufactures, and distributes power systems for aviation and other industries.

Ruth Law: Ruth Law was the first woman to fly at night, in 1913, and the first woman to loop-the-loop. Three years later, she broke the world's nonstop cross-country record, for men or women, by flying 590 miles from Chicago, Illinois, to Hornell, New York.

Ruth Nichols: In 1931, Ruth Nichols attempted to be the first woman to fly solo across the Atlantic. The flight was aborted due to engine failure but netted her the women's altitude record. Later that year, she broke Pancho Barnes's speed record. She founded Relief Wings in 1939 to coordinate private planes for emergency and disaster relief.

Silver Ghost: This Rolls-Royce name refers both to a car model and to one specific car from that series. It was originally named the 40/50 hp. The chassis was first made at Royce's Manchester works, with production moving to Derby in July 1908 and, between 1921 and 1926, Springfield, Massachusetts.

Thea Rasche: Thea Rasche was Germany's first female aerobatics pilot.

The Ninety-Nines: Established in the United States in 1929, the Ninety-Nines International Organization of Women Pilots, also known as the 99s, is an international organization that provides networking, mentoring, and flight scholarship opportunities to recreational and professional female pilots.

Tiny Broadwick: Tiny Broadwick began her career by parachuting from balloons. She was the first woman to parachute from an airplane. In 1915, she became the first person to show parachutes to the US Army.

Valentine Henry Baker (Captain): Nicknamed Bake, Valentine Baker, MC, AFC, served in all three of the British Armed Forces during the First World War. After the war, he became a civilian flight instructor and cofounder of the Martin-Baker Aircraft Company.

Wright Brothers: Orville and Wilbur Wright were two American aviation pioneers. They are generally credited with inventing, building, and flying the world's first successful motor-operated airplane.

ABOUT THE AUTHOR

WILLY MITCHELL WAS BORN IN Glasgow, Scotland. He spent a lot of time in bars in his youth and into adulthood. He's always appreciated the stories, some true, some imaginary, and some delusional. But these stories are true.

A shipyard worker, he headed down from Scotland to Yorkshire with his family to work in the steel mills. Now retired, he lives in California and has turned to writing some of the tales he's listened to over the years, bringing those stories to life.

Operation Argus

Operation Argus is a fast-paced, thoughtful, personal, and insightful story that touches the mind and the heart and creates a sense of intrigue in the search for the truth.

While sitting in the Rhu Inn in Scotland one wintry night, Willy Mitchell stumbles across a group of men in civilian clothes who are full of adrenaline—like a group of performers coming off a stage. To the watchful eye, it is clear the men are no civilians. As they share close-knit banter and beer, they are completely alert, and each of them checks him out and looks at his eyes and into his soul. Willy learns in time that the group are referred to as call sign Bravo2Zero.

Operation Argus is a story of fiction based on true events. Five former and one serving Special Air Service soldiers converge on San Francisco for their good friend's funeral, only to find his apparent heart attack is not as it seems. A concoction of polonium-210 has been used, as with the assassination of Litvinenko in London years before.

Bikini Bravo

Bikini Bravo follows the adventures of Mitch; his daughter, Bella; and the team of Mac, Bob, and Sam as they uncover a complex web of unlikely collaborators but for a seemingly obvious common good: power, greed, and money.

Many years ago, Mitchell stumbled across a bar in Malindi, Kenya, West Africa, and overheard the makings of a coup in an oil-rich nation in West Africa. Is a similar plan being hatched today?

Lord Beecham puts together the pieces of the puzzle and concludes that the Russians, along with the Mexican drug cartels and a power-hungry group of Equatorial Guineans, have put together an ingenious plot to take over Africa's sixth-largest oil-producing nation in their attempt to win influence in Africa. The cartels desire to use the dirty money for good, and the Africans seek to win power and influence.

Bikini Bravo is another book of fiction by Mitchell that masterfully flirts with real-life events spanning the globe and touches on some real global political issues.

Mitch's daughter, Bella, is the emerging hero in this second book of the Argus series.

Cold Courage

Cold Courage starts with Willy Mitchell's grandfather's meeting with Harry McNish in Wellington, New Zealand, in 1929. In exchange for a hot meal and a pint or two, McNish tells his story of the *Endurance* and the Imperial Trans-Antarctic Expedition of 1914.

According to legend, in 1913, Sir Ernest Shackleton posted a classified advertisement in the *London Times*: "Men wanted for hazardous journey. Small wages, bitter cold, long months of complete darkness, constant danger. Safe return doubtful. Honor and recognition in case of success." According to Shackleton, the advert attracted more than five thousand applicants, surely a sign of the times.

Following the assassination of Archduke Ferdinand earlier that year, at the beginning of August, the First World War was being declared across Europe, and with the blessing of the king and approval to proceed from the first sea lord, the *Endurance* set sail from Plymouth, England, on its way to Buenos Aires, Argentina, to meet with the entire twenty-eight-man crew and sail south.

Shackleton was keen to win back the polar-exploration crown for the empire and be the first to transit across the Antarctic from one side to the other.

The *Endurance* and her sister ship, the *Aurora*, both suffered defeat, and thirty-seven of Shackleton's men were stranded at opposite ends of the continent, shipless, cold, hungry, and fighting Mother Nature for survival.

This is a tale of the great age of exploration and the extraordinary journey these men endured, not only in Antarctica but also upon their return to England amid the Great War.

This is the story of the *Endurance*, the Imperial Trans-Antarctic Expedition of 1914, and all that was happening in those extraordinary times.

Northern Echo

Willy Mitchell meets an old friend in the Royal Oak, in the northern town they grew up in, for one last blast. Tiny Tim has terminal cancer, and at the end of the evening, he makes Mitchell promise to tell their story of growing up in the north of England during the punk-rock era and of their dark secret from a trip to Paris.

There were dark clouds surrounding Great Britain at that time. The Provisional IRA were actively rebelling against the English, Arabic terrorism was on the rise, and Argentina invaded one of the nation's territories in the far-off South Atlantic.

Unemployment was at its highest level since the 1930s, and whole industries were being crippled by the trade-union movement and strikes in every corner of industry. The far right was also on the rise, as was the Campaign for Nuclear Disarmament protesting the arms race that existed between the United States and the Soviet Union.

Society was on its knees; the middle class had given up, seemingly content to slide into obscurity, forgetting the victories and the pride of the past.

The youth of the time were disillusioned, with little prospect of jobs, careers, or a future, and as the punk-rock scene spread across the Atlantic from New York, it changed into a movement and a commentary on the state of the country and the mood of society.

With no future and no rules, ripping up the rule book and starting again, the punk-rock movement was an unlikely catalyst and contributor to change in Great Britain, with heaps of attitude, and it changed the nation for the better.

Mitchell, in *Northern Echo*, takes the reader on a sometimes humorous, eye-opening journey through one of the most interesting times in modern British history—a musical, political, and social revolution—and the story of two boys coming of age in their journey toward adulthood.

Gipsy Moth

Gipsy Moth is the tale of a young girl growing up with a privileged life in the north of England during extraordinary times, an era of extremes and pioneers, including the Wright brothers' first flight, the breakout of war across

Europe, and the burgeoning sadness of two parents both absent for different reasons.

Miss Boswell, the family's nanny, is the single point of continuity and has a profound influence on the lives of Nikki and her two brothers.

Nikki meets Amy, another Yorkshire lass, at school, and through their shared loneliness at home, they establish a unique and lasting friendship that takes them from Yorkshire to London and beyond, to places they've only ever dreamed of, and they encounter tragic twists and turns along the way.

Willy Mitchell tells the story his great-aunt shared with him after his own father's funeral, unearthing even more secrets in the Mitchell family history, secrets of happiness, times long gone, sadness, and tragedy.

The lives of Nikki Beattie and Amy Johnson collide as they meet through their fathers, who are successful men in their own fields of business. Their two pathways intertwine through friendship, school, university, and their discovery of the pioneering days of early aviation.

Together they get the flying bug and join the ranks of the most influential group of women in the history of British aviation. They become two extraordinary women, aviatrixes, true pioneers in the golden age of aviation.

Both are born just five months earlier than the Wright brothers' pioneering flight in 1903. Nikki's best friend, Amy, becomes not just a celebrity in the evolution of flight but also a shining light for women's rights, a national and international hero. Amy reads about her rival from across the Atlantic, Amelia Earhart, who, in 1937, goes missing during a flight in the Pacific. Her body is never found.

In 1940, Amy and Nikki both join the Air Transport Auxiliary, and in 1941, Amy mysteriously crashes and disappears above the Thames Estuary. Her body is never recovered.

Just as many have their own and family skeletons, Nikki shares her story with Mitchell, including secrets long buried.

Review of *Gipsy Moth*

Willy Mitchell's novel *Gipsy Moth: Aviatrix* is an action-packed, appealing story of adventure and romance. From an intriguing beginning to an unexpected ending, Willy takes the reader through an engaging account of the life of Amy Johnson, as seen by her best friend, Nikki.

Gipsy Moth is the fascinating tale of a young girl growing up and enjoying a privileged life in the North of England during extraordinary times. Nikki meets Amy Johnson, another Yorkshire lass, at school in Hull. Through their shared loneliness and adversity at home, they establish a unique and lasting friendship that takes them from Yorkshire to London and beyond, to places they've only ever dreamed of. They encounter tragic twists and turns along the way.

Although based on real events, *Gipsy Moth* is a work of fiction creating a gripping account of the characters' lives and times.

—Andrew Hemmings, June 2020

In Memory Of

Uncle Tommy

When I was very young my Uncle Tommy explained to me, he was going away for a long time and would be far away serving in the Royal Navy on a ship called HMS Rotherham.

He gave me a seaside bucket and asked me to fill it with smooth flat pebbles so that when he came home, he would teach me a magical trick - to make the pebbles skip across water. Upon his return, this is what he did, and I will never forget that day when the magic happened.

In memory of that first separation from now until he is laid to rest I will collect pebbles and at 2 O'clock on the 1st of October, 2020, I will be making those pebbles skip over water together with my Uncle Tommy, in spirit, and we will both send love and strength to all our family.

Someday try the magic, skim some pebbles and remember my hero, My Uncle Tommy.

Printed in the United States
By Bookmasters